*Follow the exciting adventures of Dani Ross
and her partner against crime, Ben Savage,
in two captivating novels that will
have you on the edge of your seat!*

Guilt by Association In the premiere Danielle Ross Mystery novel, Dani's faith and Ben's skillfulness are put to the ultimate test as the threat of death at the hands of a madman looms over them and eleven others held captive in a most unlikely prison. When tensions rise and the prisoners' spirits fall, Dani and Ben must work quickly. Can they solve the mystery before another hostage is killed?

The Final Curtain The second Danielle Ross Mystery brings Dani and Ben to New York City to investigate bizarre death threats against a bombastic celebrity. Dani joins the company of his newest play under the guise of costume lady and is propelled into the lead role when the star is killed — right on stage! Death threats soon yield another murder, and Dani and Ben are baffled by the bevy of juicy suspects among the cast and crew. Will they catch the villainous "Phantom of the Theater" before he strikes again?

DEADLY DECEPTION

GILBERT MORRIS

Fleming H. Revell Company
Tarrytown, New York

Scripture quotations in this volume are from the King James Version of the Bible.

Library of Congress Cataloging-in-Publication Data

Morris, Gilbert.
    Deadly deception / Gilbert Morris.
      p. cm.
    ISBN 0-8007-5419-0
    I. Title.
PS3563.D8742D43   1992
813'.54—dc20   91-36737
                                        CIP

Copyright © 1992 by Gilbert Morris
Published by the Fleming H. Revell Company
Tarrytown, New York 10591

Printed in the United States of America

"Favour is deceitful, and beauty is vain: but a woman that feareth the Lord, she shall be praised" (Proverbs 31:30).

Some children are born of flesh and blood; others come to a man through the act of living—are created by earthly laws and conventions. But a godly daughter-in-law, such as you have been to me, is not a matter of form or of legality. No, for as I have often said, I have *three* daughters, not two only. And it cheers my heart to know that there are women in this perilous age who hold fast to virtue, who are loyal, and who cling to God no matter what the circumstances. With love and admiration, I dedicate this book to my third daughter:

Monique Morris

Contents

Contents

DEADLY DECEPTION

1
The Stakeout

"Here comes another one," Ben Savage warned suddenly, his voice breaking the quietness of the night. "Better close in."

Danielle Ross had been watching the pale winter moon as it slid across the velvet sky over Lake Pontchartrain. She started slightly, then wheeled to glance at the headlights moving slowly down the narrow road that hugged the shore. "All right," she murmured and turned to face Ben. Sliding out from under the wheel of the Marquis, he moved beside her and put his right arm around her shoulders. She placed her right arm around his neck and let her left hand fall on the .38 that rested in her lap. It was cold to her touch, and as always, when she thought of actually firing it at someone, a slight shiver ran through her.

As she sat there, rigid in his embrace, listening as the sound of the approaching car grew louder, she became conscious of the firmness of Savage's neck under her hand and of his hand on her back. The faint scent of his shaving lotion floated to her nostrils, and the moonlight threw the scar over his left eyebrow into prominence. She found herself bracing her feet against the floor and was suddenly aware that she had clenched her teeth together so hard it made her jaws hurt. As the droning engine came closer, she noticed that Ben was relaxed. Somehow angered, she whispered, "Well—is he stopping or not?"

"Maybe." The car was approaching from her side, and with her face pressed against Ben's chest, she could not see it. Savage suddenly pulled her closer with his right hand and moved his body slightly forward. Dani felt his cheek press against her hair as he peered toward the approaching car. Suddenly the lights filled the inside of the car, and the engine slowed. At once Ben reached down with his left hand and pulled the .44 magnum from the holster on his right side. "Slowing down," he murmured. "Could be our little friend."

Dani's grip on the .38 tightened, and the muscles in her back grew tense. She was not at all a nervous woman, but sitting in a car waiting for a homicidal maniac who had butchered ten people caused a thread of fear to run along her nerves. As she sat there, listening hard to the vehicle as it drew even with their car, she thought of her conversation the previous Wednesday with Luke Sixkiller.

"We need eighteen teams for a stakeout, Danielle," the lieutenant of the homicide division of the New Orleans Police Department had said, his obsidian eyes studying her. "We've got his M.O. down. He always gets his victims the same way—always hits a couple parking near the lake, always sometime around midnight. And he always slices them up after he puts slugs in them both. So you and Ben be parked on Lakeshore Drive tomorrow night.

And carry plenty of heat, you hear? If the Midnight Mangler comes calling, you don't want to be bashful. Save the state the expense of a trial."

Then Sixkiller had grinned, adding, "You and ol' Ben can do some real serious necking while you're waiting."

Dani had argued hard against his plan—especially the necking part—but in the end Luke Sixkiller had shrugged, saying, "Well, Ross, if you want to cop out, that's your business. But a private investigator needs to stay on good terms with the fuzz. And the way to do that, Doll, is to cooperate in little things like this."

The car had stopped, just to the right of their own, engine faintly throbbing. Dani strained her ears, listening for the sound of a door being opened. A tremor ran through her, and she knew Savage felt it, for his right hand on her back gave a reassuring pressure.

From where she sat, her cheek against the nylon windbreaker Ben wore, she could see only the twin cones of light that illuminated the road. A strong desire to turn and look at the car came over her, but she and Ben had agreed that they had to look like a couple engaged in heavy petting, so she forced herself to remain still. Time wound down slowly, and Dani was thinking, *Why doesn't he hurry up?* when the engine revved, and suddenly the car appeared in her line of vision, ruby taillights glowing like tiny traffic lights. She automatically memorized the license number and pulled her head away from Ben's chest.

"False alarm," she noted, keeping her voice steady.

Ben put the .44 down on the seat, but kept his arm around her. "Better stay here awhile." He nodded. "He might come back."

Dani turned her head quickly and looked into Savage's hazel eyes, regarding her carefully, only inches away.

"He's gone," she exclaimed sharply. "You can let me go and get back on your own side."

He didn't move. Indeed, the pressure of his arm on her back increased, and he moved his face closer. "Can't ever tell about a guy like that," he warned. "He might be parking down the road. Might come back on foot." He was so close that she could feel his breath on her cheek. "As a matter of fact, Boss, I'm pretty sure that's what he's up to. We'd better make this business look real good!"

"Never mind all that, Ben Savage!" Dani ordered sharply. She put her hand on his chest and tried to push him away. "You just get back where you belong."

He gave her a grin, but moved back beneath the wheel. Returning the .44 to his holster, he shook his head regretfully. "Boss, you're the most single-minded woman I ever saw. You just can't do two things at once—which is a shame."

"What two things?" she asked absently, putting the revolver back into her purse. Her mind was still on the killer the papers had dubbed the "Midnight Mangler," but when she looked up and saw his grin, his statement registered, and she snapped, "Never mind! I can guess what two things you've got on your grubby little mind!"

"Sorry, Boss," Ben offered. "Guess I'm just a weak person with no character at all." She threw him a disgusted look, and he added, "Yep, put me in a parked car with a good-looking woman in my arms—and I revert to my primitive instincts." She kept stubbornly quiet, and he asked curiously, "Boss—don't *you* ever have any primitive instincts?"

"Oh, shut up!" Dani said abruptly. Bending forward, she looked at the face of the dash. "It's nearly one o'clock. Let's go home."

"Sixkiller said stay till two."

"He'll never know, and we're not getting paid for this stakeout." She leaned back and after a moment said, "I wish we *were!*"

Savage looked across at her, admiring the fine curve of her cheek and the firm line of her wide lips. Her mouth was too large, he realized, for true beauty, and her face a little too square. Lieutenant Sixkiller had ragged him about working for such a good-looking woman, but Ben had always shrugged, replying, "I never noticed."

But he *had* noticed, of course, as any healthy male would. Not only her face, but the tall, curved figure was the target of most men's eyes. She was small boned but full bodied and moved with a natural grace that was somehow sedate and sensuous at the same time. Her auburn hair fell forward, hiding her face as she glanced out the window. "Not enough business, is there?" Ben queried.

She looked at him, shrugged and answered, "It could be better." She bit her lip. "I'm not doing so good with Ross Investigation Agency."

"It'll pick up," he responded cheerfully, then put his hand lightly on her shoulder. "After all, how many women can come out of a seminary and take over a private-eye business without a few setbacks?"

Ben thought of how he had come to work for Danielle Ross. She had been preparing for the mission field, but had been forced to take over her father's investigative agency when he had suffered a heart attack. He thought of how they'd fought like cats and dogs, and he grinned slightly. "We'll be rich and famous, Dani," he promised gently. "It's just a matter—" Suddenly the sound of an approaching car broke the silence, and he caught a glimpse of headlights coming from the east.

"Here we go again," he cautioned, moving to sit beside her. He grasped his .44 and ordered, "Get that peashooter out. You'll have to watch this one, Boss. Don't let him get the jump on us."

Dani felt foolish and awkward as he embraced her, but a glimpse at Ben's face revealed that he was thinking only of the car that moved toward them. She realized that he was not as relaxed as before. They were both thinking it might be the same car that had passed moments before. She watched as the lights grew larger, and once again she began to tighten up. This was the second night she and Ben had sat in the Marquis beside the lake, and she had done the same every time a car had appeared. It was a secluded spot, often used by high-school kids for parking, but they had been scared off by the horror stories of the Mangler. The side road they were parked on was half hidden by a line of live oaks veiled with Spanish moss, and Ben had remarked cheerfully on their first night, "Just the sort of spot that ought to appeal to the Mangler."

Now the lights struck Dani's eyes, and she looked down, blinking. Pressed against Ben's chest, she felt sure he could hear the quick beating of her heart, but shook her head slightly and firmed her lips. She looked up—just in time to see the car, a dark sedan, swing into the parking area. It halted not thirty feet away from where she sat, and when the engine abruptly shut down, the sound of sudden silence hung over the lake.

Then a tiny *click* came to their ears, and Ben whispered, "He's getting out."

A shadowy form separated from the dark bulk of the car. It moved very silently, and Dani could see only a vague shape. Her fingers tightened on the .38, and her breathing grew short. She wished that Ben was in her position, for he was adept at such things—trained in the marines. But he kept his position as they had agreed, and it was up to her. Sixkiller had warned, "Don't fool with him, Danielle! If somebody sneaks up on you, cut him down!"

Whoever it was made no sound at all as he crossed the space between the two cars. Over Ben's shoulder Dani saw the figure appear at the window, his form blotting out the light of the moon. The window was down, and suddenly his hands materialized, looking ghostly white as they rested on the lower frame of the window opening. Something in her screamed out, *Now!* and Dani lifted the .38. A line of silver light formed along the snub-nosed barrel of the revolver, and she called out, "Freeze! Hold it right there!"

Savage twisted around, and as he threw the .44 level on the figure framed in the opening, a voice teased, "Glad to see you guys are keeping your mind on your work. The way you were cuddling up, I was afraid you'd gotten sidetracked."

"Luke Sixkiller!" Dani cried, torn between relief and anger. "You haven't got a bit of sense! Serve you right if I'd shot you!" She lowered the gun so that he wouldn't see how her hand was trembling and found herself wanting to cry. But she would have died before letting the two men see her reaction.

"Sorry, Dani," Sixkiller apologized, but then he leaned down, and by the pale moonlight she saw a grin on his lips. He gave Ben a quick look, adding, "You two did a good job of imitating a pair of lovers. You learn that in detective school, Ben?"

"It's a dirty job, Luke," Ben confessed with a shake of his head. "But someone's got to do it."

"I do like to see a man who takes pride in his work." The detective nodded. Then he turned and waved at the other car, which started up at once and backed out, then shot off down the road. Sixkiller walked around the car, got in beside Dani, and explained, "Debbi put me out. Said I could walk back to town as far as she was concerned."

"That so?" Ben asked as he started the engine. "You didn't overstep the bounds of propriety, I hope?"

Sixkiller shook his head sadly. "A man is a poor thing when he doesn't throw himself into his work with everything he's got. Debbi couldn't understand that it was my duty to be an ardent lover."

Dani gave him a sour look, then demanded, "I take it you want a ride back to town?"

"Let's go get something to eat," Sixkiller suggested, yawning. "The Camellia Grill is open."

Ben backed the car out and started down the road. It was not far to the causeway that spanned the lake, and soon they were speeding across the long ribbon of highway that traced a straight line across the silvery water. "No luck tonight," Ben commented. "We on again tomorrow night?"

"I guess you guys can take a break," Sixkiller said. He lay back against the seat, watching the moon's reflection on the water. "It was a long shot, but I thought it was worth the effort. Anyway, I owe you guys one for your help."

Twenty minutes later, they pulled into the Camellia Grill, and twenty minutes after that were eating thick hamburgers and crispy fries. Dani consumed hers hungrily, listening to the two men talk and noticing how the two of them were so different—yet somehow the same.

Lieutenant Luke Sixkiller was, she decided, one of the most *physical* men she'd ever met. He was no more than 5 feet 10 inches tall, but weighed 190 pounds. He seemed, somehow, more solid than other people, and his deep chest and thick limbs made Savage look almost frail. Luke had the blackest hair possible for a man to have and obsidian eyes that seemed flat and rarely showed any emotion. He was a pure Indian, untainted by a drop of white blood; and with his high cheekbones, Roman nose and wide mouth, looked very much like the Sioux who had roamed the plains for hundreds of years before white men set foot in America.

"Don't try to buy Sixkiller," the criminal element of New Orleans warned one another. They also walked around him whenever possible, for the chief of homicide had taken three bullet wounds in his career with the police department, and one blow from his fist usually ended any arguments. He was not, Dani understood, a brutal man, but his life had hardened him.

She shifted her glance to Savage, who was no taller than the policeman and weighed 175. He was not bulky, but had the smooth muscles of an acrobat—which was not strange, considering that he had once been an aerialist with the circus. He had a shock of coarse, black hair, but was not dark of complexion. With his squarish face, deepset eyes, and a brow that made a bony shelf over them, he looked Slavic.

Dani sipped her coffee, thinking of how she'd battled with Savage almost from the moment they met. They were opposites in so many ways that clashes became inevitable. While she was not an ardent feminist, Dani had set out to prove that she was as good at being a private investigator as she had been at being a CPA. It irked her that some aspects of investigative work demanded the skills of a fairly tough man, and she didn't realize that she compensated for this by trying to best Savage in other ways. They had been through some hard times together, and on a few rare occasions, Ben had let his habitual hard manner slip— just enough so that Dani could sense that he was actually a sensitive and caring man.

Once or twice he had kissed her, but though she had responded to a degree that both surprised and disturbed her, she was determined to keep their relationship on a business plane. She had the uncomfortable feeling that he knew this and was amused by what must have seemed another instance of role playing—which he insisted she did constantly.

As she took a bite of her burger, the beeper on Sixkiller's belt sounded. He got up at once, walked away, then stood planted like a rock as he took the message. Dani saw his black eyes widen, and she exclaimed, "Look at Luke! Something made him show a little feeling for once."

Ben turned to watch as the husky policeman stepped back to the table. "Let's go," he directed almost harshly. "Got to catch a squeal."

He threw some money on the table and led the other two out. Dani had to run to keep up with him, and when they were inside the Marquis, Sixkiller said, "I got no time to find a car. Head for Lanza's place—and don't worry about getting a speeding ticket."

"What's going on, Lieutenant?" Ben asked.

Sixkiller didn't answer for a long moment. He had a way of thinking over his answers before responding. Finally he explained, "Been a killing."

"Well, we have two or three of those every day," Ben reminded him.

"Not at Dom Lanza's place, we don't!"

Dani turned to stare at him. "Dominic Lanza? He was killed?"

"I don't think so. That old pirate's too mean to die." Sixkiller swayed as Ben went around a corner, his heavy body crushing against Dani. "It wasn't the old man. But *somebody* got it."

Without taking his eyes off the road, Ben recalled, "Talk is that pressure's been building up since Sal Martino got taken out." Martino was the leader of a powerful syndicate that controlled a large hunk of the illegal—and highly profitable—activities of New Orleans. What he did not control, Dominic Lanza did. There had been a war between the two factions five years earlier, with many casualties but no clear-cut victor. A truce of sorts had been patched together, so that a fragile agreement between the two warlords had prevailed.

Dani mentioned this, adding, "Could it be a gang-style killing, do you think?"

"I hope not." Sixkiller shook his head. "If that ever starts, lots of innocent people are going to get hurt." He watched the houses fly by as Ben steered the car through the light traffic, then added, "You're probably right, though. Thing that I can't figure, how did a hit man ever get close enough to blast anyone? That place is like a fort!"

He said no more, but Dani could see his mind working on the thing. He gave a few brief commands to Savage, finally declaring, "There it is. Pull up to the gate."

21

"It *is* like a fort!" Dani agreed as Savage nosed the sedan forward. She looked at the tall brick wall that stretched out for at least a quarter of a mile before sweeping backward in a curve, and noted that the gate before them was the only entrance. "And I guess these are the palace guards," she murmured as four men came to stand inside the gate, staring out at them.

Sixkiller got out of the car and walked to the gate. "Open up," Dani heard him demand impatiently.

"How about we see a little ID?" one of the men returned, and Dani stared at him, her eyes opening wide. "Ben! Look!"

Savage nodded. "Vince Canelli."

"I thought he was in Detroit!"

"So did I. But looks like he's one of Lanza's goons." He stared at the figure of Canelli, then said, "You never got Vince to hit the glory road, did you, Boss?"

"No. I never did." They both remembered a bad time when they had been confined in a barren silo by a madman named Maxwell Stone, kidnapped along with a group of people he felt he had a grudge against. Vince had been one of them. Several of their number had died, and Canelli had nearly perished. But no matter how hard Dani tried, she had never been able to break through the gangster's tough exterior.

"He'll be surprised to see us," Ben claimed as Sixkiller came back to the car accompanied by Canelli. The officer got in the front, and Canelli slipped into the backseat.

As the gates swung back, Canelli directed, "There's only one road, Lieutenant. Just follow it."

"Let's go, Ben," Sixkiller ordered, and as Ben followed the curving road through a forest of oak and pine, the policeman asked, "What's the story, Canelli? Who bought it?"

Canelli spoke tersely. "It was Phil." His voice hard with anger, he added bitterly, "He never had a chance—and they got Lorraine, his wife, too!"

"Didn't think anyone could get close enough for a killing," Sixkiller commented. His eyes moved back and forth ceaselessly. "What about your security?"

"Somebody will have to answer for that," Canelli said softly. "Never should have happened." Then he pointed out, "There's the house."

Another wall—of red brick—surrounded a large, white plantation-style house that rose up in the moonlight. "Let me get the gate," Canelli offered. He got out and spoke to someone on the other side of the heavy cast-iron gate. It swung back, and Ben pulled inside. Canelli came to stand beside the car, announcing as Sixkiller got out, "It's up there on the second floor."

Sixkiller glanced up at the facade, which caught the silver gleams of the moon, then allowed, "I guess you two can come along."

Dani got out and said, "Hello, Vince."

"What—?" Vince responded quickly, then peered at her. "Hey—it's you!" He stared at her, then looked over at Ben with wide eyes. "Savage, you here, too?"

"Let's go," Sixkiller broke in impatiently. "You people can have your high-school reunion later."

Canelli shook his head doubtfully. "You're working for the cops now?"

"No, Vince." Dani explained, "I'm still private. We were just on hand to give the lieutenant a ride."

"Well—come on then." The three of them followed Canelli up to the broad porch that spanned the width of the house. A very tall man with a shotgun met them, but Canelli ordered, "Okay, Legs," and he faded away. "Up the stairs."

The staircases were like those in Tara, Scarlett's home in *Gone With the Wind*, two curving, graceful rises leading to the second floor. Canelli led them down a long, wide hallway, then put his hand on the knob. He paused and turned to say, "Dani, it's—well, maybe you better wait out here."

"It's all right, Vince," she reassured him.

He shrugged, opened the door, then stepped back. Dani went last, after Sixkiller and Savage, but one look was enough for her. The two bodies lay in front of an open window that had been riddled with bullets. Both wore dressing gowns, and the first thing Dani saw was that the short blond hair of the woman was matted with clots of scarlet blood. Lorraine's eyes were open, and one hand was placed over her breast as she lay on her back. The other hand was flung up over her head in a strangely pathetic gesture. The front of her blue dressing gown was a mass of blood that was no longer scarlet but was dulled and heavy.

Dani took one look at the body of the man, who was facedown. A pool of blood had spread from under him, and both hands lay under his body, as if he had tried to stem the flow.

Dani looked away quickly, turning her back on the two. She studied the room, noting the immense antique furniture, the expensive pictures, and the thick carpet. Sixkiller had gone at once to kneel beside the man, and he fired a series of rapid questions at Canelli.

Finally Sixkiller decided, "Let's leave this for the lab

boys. They ought to be here any time." He walked out of the room, and the others followed. "Dani, you and Savage can go on back." He shrugged, adding, "Keep shut about this. And thanks."

Vince promised, "I'll be talking to you, Dani."

"Sure, Vince."

Dani and Ben made their way back to the car, got in, and Ben turned the vehicle around. They noticed several men with guns among the trees, and when they had cleared the main gate, Ben exclaimed softly, "A rough deal!"

Dani had been thinking of the two mangled bodies. "That was Dominic's son?"

"Yeah. The old man's sick, so they say. Phil's been running the show for the last year or so. From what I hear, he was even meaner and tougher than old Dom."

"I feel sorry for him."

"Well, he was a pretty rough one," Ben slowly justified his opinion. "I guess Phil pulled a few stunts like this himself. He wasn't a man who was afraid to pull a trigger."

Dani shook her head. "I guess so—but he's beyond all that now. And his wife—she looked so small!"

Ben said no more, but drove silently until he pulled up in front of Dani's apartment. He got out, and before she went in, he put out a hand and held her. He meant to say something, she saw, but seemed not to find the words. "Well, Boss, I'll see you tomorrow." Then he shook his head, and his eyes were sad. "She *was* a little thing, wasn't she?" He turned abruptly and got into the car.

Dani watched him drive away, shook her head, and went inside. She showered, put on a nightgown, then almost fell into bed. But exhausted as she was, for a long time she lay awake, the image of the bloodstained bodies rising in her mind. Finally as she drifted off to sleep, her last thought was of Savage saying, *"She was a little thing, wasn't she?"*

2
Family Honor

The powerful hindquarters of the rust-colored quarter horse exploded as he came out of a turn around the barrel. Dani had leaned into the turn, throwing her weight to the left, and as Biscuit shot away toward another barrel, she bent forward, moving her body in perfect time to the rhythm of his stride. She had learned long ago that poor coordination by a barrel-rider can slow her horse down by seconds, and championships were often decided by fractions of a second.

She made no attempt to guide Biscuit as he approached the barrel; the sturdy animal knew the game as well as she. The constant challenge of the sport was a matter of inches and seconds. Getting around the barrel quickly meant making as tight a circle as possible, the ideal turn being one in which the barrel was actually *touched* by the rider or the horse—but not knocked down. Turn too tightly, and the barrel went down—which meant no win. Stay too distant, and the seconds rolled away.

Once again Dani leaned far over Biscuit's heaving sides, and this time her foot touched the lightweight plastic barrel. She felt the slight contact, cried, "Blast!" under her breath, but did not even look. After the turn, she pulled the horse up, glanced back, and saw the barrel rolling slowly along the dry grass. "Oh, rats!" she snapped in disgust. The horse tossed his head, and she leaned forward and patted his neck. "My fault, Biscuit," she admitted affectionately. "I know you're disgusted with me, but I'm out of practice."

She had always talked aloud to the quarter horse, ever since her father had bought him for her, six years earlier. The horse had become sensitive to her moods and could tell when she was not herself. Now as she walked him slowly across the open field, toward the pasture fence, he gave a slight buck that almost unseated her, and she laughed in delight. "You son of a gun! Almost got me that time, didn't you?"

The late afternoon air was sharp and a little chilly, and as she slipped from the saddle and walked Biscuit to the stable, she thought suddenly how nice it would be not to have to go back to her problems. Being a CPA came in handy, but it also meant that she was at all times aware of the financial status of the agency. Even as she stripped off the saddle and threw it over the low wall inside the stable, the assets and liabilities seemed to run through her mind as clearly as if she were seeing them on a computer screen. She pulled the saddle blanket off, tossed it over the saddle, then picked up a worn currycomb and began combing the horse. He stood still, enjoying this part of their workout.

"I wish I didn't have any more problems than you, Biscuit," she muttered. A voice came from close behind, startling her, "I wish the same thing."

Dani turned with a rueful smile, and her father, who had come into the stable, added, "But maybe Biscuit's got problems we don't know about."

"Oh, pooh!" Dani sniffed. "All he does is eat and sleep and run around a few barrels." She felt embarrassed that her father had caught her off guard, and to cover that up, she tossed the comb on a shelf, poured a generous helping of oats into Biscuit's trough, then took her father's arm. "I want some iced tea," she told him and walked with him out of the dim light of the stable, into the sunshine.

He spoke little as they walked along, and Dani knew he was worried about the agency. He had been one of the most active men she had ever known before a heart attack had slowed him down, and she knew it grated on him to have to sit on the sidelines. He had been forced to ask her to leave seminary and take over the agency, but after nearly a year, he still could do no more than go to the office a few times a week.

Dani and her father were very close. Now as they approached the house, he murmured, "You're worried about money."

"Well—a little, I guess," she conceded. "But if we nail down the Consolidated account, we'll be in good shape." She glanced up at him, noting his compressed lips. "Now don't you start worrying about it," she scolded, pressing his arm. "That's what you pay *me* for."

"I wish I could do more," her father confessed quietly. From him, that brief statement was the equivalent of a scream of grief from most men, for he was not one to cry about his problems. He shook his shoulders and grinned ruefully. "You've done a great job, Daughter."

She shrugged off the compliment, saying only, "It's

been hard, Dad, but you're much better. Just a little more rest and you'll be roaring back again. And you know it's been good for Allison and Robert to have you home."

"I suppose. But it's a shame a man has to get laid flat on his back before he gives his kids the attention they deserve. I can't believe Allison is sixteen and Rob is seventeen. It's a rough world for youngsters, Dani. I don't seem to know what they're thinking."

"You don't know what I'm thinking, either." Dani smiled. "Maybe I'm having fantasies of an orgy on a desert island with a handsome movie star."

He laughed at the idea, then gave her a quick hug. "No, that would be too silly for you, Dani. You've always been the sensible one." Then he added, "You've got a visitor."

"Here? Who is it?"

"Vince Canelli. You told me about him. He's a pretty hard one, isn't he?"

"Yes, he is. I wonder what he wants?"

"Maybe he's come courting."

Dani smiled at him, but shook her head. "Not Vince, Dad. He'd run like a rabbit if a woman mentioned marriage to him. Vince is of the old school. To him a woman is sort of like—a car. A man needs one, so he goes out and finds one that looks good and performs well. Then he buys it and shows it off to his friends."

"And trades her off for a new model when he gets bored?"

"Something like that."

They reached the house, and Dani confided, "I think it's got something to do with the murder of Phil Lanza, Dad."

"Really? Well, Vince is in the den. I'll be in the study."

Dani walked down the hall, turned into the large, book-lined den, and found Vince waiting. He turned as she entered, coming at once to greet her with a quick kiss on the cheek. "Always wanted to do that!" He grinned. "Never kissed a preacher before."

"Hello, Vince." Dani smiled. "I must smell horsy. I've been riding."

He shook his heavy head. "You smell good to me." A thought struck him, and his white teeth flashed in a smile. "You smell better than you did in that crummy silo!"

"I suppose so," Dani admitted. Then she asked curiously, "Do you think about that time much, Vince?"

"Yeah, I do." He nodded. He was a thick, muscular man with a great deal of animal magnetism beneath his flashy good looks. "I nearly bought it that time. Guy can't always walk away from a thing like that." He hesitated, then said with a trace of embarrassment, "I might as well tell you, Dani—I'm going to see a shrink. Got to having real bad dreams about that time."

"Is he helping you any?"

"Well—I don't know about that, but *he's* making a bundle!" Vince said sourly. "I guess he's okay." He shook his heavy shoulders and changed the subject quickly. "You're looking real good, Doll." Dani was wearing an old pair of snugly fitting gray jodphurs and a pair of worn black riding boots. Her only jewelry was a fine amethyst ring on her right hand. The ride had put color into her face, and her oddly colored eyes—greenish-gray—were beautiful.

"You didn't come to tell me how good I look in my grubs." Dani laughed. Then she sobered, asking, "Is it about the killings?"

Vince hesitated, then nodded. "Never could fool you, could I?"

"Who did it, Vince?"

"The cops are working on it—but they know as well as we do it was a Martino job. Not Joe Martino. Probably Johnny Ring. He'd be nervy enough for it. The old man, Sal, he was smart enough to see that nobody wins in a shoot-out like him and Dom had a few years ago. But now Joe and Ring want it all." Anger smoldered in Canelli's dark eyes, and he bit his words off, "He'll go down for this little trick!"

Dani considered Vince carefully. "Why did you come, Vince?"

"Well—Mr. Lanza wants to talk to you."

"Me? What about?"

"Have to let him tell you himself, Doll."

"When, Vince? And where? At my office?"

"Like to take you to see him now," Vince interjected. "I can bring you back after you talk to him."

Dani stood there, wondering what Dominic Lanza would possibly want with her. She imagined him as a legendary Mafia type with a bloody past. Yet curiosity moved her to say, "All right, Vince. Can't hurt to hear what he has to say. Let me get cleaned up."

"Sure, Doll," Vince agreed quickly, obviously relieved. "Take your time. I'll wait right here."

Dani suddenly turned and walked to one of the bookshelves. Taking out a book, she handed it to Canelli. "Here, Vince, you can read this while I'm cleaning up."

Canelli looked down at the book, reading the title aloud: "The Holy Bible—New International Version." He grinned. "You're a piece of work, Doll—never give up trying to convert a guy, do you?"

Dani shook her head. "Start on page one, Vince. It'll do

you good." She left the room. Canelli stared after her with reluctant admiration. He threw himself in a chair, opened the Bible and read aloud, "In the beginning God created the heavens and the earth. . . ."

Dusk was closing in on Twelve Oaks, the fortresslike home of the Lanza family, as Vince pulled up to the ornamental iron gate. A smallish man dressed in a pair of white slacks and a wildly decorated Hawaiian shirt opened one of the massive gates and came to stand beside the car. He bent down, peered in, and nodded. "Okay, Vince." He stepped inside to open both gates, and Vince moved the Lincoln inside. The gates closed with a resounding clang.

As Vince drove slowly along the winding road, Dani saw men with rifles watching them carefully. "Security is pretty tight."

"Yeah. Too bad Phil and Lorraine had to get wasted to wake them up." Vince had been garrulous enough on the way, in his usual bluff fashion, but as he pulled into the circular driveway in front of the big house, he seemed nervous. Jumping out of the car, he ran around to the other side and opened the door for Dani. As he walked her up the steps, he quickly warned her, "Don't let Mr. Lanza bother you, Doll. He's an old man—and he's sick. And he's just lost his favorite son."

Dani stepped inside the door, which was opened by a tall, thin man with a pair of steady gray eyes and a shock of white hair. He was wearing a dark suit and a burgundy tie. "Miss Ross?" he asked in a low voice.

"Yeah," Vince said. "This is Thomas Rossi, Dani. He's been with Mr. Lanza longer than anyone." He glanced at Rossi apprehensively. "He ready to see her?"

"Yes. Come with me, Miss Ross."

Dani turned to follow Rossi. Vince explained, "I'll be in the family room when you're finished, Dani."

Dani couldn't repress the memory of her last visit to the Lanza house. To shake it off, she spoke comfortingly, "I know Mr. Lanza must be grieved over his loss."

The tall man nodded. "Yes. I've been with him for forty years, but I've never seen him like this." As they reached the end of a long hall, he added, "He's not young anymore—and he'd pinned all his hopes on Phil." Pausing before a huge walnut door, he knocked gently, then apparently heard something, for he nodded. "Go right in, Miss Ross."

"Thank you, Thomas." Dani opened the door, then stepped inside. It was an enormous room, larger than many apartments. Against one wall stood a long, blue couch, flanked by matching chairs and low teak tables. The east wall was a picture gallery with fine oil paintings, each carefully illuminated by a brass light. One of them, Dani noted, was a Matisse.

It probably cost more than I'll make in ten years, she decided.

Walnut bookshelves filled the opposite wall, and far to her right a massive rosewood desk gleamed richly. Beside it a complete computer system rested on a walnut-and-black-leather table that curved gracefully into a U-shape. Everything was rich and tasteful and expensive.

The man who had risen from a tawny leather chair and stood waiting for her was not nearly so impressive as the room. Dani had seen several old photos of Dominic Lanza, which had portrayed a dynamic personality. Now she saw that Lanza had lost most of the fire and drive that had enabled him to survive the savage crime wars. He was a small man, not more than eight inches over five feet, and he had the thinness of an invalid. His hair was pure white and his cheeks were sunk in. Only his dark eyes had any life, and they stared at her out of his skull-like face with a glowing interest.

"Miss Ross," he addressed her in a high-pitched voice. "Thank you so much for coming to see me." He motioned to a chair at his right. "Please sit down. Will you take something to drink—some wine, perhaps?"

"Nothing for me, Mr. Lanza," Dani said. She sat down and began at once, "I never know what to say at times like these—but I'm so very sorry for your loss."

Lanza had seated himself, and now he nodded slowly. "Thank you. That's the way, isn't it? When death takes one of us, what is there to say, after all?" He lifted the crystal goblet on the table beside him, took a sip of an amber liquid, then put it down carefully. He wore a blue silk dressing gown, and on his left hand an enormous diamond blinked, reflecting the many-faceted glow of the large chandelier overhead.

He seemed to have forgotten her. Finally he lifted his eyes to Dani's. "You are wondering why I asked Vince to bring you here, of course."

She only nodded.

His thin lips curved into a brief smile. "You do not talk much, Miss Ross. That is a quality I admire—and one I rarely find in people." He studied her with the patience that old men sometimes have and seemed satisfied.

"Vince has been trying to persuade me to hire you. I understand that you are a private investigator. Would you work for me?"

Dani asked carefully, "Doing what, Mr. Lanza?"

Her answer pleased Lanza. "Ah—you are cautious! I like that very much." He stirred in his chair, placed his hands on his lap, then confided slowly, "I built this place for security, Miss Ross, many years ago. But it was not secure enough. My son and his wife are dead." He spoke in a flat voice, but a flicker of pain reached his dark eyes as he mentioned his loss.

"You know as well as I that if an assassin wants to kill badly enough, there's no way to prevent him," Dani excused him.

"Yes, but there are *measures* that a man can take. I am an old man now, and I blame myself that I didn't take those measures. My son would be alive if I had."

"You can't carry the burden of a guilt like that, Mr. Lanza. There would always be *something* more that one could do to improve security. The security here is excellent."

"*Excellent* is not enough!" Lanza snapped, and anger lit a sudden fire in his eyes. "I have children and grandchildren in this place. They must be protected!"

Dani commented, "Well, you have money enough to hire a small army."

"Ah, that is what I would like to do!" Lanza nodded. "But my son Frank, he says the children must not grow up with armed men right beside them all the time. Perhaps he is right." He gave her a probing look, adding, "Vince has talked to me. He thinks you can help."

"I don't know why he thinks that." Dani shrugged. "You have plenty of guards. I'd just be one more."

"They are stupid!" the old man exclaimed. "Not a mind in the bunch—except for Faye and Vince. But Vince has told me about his experience with you."

"You mean about the Maxwell Stone affair?"

"Yes. He says everyone would have died in that place if it had not been for you."

"That's not true. Ben Savage got us out of there."

"And he works for you, doesn't he? Vince says the two of you are what I need."

"Ben could help you, but what could I do?"

Lanza hesitated, then leaned forward. "You could find out who in my organization set up Phil and Lorraine."

Dani stared at him. "A traitor?"

"That has to be it." Lanza nodded. "You know what's happening. Sal Martino and I circled each other for years, looking for a way to get control of this city. But both of us were smart enough to know that the other was too strong. When Sal died, his second in command, Johnny Ring, all but took over. Joe Martino hasn't even tried to control Ring. Johnny's as ruthless a man as I have ever met, and he's gotten to somebody in my organization. That's the only way anyone could have gotten to Phil."

Dani studied Lanza thoughtfully. This was not at all what she had expected, and she shook her head. "I don't think I could help much, Mr. Lanza."

"Is that what you *really* think—or is it that you won't work for a man like me?" Lanza stared at her. "Vince has told me that you have very high moral standards. Maybe you wouldn't work for a man who's done what I've done."

Dani flushed slightly, for the thought had crossed her mind. She straightened her back and looked Lanza full in the face. "I think your way of life is terrible—but that's not why I won't work for you."

"Is it money?" he asked. "I have plenty of that."

She laughed shortly. "No, I need the work—but honestly, Mr. Lanza, I'm not much good with a gun."

Lanza nodded. "We have plenty of people who can shoot guns." He seemed to think over what she had said, then got to his feet. Going over to the window, he peered into the darkness, then came back and stood over her. "Vincent has an idea. I thought little of it at first, but he's a persistent man—and very shrewd."

"What sort of idea?"

"That you come to work here not so much as a body-guard as a keeper for my grandchildren. What's the word? For a woman who keeps children . . . ?"

"A nanny?" Dani smiled.

"Ah! That's it! Vince tells me you're highly educated. We can't risk sending the children to school. Too easy for Ring to get at them. So they'll have to have tutors. You can do that, can't you? You've been to college, Vince says."

Dani shook her head doubtfully. "I'm not a teacher. It's not a matter of being smart, Mr. Lanza. Those who teach children have to have a very special sort of patience."

Then Dominic Lanza did smile, and his eyes lit up. "You'll need patience with my grandchildren, Miss Ross!" he agreed. Sobering, he added, "I want you to come here as a—a nanny. I want you here—in this house—and I want your man Savage as well. He can serve as a physical-education teacher—something like that."

Indecision moved Dani, and Lanza said impulsively, "Come with me." Dani got to her feet and followed him to his desk. He picked up a framed picture and handed it to her. "See—these are my grandchildren. I want them to live. Will you help me, Miss Ross?"

From the stiffness in his manner and an odd expression in his dark eyes, Dani realized suddenly that Dominic Lanza was not a man who was accustomed to asking favors. Dani knew he had tasted violence and lived an abysmal life—but now he was aware that not all the money he had accumulated had been able to protect his son's life. He stood there waiting patiently as she studied the picture.

It was a family portrait. The man was a younger version of Dominic Lanza—lean with sharp features and black eyes. The woman was a pretty blond with a sweet face. There were three children. The oldest was a boy of about fifteen, with black hair and dark eyes. Beside him was a girl, perhaps twelve, with a shy expression, and finally a sturdy boy not over four or five.

"My son Frank and his family," Lanza explained. "He is the oldest now that I have lost my firstborn. His wife is named Rosemary. These are Matthew, Rachel, and Patrick." He hesitated, then nodded. "To me, family is everything. I will pay any price to keep them safe. I think you can help me to do this."

Dani looked at the picture steadily, then lifted her head. Some sort of warning seemed to rise in her mind, but at the same time she was attracted by the challenge. Finally she warned, "Mr. Lanza, I'm not sure you understand what it means to be a teacher. It's not just a matter of learning dates or how to work a math problem. Children usually pick up values from their teachers—and my values and yours are worlds apart. I'm a Christian, and I can't be anything else. It's not that I would deliberately set out to convert your grandchildren—but what I believe, I must say!"

The old man studied her thoughtfully. He seemed to be weighing her words in a set of balances. Finally he nodded. "I understand. As for me, I have no religion. Some men go through a form of religion just for appearance. I could never do such a thing. I am what I am—and if I have chosen wrongly, I will answer for it before God." He paused, and another thought came to him. "And that will not be long, Miss Ross, the doctors assure me. Whatever immortality I have will be what I leave on earth in my sons and their children."

"There's more than that to being a human being, Mr. Lanza," Dani said evenly.

Again the dark old eyes fastened on her. "That may be, but it's more than I know. The honor of the family, that is my religion. Someone has killed my son. I cannot allow the honor of my family to be stained. While that is being done, I must do all I can to protect my flesh and blood. Now, will you help me? I ask for the last time, Miss Ross."

Dani nodded slowly. "I will do what I can."

"Good! But I must ask you one more question. If a man came into this house, and you saw that he was going to shoot one of my family, could you shoot him, kill him if you had to?"

The room was very quiet. Dani could hear the gentle ticking of an antique gold clock on the mantel over the fireplace. Thoughts pulled at her, and confusion disturbed her mind. Finally she nodded slowly. "I have thought about this many times, and it is a terrible decision. God has said 'Thou shalt not kill,' but he also ordained order in this world. I believe that policemen and soldiers are not wrong when they use arms to protect the lives of citizens. So if I must use a gun to protect your family, I will do it."

Lanza's expression remained unreadable, but he finally directed, "Very well, Miss Ross. You will come to my house with Savage as soon as possible. My lawyer, Max Darrow, will draw up the contract. You may name your own fee. Now, I must ask you to excuse me."

Dani stood up to leave, but as she moved away, Lanza stopped her. "Miss Ross—"

"Yes?"

Lanza seemed to have difficulty saying what was on his mind. Finally he blurted out, "Perhaps sometimes—when you are not busy teaching the children—you might have a little time for an old man. One who has suddenly become very interested in what comes after this life."

Dani smiled and almost reached out to touch Dominic Lanza but admitted only, "Yes. I would like that very much."

She left the room and went at once to Vince. "Well, are you taking the job, Dani?" he wanted to know.

Dani nodded, then smiled wryly. "Yes, I am, Vince. It looks like Dani Ross is going to be a nanny with a thirty-eight!"

3
Shoot to Kill

Dr. Jacob Strauss reached for the heavy brass doorknob, but the door swung back suddenly, striking his outstretched fingers. He stepped back quickly, and Frank Lanza halted abruptly. "Oh, sorry, Doctor." He glanced quickly at his father, then asked, "How's he doing?"

The burly physician studied the younger Lanza, shrugged, and finally grunted, "See he takes his medicine." He left the room rapidly, throwing back over his shoulder, "Don't give him any liquor."

Frank scowled at the door, muttering, "Don't see why that man can't be made to give a civil answer!" Walking over to where his father sat in a delicate Queen Anne chair, he tried again, "What did he say, Pop?"

Dominic was buttoning up his shirt with slow care. He looked up briefly, and a touch of anger tinged his voice. "Said I was dying. Bring me some of that Scotch from the bar." He buttoned the last two buttons, then gave Frank an impatient glance. "Didn't you hear me? I said bring me a drink."

"I heard what the doctor said. No more liquor."

"Blasted old fool!" Dom snorted. He heaved himself to his feet and walked slowly across the room toward the bar. "No use having him back in this house." He pulled a bottle from the cabinet, removed the top, and poured an inch of amber fluid into a glass. "Have a drink, Frank," he ordered.

"Not now—and you don't need one either." At thirty-eight, Frank Lanza was much like what his father had been at that age—on the lean side, with black eyes that dominated a narrow face. He had straight black hair, heavy black eyebrows, and sharp features. A thin upper lip and a full lower one lay under a trim black mustache, and he had the pallor of a man who lived indoors. His voice was not loud, but edged with authority. He used it now, pointing out, "That stuff will kill you."

Dominic gave a humorless laugh. "Too late for that, I'm like an animal. They always know when they're going to die." He moved across the room and stared out the window, the blinds making a pattern of horizontal marks on his ravaged face. "Don't know why a man's got less sense than an animal. People ought to go off and die in a thicket—not be a bother to anyone."

Frank stared at the old man with sudden surprise. "Don't talk like that, Pop," he objected. "You've got a lot of living to do."

Dom spoke quietly, without turning his head. "Don't be a fool, Frank. You were raised better. Didn't I always teach you to look things in the face? Well, it's my time. Not complaining. I've had some good things—more than most men."

The younger man stood there silently. There was something in Dom Lanza that he had never seen before—a surrender of the spirit, perhaps. Dom had always been the dynamic force of the family, controlling it as a man will captain a huge ship. Never had anyone doubted who would decide matters; always the small fist of Dominic Lanza held power over his family as over his business. Now, Frank realized, that was changing. It had started the moment the shotgun blasts snuffed out the life of Phil Lanza.

"You're grieving over Phil," he observed quietly. "He was always your favorite."

There was no envy in his voice, but Dom turned to give him a sharp glance. "He was the firstborn, Frank." That meant much to the old man, and he came a step closer, adding, "Now he's gone. You're the firstborn now."

"I'm not Phil," Frank warned, shrugging slightly. "I'll do the best I can."

Dom studied him, then came closer and, almost shyly, touched Frank's arm with a withered hand. "No. But you're my son—the oldest Lanza. And I'll say what I never said before—you're smarter than Phil ever was. Not as much drive as he had, but that was good. If you had had it, the two of you would have been fighting for control. Now he's gone, and you must step into his place."

"There's Eddy," Frank pointed out carefully. "I don't think you give him enough credit. He works harder than any of us."

"Eddy is a good boy." Dom nodded, but his eyes were guarded. "But he doesn't have whatever it takes to make men obey. Phil had it, maybe more than I myself. You have more than you think—but time will tell."

Frank didn't argue, but his face showed some doubt.

"Well, we'll see. But we've got to do something with Faye."

"He's on his way up," Dom said. The old man sat down in his chair, breathing heavily. "Frank, I have two new people coming."

"Not a bad idea. Security has got to be tightened. Who are they?"

Dominic smiled slightly, "I should have talked with you about it. And I think this will be the last decision I make without checking with you. But—I was afraid."

"You were never afraid of anything in your life!"

"You think that, Son?" Dom shook his head sadly. "I'm a better actor than even I thought! But I'm afraid now—and you are afraid, too. I'm afraid for you and for all the family, especially for my grandchildren. As long as old Sal was alive, things were fairly safe. But Johnny Ring—he's a different matter."

"Faye wants to take him out."

"His stock response, but it won't work this time. Maybe later." Dom told him, "Frank, I want someone with the children night and day."

"We've argued about that already, Pop. Rosemary doesn't want hoods like Louie or Legs in the house. They're a bad influence on the kids. And I think she's right. If the pair you've hired is no better than those two, forget it."

"How about this one?" Dom picked up a manila envelope, took out two photographs, and after a glance, handed them to Frank. "Not very much like Louie, eh?"

Frank studied the photographs, then asked, "What's this, Pop—a joke?"

"That's the children's new schoolteacher, Frank—they

45

call them nannys in England. She's a private investigator—and a good one. I had her checked out. Her name's *Danielle Ross*. This is one of her operatives. Name's *Ben Savage*. He doesn't look it, but he's a hard one. He'll be our physical-education teacher and part-time chauffeur. I want her to have a room as close to the family as possible. She can take the guest room in the west wing. We never have guests anyway. Savage can sleep over the garage."

Lanza was looking at the pictures. "You've got this all figured out, haven't you, Pop?" He handed the photos back. "It's fine with me. Does the woman know enough to teach kids?"

"She's a CPA. Worked for the attorney general's office in Boston." An unexpected smile lifted the corner of his thin lips. "Oh, yes, she was studying to be a preacher of some kind before she became a private cop. Not safe to have a woman that good-looking in the house, but I don't think you'd get far with her, even if you tried."

"I'm not thinking of that!" Frank corrected him swiftly. He thought for a moment, then nodded. "I like it. There's no way to secure the outside grounds—but these two will be the line of defense in the house."

"Right! But don't let this out, Frank," Dom warned. "As far as outsiders are concerned, they're just a teacher and a health guy for the kids." A tap at the door drew his attention, and he said, "That's Faye. You'll have to sit on him, Frank. He minded Phil, but he's got the idea somewhere that he'd like to move up."

"I know." Frank nodded. "I'll keep him on a short leash. Come in, Faye," he called, raising his voice.

The door opened and a man of twenty-eight entered. He was well built, with cold blue eyes and smooth blond hair. "How you feeling, Mr. Lanza?" he asked in a low, pleasant voice.

"All right, Faye," Dom said flatly. "Did you get that new alarm system in place?" he demanded.

"Sure. It's working fine. We tested it this morning." Faye shifted his feet, then his voice rose, "Mr. Lanza, about what we were talking about yesterday—"

Dom cut him off with a slash of his thin hand. "No more of that, Faye. Not now. Frank and I have decided to ride this thing out. Ring and his bunch are sitting over there like cocked pistols—just waiting for us to make a move."

"Got to be done sooner or later," Faye argued stubbornly. He gave Frank a strange look, then added, "I ain't afraid of Ring."

"Faye, it's not a matter of being afraid," Frank interjected, his voice harsh. "It's a matter of being *smart!*"

Real anger touched Faye's eyes, but the old man diverted his attention with the words, "Frank, I wish you'd go check that new system out."

"Sure, Pop." Frank saw that his father was weary. He stepped forward and said fondly, "Drink all the liquor you want. What does that fool doctor know?"

Dom laughed at that, and Frank turned and left the room, followed closely by Faye Dietrich. As they passed through the large foyer, Frank heard voices and declared, "I'll be down in a few minutes, Faye." He didn't wait to watch the other leave, but turned and walked down a side hall then took a left through a set of double doors. Stepping into the large room that served as an informal recreation area, he found his three children wrestling over a television program.

"Hey, what's going on?" he asked, stepping into the fray. "Can't you kids agree on anything?"

Patrick Lanza, aged four, spoke up at once. "It's *my* turn to pick a program!" he announced loudly. "I wanna watch 'Sesame Street'!" Pat, as he was called, was a miniature edition of his father—black hair and sharp black eyes. He was cute, smart, spoiled, and a terror to the help.

Rachel Lanza pushed at Pat's small form. "He *picked* the last program, Daddy!" she protested. "Make him take a turn!" Rachel was small and thin, with glossy brown hair and brown eyes. She had a complexion problem that gave her an even greater emotional problem. Her self-esteem was nonexistent. She wanted to run to her father, for she idolized him—a fact he never seemed to realize.

"Pat, did you pick the last program?" Frank asked.

"Yeah, but it wasn't good—I want *another* turn!"

Matthew Lanza had his father's black hair and eyes, but at fifteen was almost as lacking in self-esteem as Rachel. He glared at Pat, of whom he was fiercely jealous. "The little pig wants his own way all the time!" he spat out.

"Don't call your brother a pig, Matthew," Lanza snapped, then shook his head. "And you, Pat, take your turn. Now, I've got something to tell you." He looked them over carefully and thought how fragile they were—it made him fragile as well, he knew, and a gust of rage rose in him as he thought how a cheap hood named Johnny Ring had shaken the stability of his family.

"You're going to have a new teacher—two of them, as a matter of fact." He had their attention then, as he had expected. "You won't be going to your school for a little while."

"Hey! No more school!" Matt exclaimed. "That's cool!"

"Just a minute, now!" Lanza lifted his hand in a gesture for quiet. "I've hired two teachers to come to the house. You'll do your schoolwork here."

"You mean—have teachers right *here?*" Rachel asked. She shook her head, "I don't want them here! Why can't we go to school?"

"You dummy!" Matthew said in a lofty tone. "It's too dangerous for us to go to school. We might get killed, like Uncle Phil and Aunt Lorraine. Everybody knows the Martino gang is—"

"Matthew!" Frank ordered. "That's enough of that!"

"Well—it's true, isn't it? All the papers say there's going to be a gang war between us and them."

Frank hesitated, then told them slowly, "It's too dangerous for you to go to school for a while. Don't ask any more questions. Now, when they get here, you'll mind them just as you would your teachers in school, you hear me?"

"Yes, sir," Matthew and Rachel agreed faintly. Pat said nothing, but a stubborn look in his black eyes boded ill for the newcomers.

"All right. We'll talk about it more at dinner tonight. Stop fighting over the television. You watch that stupid thing too much anyway. Why don't you read a book?"

He left the room, and at once Pat pounced on the TV, turning the volume up as Bert and Ernie carried on a conversation. Matthew gave it only a glance, then exclaimed, "They'd better not try to pull any stuff on me! If they work for us, we tell *them* what to do!"

"I wish we could," Rachel allowed. "I hate teachers."

"Remember how we made ol' lady Reynolds leave us alone?" Matt reminded her with a laugh. "She thought she'd tell us what to do, but we ran her out, didn't we?"

Rachel nodded slowly. "I guess so—but she was just a housekeeper. These are schoolteachers."

"They'll be wimps," Matt sneered. "Just do what I tell

you, Rachel." His face brightened. "Hey, this is going to be *great!* We'll be able to do whatever we please when we get these two jokers cut down to size!" He laughed again and assumed what he thought was a tough expression. "What a time we'll have!" he chortled.

Dani stood in front of the mirror, studying herself carefully. She was wearing a pair of fawn-colored, pleated pants with front slash pockets, a bright red pullover sweater with ribbed knit trim and a round neck, and a single-breasted, oversized wool blazer with notched lapels and front welt pockets. A gold pin flashed from the left lapel, matching the gold hoops that dangled from her ears.

Slowly she turned, lifting her arms, then gave a quick half turn that caused the coat to swing with the movement. She nodded to herself with satisfaction, and with her left hand she touched the hard surface of the .38 automatic that rested high on her waist. How to carry a concealed weapon had been a problem she had struggled with ever since making up her mind she would have to do it. She had tried carrying the gun in her coat pocket, but it had been too awkward. She had attempted to rig up a shoulder holster, but could find no way of concealing the straps. Carrying it in her purse had been a possibility, but she couldn't carry a purse twenty-four hours a day.

Finally she had come up with the idea of wearing the weapon in a holster on a thin belt beneath a loose-fitting sweater. Ben had wanted her to carry a larger caliber gun. He came in one morning and tossed a package at her, saying, "Happy birthday, Boss."

"It's not my birthday," she had told him, but opened the package all the same. Inside was a new revolver. "What's this, Ben?"

"Latest thing in women's wear," he said. "That's a thirty-eight Chief Special. Takes a longer bullet, which gives you a whale of a punch, but the cylinder holds only five slugs. It's got a three-inch barrel, and it's a lot more compact than a regular thirty-eight."

Dani held the revolver, noting, "The handle is smaller, isn't it?"

"Yeah. Lots of women on the force carry them. They're compact but will put your man down every time."

She had tried the holster in different positions, finally discovering that she could wear it flat against her back. The loose-fitting sweater covered it well, and the blazer helped. *Good thing it's winter*, she thought as she peered carefully at her side. *I'd never hide that thing with a sheer blouse and skirt in summer!*

Satisfied, she turned and walked to the door. Ben Savage was perched on Angie Park's desk, and the two of them looked up as she entered the reception room.

"My!" Angie exclaimed. "You look as if you just stepped out of the pages of *Vogue!*"

Ben stood up, gave her a critical look, then commanded, "Turn around."

Feeling rather foolish, Dani did a half turn, then made a joke out of it. Moving across the room in the exaggerated posturings of a fashion model, she drawled, "And here we have an *exquisite* combination by our favorite designer, Noel Noel the Third! Isn't it just *lovely?*"

Savage stepped up, and before she could see what he was doing, slipped his arms around her waist. She tried to pull away, but he held her fast. "And what have we here?" he demanded. "Lady, are you packing heat?"

"Let me go!" Dani protested and wrenched away as he released his grip. "I wish you'd stop *pawing* me, Ben!"

51

"Sorry, Boss." He grinned, winking at Angie. "I forgot what a touch-me-not you are. Just doing some basic research. Found out something, too. You'd better not be doing any hugging while you're wearing that automatic. I was thrilled by your desirable body—but a guy hugging you is going to feel that gun."

"Nobody's going to be hugging me," Dani snapped.

"No?" Savage asked, raising one eyebrow. "Well, let's see how quick you can get that little gem out of the holster. Not going to do any good under that coat."

Dani glared at him. With her left hand she swept the coat back; then she reached behind her with her right to pull the weapon—only to discover that it was too far back—beyond her reach. Her face reddened as she stood there with her sweater pulled up, trying to draw the gun.

"Maybe you need longer arms," Ben remarked.

Dani gave a yank at the belt, brought the holster farther around on her body, and finally pulled the automatic free. "I'll have to practice a little," she admitted.

"You had better," Ben agreed. "If you need that gun at all, you'll need to unlimber it quicker than that."

Dani ignored him. "Angie, I'll call often. You've got the number to call in case of emergency, but don't call it unless you have to. Either Ben or I will check in every day." She put the automatic back in the holster, saying, "Let's go, Ben."

They left the office, and Ben got behind the wheel of the seventy-nine Marquis he drove. "Got to make a stop on the way," he announced.

"What for?"

"Little target practice. You haven't been checked out."

He avoided the main highway and said little as they

drove. When they came to a dirt road, he turned off, drove a quarter of a mile, then pulled up and shut the engine down. "All out," he directed.

Dani got out, looking around at the line of cypress trees that dotted the beginnings of a swamp. "Pretty deserted area," he said. "I come here to meditate. Now, take a few shots at one of those trees."

Dani pulled the automatic free and held it gingerly. She had never liked guns, and wearing one under her clothing went against the grain. She felt angry that she would have to do such a thing, and it showed in her face. "I hate guns!" she announced.

"Too bad." Ben shrugged. "Goes with the job. Now, blast away at that tree—the closest one."

Dani held the gun at arm's length, shut one eye, and tried to hold steady. She pulled the trigger, but nothing happened. She stared at it.

"Got to take it off safety," Ben pointed out. He reached over and moved a small lever, then said, "Ready to fire."

She lifted the gun, pointed it in the general direction of the tree, and pulled the trigger. All she got was a slight clicking noise.

"Have to put bullets in," Ben stated without a trace of a smile. "The little round things I gave you. Did you bring them?"

Dani gritted her teeth. "In my suitcase." She turned and opened the door, then yanked the suitcase out and opened it. Fishing around, she found the box of ammunition and slammed the suitcase closed. "Here," she rapped out rebelliously.

"See if you remember how to load it," he suggested. While she struggled with the clip, he whistled a little, seeming to watch a flight of egrets as they floated over-head. "All set?" he asked pleasantly. "Kill that big cy-press."

Dani lifted the gun, pulled the trigger, and shut her eyes tight as the explosion seemed to fill her ears. The gun kicked up, and she pulled the trigger again twice, firing blindly. Cautiously she opened her eyes and saw three circles spreading in the water, none very close to the tree.

"Good thing that tree's not shooting back, Boss," Ben commented. Then he shook his head. "You've got to beat that."

"I'm no gunman!"

"You agreed to protect the family, didn't you?" he snapped at her. "You can't stop an assassin by hitting him with your purse. If you didn't intend to go through with this, you shouldn't have taken the case."

"I know I shouldn't!" Dani cried. She felt miserable and wished she'd never heard of the Lanza family. "I can't do it, Ben! Kill a human being!"

"Not much danger of that, the way you shoot," he pro-claimed in disgust. His hazel eyes were bright with anger as he directed, "Well, let's go back to the office and make the call."

"What call?" she asked, lifting her head in surprise.

"The call to Dominic Lanza, telling him we won't be there."

Dani stood still, breathing rather shallowly. She had gone over and over the thing, trying to steel herself to the idea of using a gun, but now that the time had come, she felt weak and undecided. He was watching her closely, and that helped somehow. Taking a deep breath, she nod-ded. "All right, Ben. I'll try it. Show me what to do."

His lips grew less tense, and he nodded. "All right. Just three things to learn today. We'll go out and practice every day we can. But for now, just three things. First, forget holding that gun in one hand. That looks good in the movies, but no real marksman would do it. Hold the gun in your right hand and then hold that wrist with your other hand. Like this."

She watched as he took the gun. When he handed it to her, she held it as he directed. "Now, hold it on that cypress. Take one shot." Carefully she swung the automatic into position and was amazed at how steady it remained. She squeezed the trigger, and the *splat* of the explosion caused her to bat her eyes—but she saw bark fly from the right side of the tree.

"Good!" Ben said. "We'll work on firing in a pattern soon, but lesson number two. Who are you there to protect?"

"The children."

"Right. And harm will probably come in the form of a man with a gun. When you see him, the smart thing to do would be to turn your body sideways. You'd make much less of a target. But don't do that, Boss. Put yourself *in front of the children*, if you can. And stand facing him fully. Do you know why you have to stand like that?"

Dani nodded slowly. "So that if he fires, he'll hit me instead of one of the children."

"You've got it." Ben nodded. "This is the way—" He took his own gun from a shoulder holster so rapidly it seemed to Dani to *appear*, then he turned to face the tree. "That tree has a gun. It's trying to kill you." He leaped suddenly in front of her, turning his body to face the tree, and the air was rocked with what seemed to be one continuous explosion. She kept her eyes open and saw the bark flying from the tree, torn by the heavy slugs that ripped into it.

Then it was quiet, very quiet. He lowered the gun and stared at the tree, saying nothing. Dani felt almost afraid of him then. She knew he had led a violent life, in the Marine Corps and as a policeman, but she had never seen the violence explode—except once. She thought about the time the two of them had been trapped on top of the silo where they had been held prisoner by Stone. Reminded of his fight to the death with one of their captors, she wavered. "Ben, I—I'm not sure I can do it."

He turned to her, and his voice was gentle. "You can learn to shoot, Dani. I can teach you that. Remember I said three things. But one thing I can't teach you."

"What's that?" she asked.

He looked at the tree, then shrugged. "I can't teach you how to kill a man," he told her. "If the time ever comes when you have to decide—it'll be you who makes that decision. But if you shoot at all, *shoot to kill!* That's why I talked you into carrying a larger-caliber gun. That peashooter you had wouldn't put a man down, unless you got a head shot or hit the heart. This cannon I'm carrying will knock him down if it hits him in the finger!"

He swung free the cylinder of his heavy revolver, kicked the spent shells out, and put them in his pocket. Going to the car, he took his suitcase out, found a box of shells and proceeded to reload.

"Better load that clip," he ordered brusquely. "Time to get going."

Dani licked her dry lips, then took the clip from the automatic and reloaded, thumbing the safety back into position. Without a word, she got in the Marquis, and he turned the car around and drove quickly away.

Five minutes after they left, the snub nose of a curious gator surfaced, his dim brain stirred by the explosions. Finding nothing to eat, he slowly sank into the murky water, like a petrified log.

4
The Family

After the shooting lesson, Ben drove Dani to her parents' home.

Braking the Marquis, he glanced at Dani, who had not said a word since leaving the bayou. Her hands were clenched, he noted, and there was a tightness in her full lips that drew them together. "Having second thoughts, Boss?" he asked.

"What?" His question startled her, and she covered quickly. "No, of course not!"

"Oh. I thought maybe you were."

A flash of irritation ran across Dani's nerves. "Just take care of your job, Ben," she snapped. "Don't spend so much time trying to analyze me." He nodded agreeably, and that annoyed her, too, for she wanted an excuse to strike out at him. Because he was right, she *was* having second thoughts. She distrusted "hunches," considering them a device used by people who lacked the ability to think logically and clearly. There was an answer to everything, but that answer had to be found by going over the steps carefully, not by grabbing at a wild feeling.

The Lanza job should have been settled in her mind, for she had thought about it steadily since agreeing with Dominic to take it on. The money was far better than any the agency had made since she had taken over. Assuming that she and Savage would be on the case for weeks or even months, all the financial pressures that had been piling up on her would be removed.

But it didn't *feel* right—never had and didn't now. She had been troubled over carrying a gun, and the thought of shooting someone was a specter that came to her even when she lay in bed, bringing her out of a sound sleep with a wrench of shocking fear. Equally disturbing was the matter of working for a criminal figure—for that is all anyone could make of Dominic Lanza.

"Better think about this thing, Dani," Luke Sixkiller had warned when she told him she was taking the case. "These guys—they're not like people you know. You're used to folks who have some sort of moral standard. Maybe a real weak one, but at least they believe in some kind of break for other people. But you're moving in with people who don't have an ounce of pity—they live like piranhas. And no matter how you figure it, the money you get will come from drugs, prostitution—you name it."

Dani remembered he had looked at her quizzically and added, "I went down in a coal mine once. There was a woman in the group wearing a white dress. She asked our guide, 'Is there anything to keep me from wearing this white dress down into the mine?' That guide laughed at her. He said, 'No, ma'am—but there's something to keep you from wearing it back up!' So if I was you, Dani, I'd think about this real heavy before I took the plunge!"

Getting out of the car, she said, "I'll see you tomorrow. Remember, we don't know each other. Only Dominic and Frank know we're a team. Don't come running up and call me by name." She slammed the door without waiting for an answer, getting a perverse pleasure in treating Savage like a child. He would never have made such a blunder, but she was on edge.

After spending thirty minutes with her father, she got into her car and drove to the Lanza place. Pulling up to the heavy iron gate, she waited until a huge man came out of the small guardhouse, located just inside the brick wall. He bent down, peered at her, then asked suspiciously, "Yeah? What is it?"

"My name is Danielle Ross. Mr. Lanza is expecting me."

"You ain't on the list, lady."

He turned and walked away, and Dani got out of the car. "Just a minute," she cried out. "Call Mr. Lanza. He asked me to be here at noon."

The big man hesitated, then nodded. "C'mon inside. I'll check you out." He pulled the gate open, stepped back to let her pass through, then slammed it shut. The small white building was no more than ten feet square, and when Dani followed him inside, she found another man sitting in a straight chair, reading a blatantly pornographic magazine. He was very tall, with a thatch of red hair and a set of pale greenish eyes, which he fixed on her at once. "She says Mr. Lanza wants to see her, Legs," the big man explained. "But she ain't on the list. I better call."

The man called Legs stood up and tossed down the magazine. "Yeah, you do that, Louie," he agreed in an odd, husky voice. "I'll just frisk her to be sure she ain't carrying a gun."

He stepped forward, hands outstretched, but Dani quickly turned and left the house. She walked toward the gate, but it was locked. She felt his hand on her arm, pulling her around, and she called out, "Let me go!"

"Aw, come on inside, Baby! You and me got lots to talk about." He had a hold of her in his powerful grip and was dragging her toward the guardhouse when a voice hit him.

"Turn her loose, Legs." Dani tried to break away, could not evade the grip of the man. She saw with relief that Vince Canelli had appeared and was moving toward them, his eyes fixed with anger on Legs.

"Butt out, Canelli," the tall man commanded. He kept his grip on Dani, but his free hand dipped into his sport coat. "You ain't my boss."

Vince never stopped moving, but he invited the other man, "Go on, Legs. Go for that gun. I guess you've had a pretty full life."

Legs hesitated; then something ominous in Canelli caused him to drop Dani's arm abruptly. "What's eatin' you, Vince? You know we got orders to shake everybody down."

"I'd like an excuse to touch you off, Legs," Vince answered quietly. "You just get out of line with Miss Ross one more time, and as the man said, it'll make my day." He shoved Legs back, took Dani's arm, and barked, "Louie, open that gate."

Dani walked with Vince back to her car, where he offered, "Let me drive, Dani. I'll show you your parking space." She nodded and got in, and when he put the car in gear and drove past the gate, she said, "Thanks, Vince."

"Sure. I'll have a talk with those gorillas. Don't worry about it."

As the car pulled away, Legs glared after it, and Louie came to stand in the door, saying, "That Vince, he's a pretty hard cookie, Legs."

The tall man's green eyes narrowed. "He ain't as tough as a forty-four slug—and that's what he's gonna get if he pushes me again!"

Passing a grove of trees, Vince drove on a blacktop drive that led to the side of the house. He stopped in front of a long, low building, pointing out, "You'll have stall four. I'll back it in for you."

When he had backed inside, Dani got out and looked at the other cars, which included a silver Rolls Royce and a gleaming red Lamborghini. "I feel like poor Cinderella, Vince." She grinned ruefully.

He gave her his lopsided smile and took her arm firmly. "Like Hemingway said, 'Rich people are only poor people with money.' Come on. Mr. Lanza isn't feeling so good today, but Frank said to bring you straight to his office."

He led her down a sidewalk edged with contoured green hedges to a glassed-in section of the house that was broken away from the main structure. Vince knocked on the door and, when a voice called, "Come in," opened the door and stepped back. Dani entered the room, which was brilliantly lit, for there was glass on three sides, the fourth lined with books. "This is Danielle Ross, Frank. Frank Lanza, Dani." Vince spoke quickly.

"Thank you, Vince." Something in this phrase signaled to Canelli that he was no longer needed, and he turned and left the room at once. "Here, have a seat, Miss Ross," Lanza offered. "Let me fix you a drink."

Dani moved across the room to sit down in the chair indicated, but said, "Nothing for me, thank you." She saw that he expected the reply and smiled. "I don't drink, Mr. Lanza."

Something stirred in Frank Lanza's smooth expression, then a smile that made him look much younger lit his face. "That'll take a little getting used to," he finally observed. He walked over to a leather chair in front of a large rosewood desk, whirled it around, and sat down. Leaning back, he studied her as he would have examined a car he was considering buying. "My father thinks you can help us, Miss Ross. I hope so, because we need some help bad," he admitted.

"I like your father," Dani chimed in, then paused, for she had not intended to say that—in fact, she had not realized that it was true. She paused, and Lanza, noting the swift change of expression, was caught by it. She was a far more attractive woman than he had expected. His father had told him she was, but Frank thought he had meant simply that she was presentable. The young woman who sat before him was not the highly lacquered and hard-surfaced type he knew so well. Her clothing was simple, but well chosen, and the grace of her figure was apparent even in the loose fitting coat and sweater. There was a sweet curve to her cheeks that no plastic surgeon could create, and the delicate rose flush of her complexion had not come from a bottle.

Lanza suddenly shook his shoulders, gave a surprised laugh, and apologized, "Sorry, Miss Ross. I didn't mean to stare—but—well, you're not what I expected." He raised a well-cared-for hand, adding, "But that's all the better. I didn't want my kids being cared for by an amazon with biceps!"

Dani nodded, adding quickly, "I hope your father told

you that I have no qualifications for teaching, Mr. Lanza?"

"Look, let's make it *Frank* and *Dani*—except when people are around, all right? You've got a CPA, Pop says. You can handle the kids. I want you to bring in anybody you need to help. Get some high-school teacher to help with the technical stuff—history, English. . . ."

"I'll do my best."

Lanza smiled, and once again she noted how it made him seem much younger. He was an intensely attractive man, but not one who was much concerned with his looks. She saw his father's image in him, and the thought brought a serious look into her eyes. "I'm sorry about your father."

Frank dropped his head and studied his hands. Finally he looked up at her, and she saw the pain in his dark eyes. There was a hardness about him, but not concerning his father. "He's a great guy," he explained quietly. "Can't believe he's leaving us." Dani said nothing, and Lanza suddenly pulled himself out of the chair, abruptly commenting, "Well, the best thing you can do for him is to keep his grandchildren alive. I hear your man Savage is hard as nails. Are you carrying a gun?" When she nodded, he asked, "Let's see, Dani."

Standing, Dani pulled the automatic from the concealed holster, grateful that it went better than it had in her office. She held the gun loosely, and Frank admitted, "I hope you never have to use it—but I feel better about the kids already." He glanced at the gold clock on the wall. "Hey, it's time for lunch. I thought it would be good for you to meet the kids now. We can talk about procedures later, okay?"

"That will be fine." Dani nodded. "Savage will be coming in the morning. As far as possible, one of us will be close to the children at all times."

"Good! I like that very much. Now—let's go meet your pupils."

He stepped toward a heavy walnut door, opened it, then when she passed through, led her down a flagstone walk shaded by cypress trees, huge ones that towered even over the top of the house. They turned in a doorway that opened into a hall. "We have lunch in the small dining room," he told Dani as they moved down the heavily carpeted hallway. He opened a massive door, and she stepped inside the "small" dining room, which was at least fifteen feet wide and twenty feet long. Lanza closed the door and led her to a large table where four young people waited.

"All right, kids, here she is," Frank announced, leading Dani to an empty chair next to the head of the long table. He paused, then asked, "Where's your mother?"

"She's not feeling very good, Daddy." The answer came from a small girl with fine bones and large brown eyes. Her fingernails were bitten to the quick, Dani noted, and she blinked too rapidly.

Lanza interjected, "This is Miss Danielle Ross, your new teacher."

"She don't look like Mary Poppins!" Pat stared at Dani, shaking his round head with disapproval. "She don't have an umbrella!"

"That outspoken young fellow is Patrick." Lanza grinned. "I hope you can teach him a few manners. And this is Rachel—and this is my oldest, Matthew."

A young girl, perhaps eighteen, stood beside one of the tall windows. Turning, she gave Dani a quick inspection, then laughed and chimed in, "No, she's no Mary Poppins, Pat." She had an oval face with a mass of dark-brown, curly hair and a shapely body that was deliberately displayed in a tight-fitting mustard-colored top and pair of brown knit stirrup pants. "You forgot to introduce me to our nanny, Uncle Frank."

Lanza stared at her, then observed briefly, "I didn't know you intended to join the class. This is my niece, Abby, Miss Ross. She's my brother Eddy's daughter."

Dani saw the mocking light in the girl's eyes, but said only, "I'm glad to meet you, Abby. And the rest of you." All four of them were staring at her, and she laughed. "Well, Abby is right. I'm no Mary Poppins. No magic tricks—and I can't sing much."

Lanza quickly invited, "Sit down, Miss Ross. Let's eat, and then I'll leave you to get acquainted." He pulled her chair out, seated her, then sat down at the head of the table. "I guess we're ready, Mary."

A thin young woman with red hair had entered the room. She nodded and disappeared through a door, and at once another young woman, this one shapely and very pretty, entered, carrying a silver tray. As she served soup to the family, Frank performed more introductions, "This is Debbie Satterfield—And this is Mary Sinclair," he added as the older maid came back with a tray of sandwiches.

Dani spoke to them both, and they nodded as they served the food. It was an informal meal, and would have been rather stiff, but Pat kept up a steady stream of questions for the newcomer. He was a bright youngster, alert and blunt as four-year-olds usually are.

"Do you have any little boys?" he demanded at once.

Dani smiled over her soup at him. "No, I don't, Patrick."

"Why not?"

"Because I'm not married. I haven't started my family yet."

Pat considered that and asked, "How old are you?"

"Pat!" Lanza protested. "Never ask a woman that!"

"I'm twenty-six." Dani smiled.

Carefully the boy took a huge bite of his sandwich as he thought about that. Then he shook his head. "That's *old!*"

"No, it's young, Pat," Abby said. There was a calculating gleam in her almond-shaped brown eyes as she commented, "You're too young to keep this bunch in hand, Dani."

"I'm young to you, but old to Patrick," Dani noted. "What about you two?"

Matthew had been expecting something quite different. He was a shy boy, and when Dani looked at him directly with a smile, he could only shrug, saying, "I dunno. Never had a nanny before."

"Well, I've never *been* a nanny," Dani admitted, having decided to be as honest as possible with the children. "I suppose we'll have to learn how to get along. What do you think, Rachel? Are you on my side? That's asking a lot, isn't it? To side with the schoolteacher!"

Rachel had been watching Dani, fascinated by her beauty. She blurted out, "I'm not very smart."

Dani shook her head. "My first order is never say that again, Rachel. All right?" She smiled, and Rachel agreed shyly, "All right."

Dani ate little, but as the meal progressed became aware that Lanza was tense. He toyed with his food, spoke from time to time, but was obviously preoccupied—and displeased. The meal was almost over when the door opened and a woman entered. She wore a robe, and her fine blond hair had been carelessly brushed.

"This is my wife, Rosemary, Miss Ross," Frank quickly introduced her. He got up and pulled out the chair for her. "Miss Danielle Ross—the new teacher."

"Oh, I'm happy to meet you," the woman greeted Dani, seeming to notice for the first time that a stranger was there. "The children have been looking forward to having you."

"I'm sure we're going to get along," Dani replied. From the slow, overdeliberate movements and the careful pronunciation of her words, it was evident Mrs. Lanza had been drinking. She was, Dani guessed, no more than thirty, and very attractive. She had the flawless complexion found only in the south, with beautiful, cobalt-blue eyes and incredible lashes. A fine figure, as well, but she had a vague air that turned to apprehension when she looked at her husband.

Frank Lanza began to speak, as if anxious to keep his wife from doing so. "Let me say just a few things before I leave for town. Miss Ross will be obeyed at all times. I hope you all understand that. Pat, you mind Miss Ross just as you mind me or your mother. You understand that?"

"Yes, I do." Pat nodded cheerfully.

"I hope so. Matthew and Rachel—the same goes for you. You may have thought that you'd have a vacation, now that you're going to be educated at home, but it's not going to be like that. You're going to have to work hard. . . ."

Dani wished he would stop, for she could see he was building a wall between her and the children—especially in Matthew, for she saw his stubborn, rebellious look. Lanza ended, "I've got to go now. You mind your teacher and work hard." He got to his feet, looked down at his wife with a tense expression, but only commented, "I'll try to be back for dinner, Rosemary."

"All right, Frank," she answered without looking at him.

As soon as he left the room, Abby gave Dani a wicked grin. "Well, teacher, what's first on the list?"

Dani gave her a sudden direct look. The girl was an unexpected factor. Dom Lanza had not mentioned her, and Dani was uncertain of the girl's standing. She spoke firmly, "For you, Abby, nothing. I take it you're out of school?"

"They didn't tell you about me, did they? Well, I'm the black sheep, Dani." A thought tickled her, and she laughed, the bright red lips curving upward. "School? Well, I never finished high school. Expelled quite often— but never finished. I started at Tulane, but they have rules there—so I'm on some sort of probation. Grandfather told me I might learn something from you. You think you can teach me anything, Dani?"

The girl was provoking her, but Dani merely shook her head. "I'll be glad to have you help me, Abby—" Then she paused as her level gaze caught the girl's eyes. "But if you don't think you can do that, it would be better if you found something else to do."

Rebellion flared in Abby's eyes. "Grandfather said I could stay."

"As I said, Abby, if you would like to be a help, I'll be glad to have you. But your grandfather has put me in charge. I'll have to decide—not him—about what's best for all of you."

Abby flushed, rose up, and threw her napkin on the table. "I'll just go have a talk with him, then!" she pronounced and left the room, despite Rosemary's protest that her grandfather was asleep.

"Well, let's go to our classroom. We won't do any work today, but you can show me what you've learned. Would you like to go with us, Mrs. Lanza?" Dani invited.

Rosemary was startled. It was as though she was not accustomed to being consulted. A nervous smile touched her lips, and she replied, "Why—yes, I would. If I won't be in the way . . . ?"

"Of course not!" Dani got up.

Patrick announced, "I'll show you the work room. I've got my own desk, Ross."

"*Miss* Ross, Pat!" Rosemary corrected. "It is a nice room, Miss Ross," she said. "Come along and we'll show you." She let the children get out of the room, then added, "Abby—she's been having a difficult time. I wish she'd try to do better."

"I think we'll get along, Mrs. Lanza," Dani comforted her. She could smell the whiskey, which Rosemary had tried to cover up with breath mints. "You and I will have to work together," she suggested. "I'll do what I can for Abby—but Mr. Lanza is more concerned for your children. You'll help me, won't you?"

Rosemary Lanza didn't answer. Dani glanced at her and saw a tear running down her satin cheek. Dani looked away and observed cheerily, "Well, now, we've got three children, but you and I can handle the job, I think."

A large room in the east wing had been hastily converted to a makeshift classroom. Dani noted that it was a cheerful place with four desks and several bookcases.

Glancing around, she said, "This will be fine, won't it now?"

"We've all got new notebooks, Miss Ross," Rachel mentioned shyly. She added quickly, "I—I don't do math too well, but Matthew does."

"But she paints good!" Pat barged in. "Show her your pictures, Rachel!"

Dani discovered that the girl *did* paint surprisingly well and took great pains to praise the work—causing a smile to appear on Rachel's face. After an hour spent going over what they had done, Dani suggested, "It's too late to start any serious work today—what if I read you a story?"

"Yea!" Pat crowed, and both Matthew and Rachel looked relieved.

"You all sit down, we'll read as much as we can." They all settled down on the easy chairs in the room—even Rosemary. Dani began, "This book is called, *The Lion, the Witch, and the Wardrobe.* It was written by an Englishman named C. S. Lewis—and it's one of my favorite books. . . ."

5
Happy Birthday, Eddy!

A pale ray of sunshine struck Abby's eyes, and when she moved her head suddenly to avoid it, a pure sliver of pain ran through her head. It was like having a white-hot ice pick driven from temple to temple; pain so exquisite she cursed and lay as still as possible until the pain subsided. Carefully she opened her eyes and stared up at the ceiling. The memory of her conversation with her grandfather came back, and her lips drew together rebelliously. Moving slowly, she sat up in the rumpled bed, took a deep breath, then stood up. Her mouth was dry as dust, and she went to the bathroom for a drink. After drinking three glassfuls, she stared at herself in the mirror, noting the bleary eyes and drawn expression, then stripped off her nightgown and took a hot shower.

As the hot water trickled down her body, she thought with disgust of the scene with her grandfather. She had stormed into his room, demanding that she be allowed to take advantage of the new teacher. Dominic had turned his dark eyes on her with an expression that had silenced her. "You will do nothing to interfere with Miss Ross, Abby. Is that clear?" She had never been on the receiving end of the old man's stern anger, and the sting of it had driven her to drinking from a bottle she had stolen from the liquor cabinet.

After drying off with a huge, fluffy towel, she moved to a chest of drawers and pulled a new exercise outfit from the top drawer. Slipping into it, she posed before the large mirror on the wall, critically examining herself. The lavender tank top had rose insets and green piping. Capri-length stretch tights completed the outfit, both parts made of expensive Lycra jersey. It was possible to exercise in such an outfit, but it had been custom-made, in the most provocative mode, especially for Abby. Only a woman who was proud of her body and wished to call attention to it would dare wear such a thing.

Slipping into a pair of white Reeboks and a fleece jacket, she left her room and went downstairs. Voices from the large room in the east wing came to her, and she opened the door a crack, just enough to see the Ross woman and the three children in one corner at a large table. She closed the door, still sullen over her failure to get her own way, then left the house by means of an outside door in the family room.

A chilly wind touched her, and she fleetingly thought of going back inside. Instead, passing through the huge patio that lay directly behind the house, she took a wide concrete walk that passed between two walls of tall green shrubbery. Emerging into an open area, she glanced at the large geodesic dome that housed the swimming pool and turned to the right into the gymnasium, a white stucco building flanked on one end by a series of four tennis courts and on the other by a small driving range. In the other direction, just inside the eight-foot brick wall that held the house and other structures, lay a white stable with a shake roof.

An asphalt running track, six feet wide, wound around the dome and the other structures. It measured one eighth of a mile, and Abby started off at a slow jog. After one lap she stepped up the pace and was pleased with the feel of the cool air and the cold brilliance of the sun. By the time she had made ten laps, she had worked up a sweat and felt good, the hangover gone. She stopped at twenty laps, turning off the track onto the walk that led to the door of the gym, breathing a little faster than usual. She was a sleek thing; her excesses had not yet taken their toll.

The gym was small, no more than thirty by forty, but was packed with expensive equipment. Phil Lanza had been a health freak, sparing no expense on the place, but had rarely been able to draw the rest of the family into exercise. Abby used it most frequently, more from boredom than any other reason, while the kids sometimes came because it was fun to play on the equipment.

Abby passed through the door then paused abruptly, for there was a man there—a new man she'd never seen before. The security on the property was so tight that any stranger was unusual—and this one particularly so. The visitor springing up and down easily on the trampoline was male, young, strong, and not ugly. Anyone meeting these criteria automatically became a target for Abby Lanza—and the last was not really important. She moved into the building quietly, coming to stand in the midst of some Nautilus equipment. From there she saw that the man was not one of the regular staff. He was in his mid-twenties, no more, and was exceptionally built. He wore a pair of worn denim shorts, a pair of white gym shoes, and a thin white T-shirt that revealed the swelling chest and the fine definition of muscles in his back. There was not an ounce of surplus flesh on him, Abby noted. The ribbed stomach swept up into a set of swelling chest muscles of the sort one sees only in champion swimmers or acrobats.

And he was an athlete, not just a pumper of iron. As he let the round bed of the trampoline toss him upward, there was a perfect balance in his body. No swinging the arms to keep upright. No fighting gravity with the legs. Just a smooth, upward ascent—a pause at the apex—a sudden drop into the canvas—then like a coiled spring, a rise that somehow seemed to be easier than the flight of a bird.

Suddenly Abby saw him go into a crouch, and getting extra momentum, shoot upward; but this time he arched his back, did a perfect swan, and turned gracefully for the return. It was a beautiful movement and, she realized from her own attempts on the trampoline, one that had taken thousands of hours to perfect. On the next ascent, he doubled his trim body into a ball, spun like a top through three revolutions, uncoiling barely in time to land on his feet, then sailed upward.

For five minutes Abby watched as he went through a workout of turns and somersaults, never missing and always landing in exactly the right position. Finally, he came to a stop, did a handstand on the side of the trampoline, then flipped over in a smooth somersault to land on his feet. He picked up a towel from the floor, wiped his face, and turned toward the parallel bars, whistling a little. He had a pleased look on his face, and then he saw Abby, and at once his eyes grew alert.

"Hello," Abby greeted him and came to stand in front of him. "Didn't mean to interrupt your workout."

In one smooth glance he took in the sexy outfit, the bold makeup, and the saucy manner. "That trampoline's a good piece of equipment."

"You've used one before. I'm Abby Lanza." She was aware of his glance and enjoyed it. "You're new, aren't you?"

"Yes. I'm the new physical-education instructor—Ben Savage."

Abby had been expecting a forty-year-old ex-football player, and she smiled, her full lips curving upward at the corners. "Hey, that's great! Put me on your list, will you, Ben? I'd love to get into shape." She waited for him to run his eyes down her figure, then to respond in kind to her remark, but he merely nodded.

"Sure. That's what I'm here for, Miss Lanza."

"Call me Abby," she invited, studying his face. He reminded her a little of a younger version of some movie star—one who always played tough-guy roles. Some quality about Savage excited Abby; she felt that he could be *dangerous* somehow.

"Could you begin now? I've tried that trampoline, but it's hard," Abby complained. "Just a few pointers would get me started."

"Sure." He tossed the towel on the floor and turned to the trampoline. "Hop up, and we'll see how it goes." He watched while she got into position, then with a simple move, leaped up and stood balanced on the outer rim. "Just start bouncing. Nothing fancy."

As the girl began bouncing up and down, Ben ran over the information he'd gotten on her from Dani: *Abby Lanza, age seventeen. Only daughter of Edward and Irene—that's Dominic's youngest son. Abby started going wild when she was thirteen and hasn't stopped yet. Thrown out of school so often the officials finally asked the family to take her out. Tried a semester at Tulane—same thing. No, worse, because she was in the dorm with no one to watch her at all. Finally expelled for academic reasons—which wasn't the case. She was corrupting some of the students and headed for a crash. A real sexpot, Ben, so watch your step!*

"You're doing fine, Miss Lanza," Ben commented. "Good balance you've got there." The girl was, he realized, dressed to tantalize, and she was a tempting sight in the revealing costume. She knew exactly how to use her body to attract men.

Finally she came to a stop, turned her eyes on him, and challenged him, "Come on, Ben, show me something harder. How about a somersault?"

"Just try a few sit-downs." He nodded. "Then a lay-out. Go down flat on your back, let the power of the net do the work. Try to come up smoothly into a standing position."

She had done some of that and soon was ready for something more difficult. "You did *three* somersaults, Ben," she pouted. "I can do *one!*"

"There's a few people stuck in wheelchairs for life because they missed a somersault on one of these things. If you catch this rim on the back of your neck, no more dancing for you. Look, just do some more falls. Next time we'll do something harder."

"Oh, all right!" she allowed and began jumping again. But she drove herself as high as she could—so high that Ben said sharply, "Not so high!"

Abby, by accident or by design, seemed to lose herself

at the apex of a jump. She screamed and threw her arms wildly to the side. Savage saw her headed for the side of the circle and leaped to catch her as she came down. Her weight caught him off balance, but he managed to pull her to the center, both of them falling. They took a wild bound, turned once, and he came down on top of her.

"You all right?" he asked quickly.

Abby reached up and pulled him down. Her eyes were half closed and her grip on his head was firm. "Yes—I'm just fine, Ben!"

Savage was awkwardly placed, lying half across her body, where he had fallen at right angles. He was pressing against the soft curves of her body, and her hands were locked behind his head. She smiled slightly, and there was nothing childish about the expression in her eyes at that moment.

Despite the sudden impulse to take the kiss she offered, his next impulse was to get away. A warning came to him in the form of a question, *What will she do if I brush her off?* She was holding his head so firmly that he could not shove her off without being obvious. For the moment he simply froze, his face not six inches from Abby's.

"You're not bashful, are you, Ben?" Abby murmured and increased the pressure on his neck.

What might have happened, Savage never knew, but suddenly a sound came from the direction of the door. Abby heard it as well and turned her head to see the new nanny and all three of her charges standing not twelve feet away, staring at them. She released her grip on Ben's neck, and at once he came to his feet. He offered her his hand, but she ignored it, descending to the floor and snatching up her jacket.

"I hope we're not interrupting anything," Dani stated innocently. "We came to get our exercise program from the new instructor."

Abby glared at her as angry words reached her lips, but there was no sign of mockery on the older woman's face. "I was just leaving!" Abby snapped and turned to walk away.

"Perhaps you can introduce us to our physical-education instructor before you leave, Abby?"

Abby bit off the words, "This is Ben Savage." Then she walked out of the gym with her back straight.

Dani said, "Mr. Savage? I'm Miss Ross. And these are Patrick, Rachel, and Matthew. Children, would you like to welcome Mr. Savage?" Her voice was sweet, but a steely glint in her eye warned Ben that sooner or later he would hear more of the incident.

He was not wrong, for later that day he met Dani in the room where she taught. Ben had sat down at one of the desks while she finished her final instructions to the children. He was looking down at a piece of paper with something written on it, and as she came to stand in front of him, he questioned, "Who wrote this? It's pretty good, isn't it?"

Dani ignored the paper, which contained an exceptional poem written by Rachel. There was an ominous rigidity in her back, and after carefully shutting the schoolroom doors, she clipped her words off sharply, "All right, Ben, what were you doing with that girl?"

Savage looked up, and taking in the suppressed anger in her face, asked, "Don't suppose you'd believe she got something in her eye, and I was trying to get it out?"

"I'm not kidding, Ben. This is serious."

"You want the truth?"

"I'm going to have it!"

"Well, here it is. The girl is man crazy. She'll make a play for anything in pants."

"So she threw herself down and pulled you down on top of her and was forcing you to make love to her when we so inconveniently happened by. Is that it?"

"Well, I did make a mess of it," Ben confessed ruefully. "I knew she'd make a play, but I didn't think it would be so soon." He looked at Dani and admitted, "All right, I didn't handle it well. I'm sorry, what else can I say?"

Dani was angry, but forced herself to say only, "You'll have to be more careful in the future. That's all we need, you getting mixed up with a member of the Lanza family."

"I'll watch it." Ben stood up and wondered, "What do you think? Are we going to do any good for the old man?"

"I don't know. But sooner or later Johnny Ring is going to make another try. From what I hear, he's completely ruthless."

"So they say. You think there's some kind of leak? Maybe Ring's bought off somebody?"

"I don't know, but we can't discount it. So keep your eyes open. And be careful."

His eyes opened wider and he warned, "You, too, Boss. If Ring's goons start slinging lead, you're in a good position to take some of it. This thing pays good—but let's be sure we don't become casualties."

The following week, Mardi Gras possessed New Orleans—a demented time, when responsible men and women threw off all semblance of decorum. A vacation from reality—and from morality.

But Mardi Gras did not come to Twelve Oaks. The drawbridge did not lower, and the fortress created by Dominic Lanza kept close watch. Some of the hired help took time off to join in the madness, but by executive order, none of the family went to observe the sickness.

"It would be too dangerous," Frank stated when the children begged to go. "We'll make it up to you. Maybe a trip down to Palm Beach."

Such a promise never brought balm to a youngster, and Dani had to put up with sullen, rebellious behavior from Matthew, though not from Rachel. She had made a separate peace with Rachel and Pat. The girl was so starved for attention that anyone could have won her. It had not taken two days for Dani to discover that a little attention from her father would have given Rachel the confidence she needed. As for Pat, he was such a cheerful little rebel! But it was not a surly rebellion; it was simply the result of a determined spirit, which would, if properly channeled, make him into a man of firm resolution. This bothered Dani, for Pat was like his grandfather, whom that same independent spirit had led into a life-style that was now in danger of collapsing under its own weight.

But Matthew hid behind a wall ten miles high and almost as thick. He challenged Dani's authority with a dogged persistence, and it was almost impossible for her to show the love she was convinced he needed. Matthew's need for his father was even greater than Rachel's, Dani realized. But what could she do with her knowledge? Instinctively she knew that to go to Frank Lanza with the accusation that he neglected his children would be disastrous. It was not that he didn't have affection for them, for he did. He was able to show this more to Pat than to the others, perhaps because of the child's open nature. Had Frank become so bitter in his marital relationship that he identified the children with Rosemary? Or maybe, she thought, Rachel and Matthew were complicated, with complex problems, while Frank had learned to treat problems head-on. But you could not attack the sensitive areas in Rachel or in Matthew as you would a problem in business.

In any case, Dani soon was caught up in the Lanza family problems. Against her will she was drawn in, as a swimmer is drawn into a whirlpool. And who was to blame? Was it Rosemary's fault? Her drinking disgusted Frank, and the children were ashamed of her, though they tried not to show it. But soon Dani decided that the drinking was not natural to Rosemary. She had discovered this when Rosemary had come, as she often did, to observe as Dani taught the two older children some basic math. Pat had crawled up in his mother's lap. He did not understand, had not learned, that his mother was weak, so he treated her in a greedy manner, claiming her love—which she poured out on him.

After Rachel and Matthew left, Rosemary sat there holding Pat, and the two women talked for a long time. Rosemary, so silent when others were around, seemed to forget that she was talking to one of the hired help. In between all the unimportant and mundane things she said, Dani picked up something.

Rosemary had been talking about her youth and let fall: "I was taught to do what was right. But when I married Frank, all I had been taught I had to throw away. My mother had tried to tell me that the Lanzas were not for me, that they were in criminal activities, but I was so in love with Frank, I wouldn't listen." Rosemary sat there stroking Pat's hair and added, as if in a dream, "I've been afraid since the day I came to this house as a bride. I'm always afraid, Dani. And I still feel so—so *shamed* by the way we make our money!"

Dani said nothing, but from that moment, she had known that Rosemary Lanza's drinking was her only way to escape the shame and fear that must have made her life a hell. But how could she tell Frank Lanza that?

She talked little about these things with anyone, not even speaking of them to Ben. They spent much effort on security, taking such precautions as were possible. But they both felt edgy, as if they could hear the almost inaudible sound of distant thunder—the warning of a coming storm that would tear down the treetops.

Eddy and Irene Lanza had been to the West Coast on business, and they came back the day before Eddy's birthday.

"We'll have a party," Dominic had announced at dinner on Monday. He felt better, and the color had come into his pale cheeks. "A birthday party for Eddy. Take care of it, Frank."

Tuesday, the house was filled with activity. When she came down for breakfast, Frank rose to greet Dani. "I have someone for you to meet." He smiled. He turned to the couple at the table, saying, "This is my brother Eddy and his wife, Irene. And this is Dani Ross."

Eddy Lanza got to his feet and stepped forward to meet Dani. "Pleased to meet you, Dani," he greeted her. He was only two years younger than Frank, but he looked older. He was very thin, and his brown hair was receding. Dani didn't look at his foot, for she knew he felt terribly sensitive about the built-up shoe a bout with polio had forced him to wear. His hand was thin, but he had a nice smile.

"I'm happy to meet you, Mr. Lanza—and you, Mrs. Lanza."

"Abby has said such nice things about you," Irene commented. "We're grateful for the help you've given her." She was a sharp-featured woman, wearing the best clothing money could buy. There was a somewhat cold light in her eyes, but she seemed pleasant enough.

"Abby is very bright," Dani observed quickly. "She's been a big help to me with the children."

Both of them had seemed pleased with that, and Dani had said later to Ben, "They don't seem like big-time racketeers, do they, Ben? She's a little sharp, but Eddy's just a nice man."

Ben had been more skeptical. "Maybe so—but I think some of that's a front. A few stories about him I picked up seem a little strong. I guess Eddy's old Dominic's son. But he's always had to live in Phil's shadow—and now it's Frank's shadow."

The party was expensive, but not crowded. Except for the family, there were only ten other people, close family friends. Frank had insisted on Ben and Dani's attending.

They met at seven in the dining room, and the meal had lasted for two hours. A string quartet, placed at one end of the room, furnished the music, and Mrs. Bennett, the housekeeper, along with the two maids, did the serving. Thomas Rossi played the role of butler, moving about his duties with one eye always on Dominic Lanza.

As a treat for the children, Frank had engaged the services of a clever magician—one Dani had seen on local television several times. He was witty and entertaining, managing to keep the adults laughing throughout his act. After he was finished, Frank announced, "Well, it's time for the gifts. Eddy, come up here."

Protesting but obviously pleased, Eddy limped to the front and, at a sign from Frank, Ben and Vince Canelli entered, carrying a table piled high with presents. "You guys shouldn't have done this," Eddy kept saying.

It was a time for family, and Dani sat quietly as the opening of the gifts went on. She ran her eyes around the table, thinking how in such a short time her life had gotten involved with this strange and powerful family. The faces of Matthew, Rachel, and Pat were intent and happy; yet she knew all three faced futures fraught with danger and unhappiness. Rosemary and Frank sat side by side, but emotionally the width of the Grand Canyon lay between them. Beautiful Abby was on a one-way trip to a bad end. Irene watched her husband with a mixture of pride and a faint touch of some sort of anger.

She must be jealous of the favoritism Dominic's shown to Phil and Frank, Dani thought.

At the moment Eddy's thin face, flushed with wine and pleasure, seemed happy, but Dani had heard talk that he had moments when a jealous rage came on him, when he even faced up to his father, accusing him of showing partiality toward his brothers. Dominic Lanza's thin lips smiled, but a shadow lined his cavernous eyes. What was he thinking, now that he had received that last summons? Dani could not read the man; indeed, she doubted if anyone could—unless it were Thomas Rossi.

Frank had been reading the names from the tags on the gifts and handing them to Eddy, who unwrapped them. Each time this happened, Frank would say something about the giver, and when Eddy unwrapped the gift, he would try to say something funny. Usually it was not very amusing, but at times such as these, people were ready to laugh, so there was considerable noise in the room.

Frank had handed Eddy a package about the size of a cigar box, and said, "And this is from your old friend Brad DeVito. Brad couldn't come but he says he's sending you the best King's has to offer. Happy birthday, Eddy, from Brad."

Eddy reached for the package, and a bell went off in Dani's head. She acted out of pure instinct; leaping to her feet, she cried out, "Don't!" as loudly as she could. Pushing her chair back, she ran around the table, her face pale and her eyes wide.

Eddy had taken the package from Frank, had even started to make a joke—but Dani's cry cut off every sound in the room. He stood there as Dani came to a halt in front of him and stuttered, "W-why, what's wrong?"

Dani reached out and took the package from him. Carefully she turned and looked at Frank, who was stock still. It was as if everyone in the room were frozen, even young Pat, whose eyes were like moons.

"This package didn't come from King's," Dani observed evenly.

"How do you know that, Dani?" Frank asked quietly.

"King's uses only one kind of wrapping paper," she answered, staring down at the package. "A light lavender with gold crowns on it. They won't use anything else. It's a status thing. They've had the paper patented. This didn't come from King's Gift Shop."

The room was as still as a candle in a crypt. "Please have everyone leave the room, Mr. Lanza," Dani directed.

It was Dominic Lanza who instantly commanded, "Everyone out—now!"

Everyone left, and Dani put the box carefully down on the banquet table, then walked outside. There was a great deal of talking, and Dani voiced her concern to Dominic, "I may be wrong. It may be just a present."

Old Dominic's eyes burned, and he took her hands. "You are doing your best to take care of us. I will rejoice if it *is* just a present. But if it is *not* . . . !" He said no more, but shook his head. Frank came up, informing his father, "I called the police. They're sending the bomb squad."

Dani left as the guests were being shown out and, as soon as she got to her room, had an attack of nerves. She called herself three kinds of a fool and finally took a shower. She had just come out, wearing her gown, when a faint knock at the door jarred her. Snatching her gun, she threw on her robe, pulled it together, and opened the door.

Frank Lanza stood there, a pallor on his thin face. "It *was* a bomb," he whispered. "Sixkiller called. He said there were enough explosives in it to have blown the room apart."

Dani began to tremble, and Lanza saw it. He stepped forward and took her hands. He seemed to struggle for words, and finally he came out with, "We Lanzas—we're very cold. We don't like to owe favors."

Dani could feel the strength of his hands, but tried to lighten the moment. "No extra charge, Frank," she whispered and tried to smile. "It's what you pay me for."

He shook his head. "No, this is different. This is—this is *life!*" Suddenly he took her hands and raised them to his lips. His kiss seemed to burn her skin, and he added huskily, "Dani! Thanks—for me and for my family!"

She couldn't speak, and for one moment she felt the power that was in the Lanza men. It was so strong that if he had tried to kiss her, as she thought he meant to do, she was not at all certain that she would be able to pull away.

But he only stared at her for a moment, then dropped her hands. "Money won't pay for this. I must find another way," he exclaimed then turned and walked quickly away.

Dani stepped inside and shut the door, holding her hands together to stop the trembling. Death had been in the room below, and her fertile imagination could see the mangled corpses of Pat and Rachel and Matthew, of Ben—and of herself. She walked to bed, kneeled, and began to pray, not for anything that God could give, but for what He had already given that very night.

6
Matthew

Matthew watched the black Lincoln pull up to the front door. Perry got out, held the door open for Dani, Rachel, and Pat, closed it, got in, and drove off. "I don't care!" the boy muttered angrily. He flung away from the window, crossed to his desk, and stared down at the sheet of paper half filled with math problems. "Who wants to go to the stupid aquarium anyway?"

You do, Stupid! a disgusted voice spoke deep inside. True, his only visit to the fabulous new aquarium *had* been wonderful.

Matt suddenly scooped the sheet of paper up, shredded it into strips, and threw them on the floor. "See how you like that!" he cried out defiantly and, with his shoulders squared, turned and dashed out of the room. He left the house, slamming the door, and rapidly headed for the geodesic dome that housed the swimming pool. As he went through the door he exclaimed under his breath, "Let's see if she can stop me from having a swim!" In short order he changed into a suit, then walked down the short hall that led from the men's dressing room to the pool itself.

Matt looked up at the arching ceiling, as always admiring the space and the way the sun filtered down. The pool's heaters kept the chill out of the air, and the water was a tepid seventy-one degrees.

He saw Savage vacuuming the pool. "Hey, what's going down, Matt?" Savage asked.

"Oh, nothing." He hesitated, and Savage saw the petulant expression on the boy's face. "Thought I'd take a swim."

"Sure. But I thought all of you were going to the aquarium with Miss Ross."

"Aw—who needs it? Bunch of stupid fish!"

Ben shook his head. "That bad, is it? I was thinking you and I could sneak off some afternoon and take it in. I've always loved those things!"

Matt objected, "I didn't know you liked stuff like that."

"Well, if you think it's dumb. . . ." Ben shrugged. "Guess it wouldn't be too good an idea."

Matthew opened his mouth to protest, then confided, "I really *wanted* to go, but Miss Ross wouldn't let me."

"Why not?"

"Well—" His young face was as easy to read as print. It made Savage think of his own boyhood and the troubles that had gone with it. "I—I was supposed to do some work. Shoot! I could have done it when we got back— wouldn't have killed her to let me do that!" He dropped his head and stared down at the tile, muttering, "She's a drag! You don't like her, do you, Ben?"

"Well—I kind of do." Savage nodded. He saw the disappointment written on the boy's face, and added, "She reminds me of the drill instructor I had in the marines. If you think Miss Ross is tough, you should meet up with W. A. Pendergast! He just about peeled my potato, Matt!"

"And you hated him?"

"I did until we got in the jungle and started getting shot at," Savage said. "Then you know what I thought, Matt?"

"What?"

"I thought, *Thank the good Lord for W. A. Pendergast!* I all of a sudden realized that he wasn't being rough on me just because he was a bully. He was trying his best to get me ready for something he knew was coming. There's no real easy way to do that—in the marines or anywhere else."

Matt struggled with the idea, hating to admit he was wrong. But a streak of honesty in him finally forced him to remark, "I—I guess she's not so bad. I could have done that old math easy!"

"Just didn't want her to push you around, I guess."

"How'd you know *that?*" Matt stared at the man with a mixture of shock and admiration.

Savage put the wand down, not wanting to turn the talk into a lecture. "Because, buddy, there's something in us men that works like that. Don't know why it is, but we just got to prove how tough we are. I have several unnecessary scars I collected showing people how Ben Savage couldn't be pushed around, no, sir!"

"You have?"

"Sure. Come on, and we'll work on that back dive. I think you've almost got it." He let his hand drop on the boy's thin shoulder as they walked along. "Us guys have to give in to women, Matt. They're kind of fragile." His words did what he expected, for by speaking of the two of them together, he gave Matt a way to save face.

"Yeah, Ben, I guess that's right. I'll try not to be so rough on Miss Ross." The tension flowed out of him, and soon he was happily flinging himself off the one-meter board, satisfied and content.

Matthew's entrance into the dome had been observed by Legs Thomas. The tall gunman had been in the living quarters built over the garage, playing poker with Faye Dietrich and Louie Baer. The apartment consisted of three bedrooms, two baths, and a large combination living-room/kitchen/dining area. Legs and Louie shared one bedroom, Faye Dietrich and Frenchy Doucett, a second, and Savage shared the third with Perry Miller, the chauffeur.

"There goes the kid," Legs commented. "Guess he's going for a swim."

Faye glanced up with irritation. "You want to play cards or not?" He shuffled the deck adroitly, dealt the cards, and won the pot. His face was moody, and Legs asked, "You get any more flak from the old man or Frank about that bomb, Faye?"

"No!" Dietrich shuffled again and threw the cards down with unnecessary force. His eyes were hooded, but the anger in them didn't go unnoticed by Thomas. Faye Dietrich had a terrible temper, and the scalding tongue-lashing that Dominic Lanza had administered to him after the night of the birthday party had left a raw scar on his ego. He had never taken such words from any man, and when it was over, he had burst forth, "Mr. Lanza, I'll take the rap for the bomb—but I'm telling you what I've said all along. We've got to hit Martino! You know better than anyone a guy like Johnny Ring can only be stopped one way. Don't waste your time on anything else!"

Dominic had responded angrily, "I will decide when

there's something to be done, Faye! You keep this place secure—or I'll find somebody who will!"

The shame of being dressed down by Lanza had burned in Dietrich's soul, and he had taken it out on the men who worked for him. Legs and Louie had caught their share of his acid tongue and glanced at each other nervously. The game went on for fifteen minutes, and when Louie got up to get a bottle of beer, he glanced out the window. "Hey— there goes Abby," he gloated. "Going swimming, looks like."

Legs was still smarting over the harsh words that Faye had laid on him and could not resist a smile. "Seems like everybody's become a health nut since that guy Savage got here, don't it? Abby's been spending so much time in that pool, taking swimming lessons, she must be trying for the Olympics, right, Faye?"

"Shut your mouth, Legs!" Faye ordered. Getting to his feet, he threw his cards down and walked to the window, then stared at the dome. He had been after Abby for a long time. It wasn't just her sultry good looks that drew him, though that was a factor, but sooner or later whoever married Abby would be Eddy Lanza's son-in-law. And Eddy Lanza was a weakling. It wouldn't be hard, Faye had recognized long before, for the right man to handle Abby and her father. And the old man was dying. That left only Frank Lanza. Phil had been a different matter, as Faye had known—a tougher man than Frank, one who would crush anyone who tried to move him out. But Frank had not been on the rough side of the empire; he had a sharp mind, better than a lawyer's, really, and it had been Phil who had done the dirty work.

But Savage's coming had changed things, and Faye

stared balefully at the dome, hating Legs for hinting that Abby was drawn to Savage—but knowing it was true. *Got to break Savage down!* The thought had rattled around his mind for days. Suddenly he turned, insisting, "Louie, come with me."

"Me, too?" Legs asked.

"No. Just Louie."

The two men went downstairs, and as they crossed to the dome, Faye made up his mind. He was clever, and he knew that he had to keep himself clear. But he was adept at manipulating others—and Louie Baer was a tool that he could use. "Louie," he announced suddenly. "I don't like what this guy Savage has been saying about you."

"About me?" Baer's thick features showed surprise, and his little eyes stared at Faye. "What do you mean, Faye? He ain't said nothin' to me."

"No, but he's done some talking *about* you, Louie," Faye reported. "He's telling it around that your fights were all fixed—and that you took a lot of dives."

This simple man—childish actually—had not been very bright to begin with, and his long career in the ring had blunted his features and slowed down his thinking. He was a hulking man, but good-natured and willing to please. Louie had pride in one thing—his record as a fighter. He had never been very good, for he had been too slow for the great ones. But he had been tough and a crowd pleaser—a good show for six rounds before the main event. He had never taken a dive, and he had never been involved in fights big enough to have one fixed.

Now he stopped dead still, his cloudy mind struggling to take in Dietrich's words. "Savage said that, Faye?" His brow wrinkled and a trace of anger lit his small eyes. "He's a liar! I never took no dives!"

"The guy is no good." Faye nodded. "I don't like him around." He saw that Louie was chewing on the thing, and quickly added, "Come on." He walked inside and saw at once Savage on the low diving board, with the kid and Abby standing on the side of the pool, listening as he explained something.

Ben looked up as the two men entered, and he walked back, leaping to the tile floor. "Anything wrong?" he asked quickly.

"Just checking," Faye barked. He cast a glance at Abby, noting the bikini, a new one, and his lips tightened. She was watching him, enjoying the whole thing, which did not surprise him. She was a teaser. Always had been—but that would change pretty soon, he thought.

Louie had followed Faye into the pool area, his mind working slowly. He had had no grudge against Savage, had felt rather friendly in his foggy way, but the lie that Faye had planted was growing. It seemed to become a living entity, and suddenly one thing seemed clear—he had to show Savage that he was wrong and shut his mouth from telling any more lies.

Louie suddenly moved toward Savage, brushing against Faye in his single-minded hunger for action. Knocked to one side, Faye called out at once, "Hey, what you think—?"

But Louie interrupted him, hoarsely grunting, "You lied on me, Ben!" And before Savage was aware of his intention, Louie caught him high on the head with a straight, hard left.

The blow was a disaster to Ben, sending a shower of sparks in front of his eyes as he was driven back, sprawling on the cold tiles. He was vaguely aware that Louie was coming at him, and he heard Faye gasp, "Cut that out,

Louie!" Without being in the least aware of it, driven by pure instinct and a thousand hours of training and instruction, he rolled to one side and came to his feet. Louie came at him at once, right hand cocked, left driving hard, but Ben moved his head two inches and slipped the blow. The force of it carried Louie into him, and both of them staggered, trying to keep their footing.

Everything suddenly jumped into focus for Ben as he threw the big man away. Baer staggered, caught himself, then put his hands up in the professional manner. "I'm gonna hurt you, Ben!" he mumbled. He was overweight and slow, but there was a ponderous power in his massive arms, and hundreds of professional brawls had given him craftiness and confidence.

Ben cried out sharply, "You're out of line, Louie. Slack off!"

"You said my fights were fixed," Baer insisted doggedly. "I got to show you what I can do, Ben."

He came forward, and Abby screamed, "Faye—stop him!"

Faye moved forward a step, mouthing, "Come on, Louie, cut it out!" But he knew that the hulking man moving forward would not hear—and would not obey if he did.

Matthew watched, his face pale as paper, as the huge form of Baer moved toward Savage. He had longed to grow up tough, but now that actual violence was in front of him, he had a sickening feeling in his stomach. Ben Savage looked almost frail next to the bulk of Louie Baer, almost like a young boy. He was wearing cutoffs and a thin T-shirt, and the trim form looked fragile, measured against the other man. Baer was six feet two and weighed two hundred and twenty-five pounds, while Savage, at five feet ten, weighed no more than one seventy-five.

Then as Baer lunged forward, throwing another ponderous left that would have ended the fight, Ben suddenly twisted to his left. He pivoted on his left leg, and the right leg—merely a blur of motion—shot out and caught Louie directly in the stomach.

It caught the big man coming in and stopped him as abruptly as if he had run into a brick wall. A hoarse grunt came from his lips, and he stood there staring at Savage, his eyes rolling. But he had taken many blows, and it was his pride that he never went down until he was out. With a cry of mindless rage, he rushed at Savage, fists high.

Matthew had seen the movies featuring martial arts, loved them, in fact. But they left out something—the pain and tearing violence of the act. They were drama, with catsup for blood, and he had always known that it was not really so. It was like watching a ballet, with the victims falling to the floor, not really hurt, just completing the choreography.

But as Savage's hands sliced at Baer's neck, then at his cheek, the sudden rush of scarlet blood that splattered down the puffy face was not catsup—it was real, as was the pain that filled the boxer's eyes.

Ben hated what he was doing, but he knew that this big man would never quit. He had stopped Baer with sledging blows to the head, but they were not enough. Again he swiveled, and again a fierce kick caught Baer in the stomach. It *boomed* audibly, and the air gushed out of the chest. Louie's eyes rolled upward, and he collapsed forward in a final and boneless manner. Savage broke his fall, not able to hold the big body, but turning him so that the face was not battered against the hard tiles.

The suddenness of Louie's collapse and the almost tangible silence that followed were disrupted only by the sound of the gurgling of the water as it was sucked in by the pumps. Faye stood as if frozen to the spot, his eyes fixed in disbelief on Louie. Then he lifted his gaze and said in a strained tone, "Don't know what got into him!"

Savage studied Dietrich, then bent and helped Louie into a sitting position. Soon his eyes fluttered; then they opened. He was sucking in air greedily and finally croaked, "Hey—Ben!"

"Take it easy, Louie," Savage directed. "Don't try to get up."

Dietrich suddenly turned and walked rapidly from the scene, his head held high. As soon as he left, Louie groaned but started pulling himself to his feet. His face was still a putty color, but he was not angry. "You shouldn't of told them lies about me, Ben," he gasped. "I never took no dives."

Savage was still holding his arm. "Why, Louie, I've never said a word about you."

"No kidding?" Louie touched his stomach gingerly, then shook his head. "Somebody said you did." He shook his shoulders together, then asked anxiously, "I didn't hurt you, did I, Ben?"

"No. I'm okay, Louie."

"Well, that's good. Guess I'll mosey along." He shuffled out, his feet half dragging, and disappeared through the door.

"Gosh, Ben!" Matthew came to stand close to Savage, staring up at him. "He's so big—and was a fighter! And you just—you just—"

"I took him, Matt," Ben pronounced quietly. "And there's guys who can take me. And I know guys who can take them."

But Matt was not listening. "Will you show me how to fight like that?"

"You may get through your whole life without a fight," Savage said. His face was sober, and he was staring at the boy with an odd expression. "I hope so. Anyway, no more diving lessons. You better shower."

Matt nodded, turned at once and left for the showers. Abby was silent, and when Ben turned to her she admitted, "I was scared, Ben."

"So was I."

"No." She shook her head, and there was no craft about her at that moment. "No, you weren't afraid. But you'd better be."

"Of Louie?"

"Of Faye," she warned. "He set it up, didn't he? He's jealous of me."

"Go take a shower, Abby." Ben suddenly felt tired and a little angry. "Stay away from him. He's no good."

Abby blinked, and then her lips drew together. "Well, that makes a pair of us, doesn't it now?" She walked away, leaving Savage alone. He looked at the great curved space over his head, then went back, picked up the wand, and began cleaning the pool.

When Louie found Faye, he said, "He didn't tell no lies on me, Faye. Somebody must of told *you* a lie."

"I guess so, Louie." Faye was looking at the big house, and after a while he ordered, "Go get Legs and Frenchy."

"What you want with them, Faye?"

Faye Dietrich spoke slowly. "To do a job, Louie. A job that should have been done a long time ago!"

At dinner that night, Ben and Dani ate with the family. Pat dominated the talk, giving a fish-by-fish account of the trip to the aquarium. When he ran down, Eddy broke in, "Oh, by the way, Ben, I'd like to have you drive Abby to a concert tonight. She's got a date, but I'd feel better if you went along."

Ben raised one eyebrow, a quizzical look in his hazel eyes, only commenting, "I'll take care of it, Mr. Lanza."

"It's one of those wild rock concerts, I'm afraid," Eddy noted ruefully. "But you won't have to go in and listen to it. Just see they're safe on the way and back."

After the meal was over, Dani whispered to Ben, "How does it feel, being a chaperone?"

"Rather have a root canal."

Matt came up just then, confessing, "Miss Dani, I—I'm sorry about today."

Dani blinked at him in surprise and recovered quickly. "Why, I'm glad to hear you say that, Matthew. It wasn't much fun without you."

Matthew blushed, then winked at Ben before leaving.

"Did you have anything to do with that?" she asked.

"Not me. His own idea. He's a good kid."

At that moment, Abby came up to announce, "Well, I've been stood up. He just called. Daddy said I could still go, if you'll sit through the concert with me." Abby smiled and pouted. "You will, won't you, please, Ben?"

It was Ben's turn to blink. He didn't dare look at Dani, but allowed, "I guess so, Abby."

She laughed and left at once—and then he did look at Dani, who advised, "Ben, I don't think that's a good idea."

"Can't keep a kid locked up all the time," he responded weakly.

Dani's voice was pure polar ice. "She—is—not—a—kid!"

"I promise to obey all the scout laws."

"Ben—you know what she's like. You're playing with fire."

"You tell me not to go, I don't go. You're the boss."

Dani gritted her teeth, longing to say, *All right—don't go!* Instead she took a deep breath, bit her lip, then nodded. "You have a charming way of worming your way into doing exactly what you want to do, Ben Savage."

"Spoiled rotten," he agreed. Then he smiled. "Not to worry. But Eddy is right. Every time one of these kids leaves these grounds one of us ought to go along. Now, would you like to go see Sting with Abby?"

"I'd rather die! But be careful."

"You, too, Boss."

She said no more but was watching an hour later when the pair of them left in the Continental. It was, she knew, a special car, originally made for a nervous racketeer in Chicago. The most interesting thing about it was that it was bulletproof. "I wish Ben had on something made of the same material to protect him from that—*kid!*" Dani muttered.

Night was beginning to fall, and she was about to leave the window, when a movement caught her eye. She peered through the glass, then suddenly wheeled and left the room. Leaving the house, she ran quickly to the front, and there, under one of the massive oaks, found Rosemary Lanza struggling to get up from where she had fallen.

"Rosemary!" Dani cried, and stooping over to grasp the woman's arms, she smelled raw whiskey. Shaking her head, she said, "Come on, Rosemary. Let's get into the house."

"Dani—'zat you?"

"Yes. Now come along."

She half led, half carried the drunken woman around to a side entrance, hoping that the children were still in the den, watching TV. She was thankful to see nobody and had just reached the foot of the stairs with her burden, when Dominic Lanza suddenly appeared. He stared at the two women, saying nothing, his face a mask.

"Rosemary isn't feeling well, Mr. Lanza," Dani explained quickly. "I'll take care of her." He said nothing, did not move, until Dani started up the steps. Then he turned and walked back down the hall, his back bent.

Dani got Rosemary up the stairs and into her room. Frank Lanza was out of town, so there was no danger of encountering him. She helped Rosemary undress, got her into a gown, and led her to the bed.

"Dani?" Rosemary's blue eyes were open, and she suddenly seemed afraid. "Who is it?"

"Lie down, Rosemary. It's Dani."

"Dani?" Rosemary reached out as she lay back, groping for Dani's hand. "Don't leave me—please!"

"I'll sit here for a little while," Dani told her quietly.

The woman lay still, but her grip was still tight on Dani's hand. Finally she whispered, "I'm so sorry!"

"Don't think about it, dear," Dani said. "Go to sleep."

"I—don't want to! I have such awful dreams!"

Dani sat there in the semidarkness for a few moments. Something was coming to her, and she waited until she was sure. Finally she said, "Rosemary, God can give you a great gift. The Bible says, 'He giveth his beloved sleep.' "

Rosemary shook her head. "God doesn't—love me!"

"Oh, yes!" Dani continued quickly. "The whole Bible is saying that—God is love."

"I've been so awful! I—I can't—!"

"Let me pray for you, Rosemary. That God will do two things. Can you understand me? First, that you will sleep with no bad dreams. And more than that, that you'll be shown that God *does* love you." She waited, then began to pray, "Lord, I ask that you give my sister a sound rest. Take away all the bad dreams. She is your beloved. Show her your love. I ask it in the name of Jesus."

Dani sat there, not sure if the woman were awake or asleep. Finally the breathing grew even, and the tight grasp on her hand relaxed. By the small light on the vanity she saw that Rosemary's face was still, as though carved in marble. "Thank You, Jesus!" Dani breathed, then rose and left the room.

7
"London Bridge Is Falling Down . . . !"

The parking lot of the Black Orchid was eclectic. A four-wheel-drive Ford pickup with a 30-30 across the back window was bordered on one side by a sleek red Jaguar and on the other by a muddy CJ-7 Jeep. A small covey of Japanese imports was offset by a scattering of Town Cars, Imperials, and Caddies, and the lone Lamborghini seemed to stare balefully at the ancient Pinto with the crushed fenders, parked directly in front of it. Across what was left of the Pinto's bumper, a tattered bumper sticker proclaimed: SO MANY PEDESTRIANS—SO LITTLE TIME!

The Black Orchid itself, the building, was a study in pragmatic and utilitarian architecture. It had been built for one purpose—to provide a dark, private place in which people could get drunk; if there were a prize for Ugliest Building, the Orchid would have been a hot contender— except for the fact that it was merely one of a hundred or so "clubs" sown over the city—clones that were old the day they opened and reeked of corruption within a week. The low, flat-roofed, cement-block structure had no windows, and a double door in front. Perched on a paved lot on the fringe of New Orleans, the Orchid began to ingest its clientele in earnest when the sun went down, masticated them inside the blind walls until two o'clock, then began to vomit them forth, usually in a most reprehensible condition.

Inside the Orchid was a small foyer that one passed through to the bar itself. The details of decoration are never significant in places like this, for it is always impossible to see them through the murky darkness, the eternal half-light through which waiters, drunks, businessmen, hookers, football players from the local university, discontented housewives, truckers, and denizens of all sorts eat, drink, whisper, yell, fondle, fight, scheme, and pay a king's ransom for an ounce of alcohol, which numbs their brains and ruins their livers.

Like all others of its breed, the Orchid had private rooms used for sundry and nefarious purposes. In one of these, a smoke-filled cubicle ten feet wide and twelve feet long, five men sat around a circular poker table. Like the famous Round Table of good King Arthur, there was no "head" where the highest might sit, but from one of the five emanated that force no man can define, imitate, or cultivate— whatever it is that makes people stare when the man possessing it comes into the room. Napoleon, Lincoln, Peter the Great, and Al Capone had it and used it for widely differing purposes.

Johnny Ring had this power to command attention. He was no more than five feet nine and seemed fat. But the

105

rotund shape was hard with muscle. He had dark eyes, a round face, and a small mouth, which he opened only enough to let his words escape.

The man on his right, Joe Martino, was a pale imitation of his father, Salvadore Martino. Sal had been even harder than Johnny Ring, but the genes had backfired, and before Alzheimer's disease had wasted the old man away, he had recognized that it would be Ring—not his own flesh and blood—who would control the empire he had created. If he had been a younger man, Sal would have eliminated Johnny Ring, but he had waited too long. Though Joe Martino had the name, everyone in New Orleans understood that the iron fist that controlled the Martino organization was attached to the right arm of Johnny Ring.

On Ring's left sat L. D. Burger, a tall, heavy man of fifty-six. This lawyer had a tanned face, a pair of sharp gray eyes, and the tastes of a Roman emperor.

The other two men, Duke McCord and Ray Snyder, were hirelings. McCord was dark of hair and skin, while Snyder had thin blond hair and blue eyes, but they were Tweedledum and Tweedledee of a deadly, ruthless, and easily replaceable variety. Many young men envied McCord and Snyder, so many that L. D. Burger once asked in wonder, "Is there some sort of training school out there somewhere, turning out assassins?" With a sharklike grin on his small lips, Ring had replied, "Yeah, it's called the Quarter."

"What time is it?" Burger asked. "I've got to be in court early tomorrow."

Ring glanced at the heavy gold watch on his thick wrist, a Rolex. "Only eleven." He grinned at the lawyer. "You're not thinking about court, L. D. You've got that little dancer at the Stardust on your mind."

A knowing laugh ran around the table, but Burger seemed not to care. "She's better than losing money to you, Johnny. I haven't won a pot in the last two hours."

"Maybe your luck will change." Ring dealt the cards, and the game went on. Picking up his cards, Joe Martino blithely commented, "Things are going good, Johnny. I told you it would. Old Lanza's given up."

Ring gave him a straight glance out of a pair of close-set eyes. "He didn't get where he is by letting people take things away from him, Joe."

"Phil was his strength, though," Burger suggested. The lawyer studied his cards and snorted. "What a mess!" He threw two cards down, took two from Ring, and added, "Maybe Joe's right, Johnny. Phil was like a cobra. I never slept too well when that man was alive. But I don't think Frank is so much along those lines."

"Who'd he ever put down?" Ray Snyder shrugged. "He's a bookkeeper."

"He's a Lanza," Ring insisted stubbornly. "And Dom Lanza may be sick, but he's got an arm as long as this state. When he decides to get someone, there's not a hole in the country deep enough to hide in."

They argued back and forth, drinking and smoking the long cigars. Finally at a quarter to twelve, Ring exclaimed, "Enough already!" He threw his cards down and got to his feet, and the rest began to pull themselves out of their chairs. "We all straight on everything? Duke, you know what to do with Mattox? And you got the word on that clown at the Skylight who's out to buck us, Ray?"

"Yeah, yeah," Snyder said, getting to his feet. He picked up the shoulder holster draped over one of the extra chairs, slipped it on, then put his coat on. "No problem, Johnny."

"I still say we can't risk a hearing with the DA over that Matson thing, Johnny," Burger cautioned, shaking his head. "Let me delay it. Cost a little—but better safe than sorry."

Ring stared at him. "Okay. But I want it wrapped up quick."

"Sure." Burger got up and put on his coat. He wore no gun, nor did Joe Martino, but the other three did. Suddenly he snapped his fingers, frowned, and recalled, "Joe, you've got to sign those papers on the Conway matter. They're in my car."

"Can't it wait?" Martino complained.

"Won't take but a minute. I'll get them."

"Come on. Let's get out of here," Ring ordered as he took a wad of bills from his pocket, extracted two fifties, and threw them on the table. Snyder and McCord followed him closely as he threaded his way through the dark room. Several men recognized him, but nobody did more than nod, and the three men left the Orchid.

"Going to be cold tomorrow, the paper said." Ring pulled his coat together, lamenting, "I hate cold weather!"

"Be glad we're not in Chicago," Snyder remarked. "They got sixteen inches of snow today."

"People are crazy to live in a big freezer like that," Ring asserted. "Come on, let's get in the car."

They walked across the lot, threading their way through the cars until they came to a dark Cadillac sedan. "You drive, Ray," Ring directed, tossing him the keys. "And get the heater going."

Snyder slid behind the wheel, and Ring sat beside him. Duke McCord got into the backseat. The engine started at once, and Snyder noted, "Take a few minutes for the heater to warm up, Johnny."

"Go on—let's get started."

The heavy car moved forward, Snyder steering carefully between the rows of vehicles. When he came to the central drive, he turned left. As he did, a car that had been parked in the main driveway began to move, its lights suddenly throwing out twin beams that picked up the Cadillac.

Ring, huddled on the right side of the seat, paid no attention, but Snyder yelled, "Hey—what's that guy doing?"

At once Ring sat up, throwing a glance through the back windshield. He got a glimpse of the car, which was swinging out to pass them, but the lights blinded him momentarily. Because Johnny Ring had survived in a world that teemed with predators, he had developed a sense of danger that went beyond the brain. His nerve endings or some part of the chemistry in his body sent some sort of signal that he did not analyze. With one motion of his right hand, he slapped the door handle; then he threw his weight against the door. It flew open, and he rolled out of the seat, his right shoulder taking the force of the fall. His face scraped the rough concrete just as the chatter of automatic rifle fire sounded. Slamming to a stop, Ring saw the fiery muzzles of two weapons belching flame and lead into the Cadillac. The driver of the attack car, he noted, was good! He kept pace with the other car perfectly, allowing the gunmen to rake the car with a stream of bullets.

The Cadillac swerved, ran through the steel cable that marked off the parking lane, and came to a halt. The other car accelerated, turned off onto the main highway, and did not make the mistake of tearing down the road at a breakneck speed—a tactic that had proved fatal by attracting the attention of police and others. It was just a car moving down the highway at a reasonable speed, no different from any other on the road.

Ring got to his feet, wiped the trickle of blood from his cheek, then walked over to the Cadillac. It seemed very quiet, and when he looked inside, he noticed the side windows were slivers of glass, and the doors were patterned with hundreds of round holes. Ray Snyder lay across the seat, his face a bloody mask, and the still form of McCord filled the floor below the backseat.

Quickly, Ring wheeled, for the doors of the Orchid had swung open. He moved to the parking lot, waiting until two men came hurrying toward him. He recognized Burger's voice as the lawyer cried, "We've got to get clear, Joe! The police—"

"Burger—," Ring called out, and the two men halted abruptly.

"Johnny?" the lawyer gasped. "I thought you were in the car!"

Ring shook his head. "Ray and Duke got it." He could not help throwing a barb at the two men. "What do you think of your nice little theory now? Still think Dom Lanza's in his grave?"

"Johnny, let's get out of here!" Martino bleated. His face was pale and his hands were trembling.

"You two get out. It's my car, and the cops will pick me up. I'll stick around. Get out."

The pair scrambled into their cars and left, and even as they did, Ring walked quickly inside. The crowd was packed in the entrance, and he shoved through, going at once to the manager's office. Picking up the phone, he dialed a number and waited. "You know who this is?" he asked. "Okay, I'm ready to deal." Ring paused and said in a tight voice, "I didn't think you'd have the nerve to hit us." He listened then, and finally said impatiently, "Yeah, yeah, I got you straight. Two of our guys are dead—and nearly me! So, we work together. You're on the inside, and if Dom ever finds out you've got a deal with me, he'll nail you to the wall! But that's your lookout. We've got a deal. Here's what I want you to do—and there'd better not be any slipups!"

He spoke rapidly, slammed the phone down, and went out of the office. Faintly he heard the sound of sirens, and he stopped at the bar, took a bottle, then sat down and waited for the cops.

"Let's stop and have a drink, Ben. We've got time."

"I guess not, Abby," Ben said. They had left the concert a little after 11:30, and as he drove along the highway his eyes moved continually, checking each intersection and every car that moved in their direction. "It's pretty late."

Abby moved closer and put her hand on the back of his neck. "Oh, don't be such a drag! It's the first time I've been anyplace for two weeks, Ben. Just thirty minutes— please?"

Her hand stroked his neck, and he could feel the pressure of her thigh against his, but he repeated cheerfully, "Just can't do it, Abby."

She grabbed his hair and gave it a painful tug. "What's wrong with you, Savage?" she demanded. "Don't you like girls?"

"Like them fine. But Mr. Lanza didn't hire me to take you dancing."

"He won't know."

"Maybe not—but I will."

Abby stared at him, then released his hair. She threw herself angrily to her own side of the seat and stared out the window. Ben insisted, "Come on, Abby. You've got a dozen boyfriends. Why would you need the scalp of a run-down P.E. instructor and third-rate chauffeur on your belt?"

"You don't know!" Abby turned to glare at him. "What kind of guy could I get? If I get one I like, he finds out about my family and runs like a rabbit. So I run around with those I don't like, just to have some fun. Then I get locked in the castle."

"That'll change," Ben reassured her. "You'll go back to college and marry the star football player and live happily ever after."

Silently Abby turned to stare blindly out the window. Finally she turned back to him. "Are you married?"

"Nope."

"Ever been married—or engaged or anything?"

"Just the last—anything." Savage watched a brown station wagon pull out to pass them and put his hand inside his coat and kept it there until the vehicle was in front of them. He took his hand out, then asked, "You know what I like about beer?"

She stared at him, then laughed. "I guess to drink it."

"No, I hate the taste of the stuff. To me, it tastes like the antiseptic you put on mosquito bites. What I like is an old commercial that was around a few years ago. Was on television all the time. There was always this scene with this guy and this girl in a beautiful setting. And some oily-voiced announcer would encourage people to go for all they could get in this life. I always thought that was pretty good."

"Hey—I saw that commercial! And it's right on, Ben!"

"Well, I didn't much agree with the implication. It was saying, drink all the beer and liquor you can hold, make out all you can, and have fun, because the time comes around when you die and won't be able to have fun anymore."

"That's the way it is!"

"Only for dogs and cats, Abby. I'm not much of a philosopher, but a man or a woman—there's a little bit more to life than having fun."

"Working yourself to death, you mean? Or going to church with a long skirt and never doing anything the preacher says is wrong?"

"I hate oversimplifications." Savage grinned. "The old either/or trick. You've *either* got to be a drunk—or you've got to be a plaster saint in a monastery somewhere."

Abby was intrigued by Ben's strange outlook. His adamant refusal to make a play for her had puzzled her, then angered her. Now she stared at him and asked, "Well, what are *you* going to do on your 'one time around,' Ben?"

He turned off the highway, onto the private road that led to Twelve Oaks, and stared at a clump of trees set off to one side. When he passed them, he admitted, "Don't know for sure, Abby. Guess both of us are looking around for the best buy. Who was it who said, 'It would be terrible to come to the end of life—and discover that I'd never lived' "?

He pulled up to the gate and was admitted by Louie, who passed on the message, "Mr. Lanza wants to see yuh, Ben." He looked more closely at Savage and continued, "I was outta line today—at the swimming pool. Okay, Ben?"

113

"Sure, Louie. We'll go out and get a steak at Maxie's pretty soon, right?"

As Ben drove on, Abby was quiet. He parked the car, and the two of them moved toward the house. When they walked up the steps, Abby stopped at the door, turned to him and said, "Thanks for taking me." She waited for him to try to kiss her, holding herself ready. But when he replied, "I enjoyed it," she shook her head and ran inside.

Ben went upstairs and knocked gently on Lanza's door. It opened. Thomas Rossi nodded. "Come in. I've got some things to do."

Rossi left, and Ben walked over to where Dom sat in a chair. The only light was the lamp on the table beside him, and it threw his face into cavernous shadows. He was, Savage saw, being planed down day by day, the flesh retreating, leaving the outlines of the skull more visible.

"Sit down, Savage," Dominic commanded. "Or fix yourself a drink if you want one."

"No, thanks."

Lanza waited until Ben was seated, then asked, "You took Abby to some sort of concert?"

"A rock concert, Mr. Lanza."

"Did you enjoy it?"

"No. I hate rock music."

Lanza spoke expressionlessly, "Abby is a difficult girl. She has been in trouble with men several times."

Savage gave Lanza a level stare. "She won't be in trouble with me."

A light that could have been humor flickered in the old eyes. Lanza considered Savage, then nodded. "I believe that is true. In my day I could read men pretty well. I take you for a smart man—and it wouldn't be smart to take advantage of my granddaughter."

114

"I never have anything to do with the women on a case."

"A good policy." Lanza shivered and pulled his robe about him. "I can't seem to get warm. That's part of it, I suppose. Dying is an inconvenient business!" Then he queried, "What do you make of this business? What's going to happen next?"

Ben shrugged. "Right now it's like two big dogs circling each other, each waiting for the other to blink. Sooner or later one of you will, and that'll set the thing off."

Lanza nodded. "I need a man like you," he asserted. "I could pay you much more than Miss Ross does."

"Thanks, but I'm not interested."

"I knew that. Are you in love with her?"

Lanza had been trying to get some sort of a reaction, to break through Savage's iron control. He always did that with a man, tried to break him, find out what made him flinch. Now his lips pulled back in a thin smile as he saw Savage suddenly out of words. "It wouldn't be surprising, Ben," the old man told him. "She's quite a girl."

Savage pulled his lips together, a frown forming on his forehead. He almost told Lanza to butt out—then suddenly laughed softly. "You old pirate! It's none of your business, but I just work for her."

"Ah. Well, that's as may be." Lanza nodded. Then he sobered, continuing without emotion, "Two of Martino's men were gunned down tonight."

Ben stared at him and shook his head before lashing out, "I hope one of them was Ring."

"It was not."

"Too bad."

"My thought exactly." Lanza spoke in a spare tone, but anger lit his eyes. "I did not order it done."

"Ring will never believe that," Ben stated flatly. "I suppose it was Faye?"

Lanza nodded slowly. "Yes. He's been trying to get me to hit Martino for a long time—ever since Sal died."

"You going to fire him?"

"No. I can't spare him. If Phil were alive, he could control Faye. But now we need him. He's hotheaded and rash, I know."

"And ambitious," Ben observed.

"You see that? Well, it's true enough. When I die, there will be only Frank and Eddy. Neither of them are what Phil was—so there has to be a man like Faye." Lanza hesitated, then leaned forward. "I never learned how to ask favors, Ben, so I don't do it very well. . . ."

He paused, and Ben interjected, "I can't speak for Dani. I hope she'll keep us both here as long as you need us."

Lanza did not smile. He stared at Ben with a quizzical look. "I have missed something in life. I have only had faith in family. Now that it is too late, I discover that some men are to be trusted—just because they are what they are."

Ben was embarrassed by the scene. He knew that the old man before him had been guilty of breaking every law of God and man—yet now that he was old and helpless, he was finding out what it was like to have to lean on others. It was something, Savage knew, that he himself did not do well. To head off any expression of gratitude, he interposed, "Oh, knock it off, Dom! You'll have both of us crying in our beer about how noble we are!"

Lanza blinked, then saw what Savage was doing. "Very well, I will not speak of it."

"Want me to do anything special?"

"Yes. I have talked with Dani. The two of you are the last line of defense. I think Ring will react very soon. And I am afraid that he will get inside our defenses."

"You think he's bought somebody in your organization?"

"It would be the way to do it. It is exactly what I would do myself."

"Any ideas?" Savage asked.

"You're the detective, Ben, not me," Lanza pointed out. He leaned back, and Ben noticed that he looked exhausted. "Send Thomas in as you leave. And thanks."

Ben left the room and found the tall servant in the kitchen, eating a sandwich. "I guess he's ready for bed, Thomas," Savage reported. He hesitated, then added "He's not doing so well."

"No, he's not. I think he's keeping himself alive just to do what he can for Frank and Eddy." Rossi drained the glass of milk, then washed the glass. He turned to the door, but paused long enough to comment, "It's like the old nursery rhyme, 'London Bridge Is Falling Down,' isn't it?" He didn't explain, but exited the kitchen, leaving Ben alone with his thoughts.

Ben left the house, and as he crossed to the garage, the old melody kept going through his mind: "London bridge is falling down, falling down, falling down. . . ." He went to bed, and for a long time he lay there, trying to see some way to stop the thing, some hope that the Lanzas would come out of it and live happily ever after. But he saw no solution and slept poorly all night.

8
Another Birthday Party

Lieutenant Sixkiller arrived at the mansion unannounced on Friday morning, three days after the killing at the Orchid, and practically forced his way past the gate. Legs had thoughts of trying to bluff the bronzed policeman, but one look into Sixkiller's chilling gaze, and he quickly fumbled with the phone. After a quick call, he instructed in a surly tone, "You can go on up to the house."

A short meeting had taken place in Frank Lanza's office. After greeting Dom and Frank, Sixkiller had rapped out, "Thought I'd give you the word about that bomb. And the word is that the lab can't help. Nothing in it we can trace. Mostly stuff that can be bought over the counter or swiped pretty easy."

Dominic Lanza nodded. "I thought it might be like that."

"Yeah, well, as long as I'm here," Sixkiller spoke as if an afterthought had come to him, "I may as well mention one other little thing. I guess you read about two of Martino's men getting blown away earlier this week."

"Yes, I read about it in the paper."

Sixkiller's lips turned up in a very slight grin, as if he was enjoying the conversation, but he replied evenly, "Well, here's what it looks like, Mr. Lanza. There are two rival gangs in New Orleans. They've been in a war before, and only last week one of them tried to bomb the other one. Now the one that tried to bomb the other gang out is hit in a gang-style killing." He looked at Frank Lanza, who stared at him expressionlessly. "Some of us at the department are beginning to suspect a connection."

It was Dominic Lanza's turn to reveal a trace of humor. His eyes glinted at the policeman, but he only replied, "I can see how you might come to that conclusion, Lieutenant."

"Wonder if any of your men were out of pocket on that night—say at about midnight."

Frank informed him, "The men work in shifts. Some of them were off. We don't keep a record of what they do when they're off duty."

"That would be a violation of their civil liberties, wouldn't it?" Sixkiller nodded. "Well, just wanted to pass the word along. The mayor is nervous. So's the DA. You know," he observed idly, "the next time we have a killing, it wouldn't surprise me a bit if those two didn't get together and tell the department to crack down on both organizations. You know what pests we can make of ourselves when we set our mind to it, don't you, Mr. Lanza?"

"We'll all hope that it won't come to that," Dom commented smoothly.

Sixkiller got up from his chair with an easy motion. "Like to see Miss Ross, while I'm here."

"I doubt if she knows anything about the shooting," Frank observed.

"No, but she might agree to go out with me on her night off," Sixkiller confessed. "I've tried everything else, now I'm going to threaten to pull her license if she turns me down again."

"I seriously doubt if that will work." Dom smiled. "She's a very firm young woman."

"Tell me about it!" Sixkiller grinned. "Where can I find her?"

"She's with the children," Frank told him. "I'll take you to their classroom."

"I'll be in touch, Mr. Lanza," Sixkiller promised, then followed Frank out of the room. The two men said nothing as they walked down the hall, but when Frank paused outside the door, he turned and asked, "I know you've already checked out our men. Are you going to make any arrests?"

"Nope. In the first place they've all got iron-clad alibis. Even if they didn't, I wouldn't waste time with them. My theory is a lot more simple than the mayor's. I'd just let the Lanzas and the Martinos whittle each other down. In a good gang war as many as twenty or thirty cheap hoods can get wiped out."

Frank Lanza stared at the policeman, letting nothing show in his face. "This is where Dani teaches the children," he indicated quietly. He opened the door, and Sixkiller gave him a quizzical look, thinking, *If I'd said that to Phil, he'd have tried to open me up!* But he had always known that Frank and Phil were vastly different.

Dani was standing at a blackboard, diagramming a sentence, as the two men walked in. Matt and Rachel were

120

seated before her, and Abby was lounging beside a table where Pat was pushing toy wooden cars around.

"Well, class, we have visitors." Dani smiled.

"The lieutenant wants a word with you, Dani," Frank announced. "I'll fill in for you, if you want to go to the living area."

"Why, thank you, Mr. Lanza," Dani replied. She walked outside, but demanded at once, "What is it?"

"I told the old man I was going to ask you to go dancing," Sixkiller said. "How about it?"

"I'm not much of a dancer, Luke," Dani objected. "And that's *not* why you want to see me."

The burly officer shrugged, then informed her, "We're not going to be able to put anybody away for knocking off those two Martino guys. Just wanted to warn you: Ring won't let it alone. Sooner or later he'll try to even the score. Keep your guard up, Dani." He blinked, then advised quietly, "Get out of it. These people are going to kill each other off."

"What about the children? Do I just write *them* off?"

Luke stared at her hard, then shook his head. "I knew it was a waste of time—but I thought I'd give it a shot." He grinned, asking as he moved to go, "You sure about not going out with me?"

Dani liked him, but she shook her head. "Maybe when this is over. You'll have to come and ask my father, though. He has to approve all my dates."

"Yeah, I'll do that." He turned and left, and Dani returned to the classroom. At once she saw that something was wrong with Rachel. She came to stand beside the girl and threw a quick look at Frank.

Lanza met her gaze and reported, "I can't make it to the

circus tonight. I was just telling Rachel I'll make it up to her."

"It's all right, Daddy," Rachel whispered. She tried to smile, unsuccessfully.

Dani stared at Lanza, anger building up inside her like a thunderhead. "Well, you kids have a good time at the circus," their father urged. He turned and walked out of the room without looking back.

Dani glanced at Rachel, and the sight of the effort the child was making to keep from crying made her furious. "Abby, stay with the children, will you?" She started for the door, her back rigid and her lips thin.

She caught up with Frank downstairs and addressed him in a spare tone, "I want to talk to you."

Frank looked at her strangely, but only offered, "We can go to my office." He led the way, and when they were inside, he attempted to head her off: "You're upset because I can't go to the circus. Well, I'm sorry, but it can't be helped. Something's come up that I can't get out of."

Dani bit off her words carefully. "Whatever it is, it's not as important as keeping your word to your daughter."

Lanza snapped back angrily, "I don't have time to listen to this! Is that all you have to say?"

"Oh, no, Mr. Lanza!" Dani pulled herself up, her eyes flashing, and there was no gentleness in her voice as she tore on, "No, it's not all I have to say. What kind of a man are you, anyway? You have a daughter who's starving for a little affection from you. It's her birthday, and you're the lad who said, 'Pick any place you want to go, Rachel, and I'll take you on your birthday.' So now, after you've let her build her hopes up all this time, you come marching in with 'I have something more important to do. Run along and play'!"

Lanza was not a man used to being talked to in such a fashion. A flash of color touched his cheeks, and he ordered, "Get out of here! Just do what you're paid to do!"

Dani didn't move. "What am I paid to do? Keep someone from shooting your children? That's all you care about, isn't it? Just feed them, buy their clothes, and keep somebody from killing them! Never mind that Rachel is going to pieces—and Matthew as well! The big man has *important* things to do!"

Only twice in her life had Dani slipped out of control. She knew exactly what she was saying, but couldn't stop. Though she realized that Frank Lanza would never let his hired help talk to him in such a fashion, the words came spilling out.

"Do you know two of your children are afraid of you? You're a stranger to them. Do you think they don't *know* there's death in this house? They do! And you're the one, their father, who should be holding them up. But not Frank Lanza! Oh, no! You come floating by and give Pat all the little scraps of attention you have in your miserable soul and let Matt and Rachel see how much more you think of him!"

"Get out!" Frank cried hoarsely. "You're fired!"

"No, I'm not fired," Dani shot back. "You didn't hire me. Your father did. And I'll leave when he tells me to."

Frank's face was pale and set. He turned and walked around her, saying, "Pack your things." As he strode to his father's room, he found himself trembling. He was filled with a sense of rage and indignation such as he had rarely known. It was so severe he had to stop outside his father's door for several moments, waiting until he could breathe more evenly.

He knocked, entered, and found his father reading. "I just fired the Ross woman," he announced abruptly. "We'll have to find somebody else."

Dom put his book down and stared at his son. "Why?"

"She's—she's getting insolent!" Frank shook his head, then knowing he'd have to explain, told his father what had happened. "She'll have to be replaced," he defiantly proclaimed.

The silence ran on, and Frank grew more nervous under the heavy weight of his father's eyes. Finally Dom asked, "Did you promise to take Rachel to the circus?"

"Well—yes," Frank admitted. Then he added quickly, "But you know how it's been since Ring got hit, Pop. It's a bad time."

"And your word, it's not good, Frank?" Dom stared at his son, his old eyes sad. "I have done so many things that I am not proud of. But I have never broken my word to you, have I? Or to any of my family."

Frank dropped his head suddenly, remembering. "No, Pop—you never did."

The old man rose and came to stand beside his son. He put his hand on the younger man's arm and waited until Frank met his gaze. "Frank, you are my son. There is nothing I wouldn't do for you. But I have to be honest." Dom hesitated, then continued very softly, "I know your pride is hurt. We Lanzas—we have a lot of pride. Too much, I think, at times. But isn't the woman right?"

Frank could hardly meet his father's eyes. He had known when Dani was slicing at him with her accusations that she was telling the truth. He had always known that he was not the father he ought to be. That was why he had reacted with such anger. Now as he stood there, thinking of her words and trying to meet his father's eyes, a razor was doing fine work on his conscience. Finally he nodded, and whispered: "Yes, Pop, she was right." He tried to grin and could not. "That's why I got so mad, I guess."

Dom observed, "You are a good father in many ways, Frank, but even I have seen that your children need more of you." He shrugged his thin shoulders. "I was the same way. I favored Phil. I didn't give you and Eddy the attention you deserved. That—has been heavy on me, my son. It has hurt me much worse than the thought of dying."

"You were always a good father!"

Dom looked at him eagerly. "Do you really mean that, Frank?"

"Yes! Eddy and I knew Phil was your favorite. But you didn't cut us out. Remember the trips to the beach every year? And how you taught us all to play golf? I've never forgotten—"

Frank cut his words off sharply, then stared at his father. "That's what I remember most—the *time* you spent with me. And that's what Dani said I haven't been giving the kids—and she's right, Pop. But I just don't seem to know how to talk to them."

"I really don't think it matters much what you say," Dom advised slowly. "What matters is that you are *there*. I wish all our problems had such an easy solution. Rachel and Matthew will be happy if you just spend a little time with them. Can you do that? And I suppose you'll have to apologize to Dani." He gave a semblance of a smile. "Another thing we Lanzas never learned to do—apologize."

Frank gave a nervous laugh. The tension of the moment had raked across his nerves, but he responded, "I'll try— but she might pull that gun she wears and shoot me before I have a chance!"

She is a fiery woman, isn't she?'' Dom nodded. "But I am glad she is here. Now, go eat your words. It will not be as bad as you think.''

"All right.'' Frank left the room, and Dom went to the chair and sat down abruptly. The pain in his stomach burned like a fire, but he ignored it and smiled as he pictured the scene that would be taking place between his son and the nanny.

Dani had gone back to the classroom after the confrontation with Frank. Abby stared at her curiously, but said nothing. Pat had pulled at her slacks, and she had gone to sit with him as he pointed out the function of each of his cars. Dani wanted to go to Rachel—who was sitting at her desk, a book before her, her head down—but thought, *I'll wait until later, when we're alone.* Matt was joylessly working on the model of an aircraft carrier.

Ten minutes later, the door opened, and Dani looked to see Frank. He didn't even glance at her, but went directly to Rachel. He stood over her, but she kept her head down, eyes fixed on the book. "Guess what, Rachel?'' he asked.

"I don't know, Daddy.'' Her answer was faint, and when she looked up, he saw she had been crying.

"Well, I've been talking to your grandfather—'' He did glance at Dani then, but quickly continued, "He told me something about promises—something I'd forgotten. Can you guess what?''

"No, Daddy.''

"He told me that if a father ever makes a promise to one of his children, he has to keep it—no matter what!''

"Did he really say that?''

"Yes—and you know what? He's *right!* So if you won't be mad at me, I'd like to come along to the circus with you. Is that all right?''

"Oh, Daddy!" Rachel leaped up and made a grab at her father. Lanza caught her and picked her up, and she pressed her face against his chest. Lanza thought how long it had been since he had picked her up and felt amazed at how thin and light she was. He looked at Dani and cleared his throat. "As long as you're all here, I might as well just tell you all. I felt very bad when Pop showed me how wrong it was to break a promise. He told me to say I'm sorry—so, I'm saying it—to all of you."

Dani had been prepared for the worst, and when Frank's eyes met hers, after the speech that must have cost him a great deal, tears stung her eyes. She managed a smile, then commented, "Not many fathers would do what yours has just done, Rachel. I think we'll all have to be *very* nice to him, to show how we appreciate it."

Lanza gave Rachel a hug, set her down, then walked toward the door, calling out, "Bring on the elephants! I'll tell Ben we'll need the van for this bunch!"

"What'd you do to him, Dani?" Abby asked in awe. "I didn't know anyone could make Frank do a thing like that!"

"Oh, I didn't *make* him do it, Abby," Dani protested. "I think deep down he's wanted to do something like that for a long time."

Abby shook her head in disbelief. "How much do you charge for teaching how to make a man do what you want him to? I'd pay big bucks for *that!*"

Dani thought, *I wish it were as easy to make a dent in Ben Savage!* But she only warned, "It's pretty dangerous to try to change people, Abby. I don't much like to do it."

*   *   *

"You all go get in the van," Frank poked his head into the den and yelled over the sound of the stereo. "We'll be right there." He ran upstairs, amused at his own excitement about going to a circus, and entered the bedroom calling out, "You ready, Rosemary?" He pulled off his coat, slipped out of his slacks, and changed quickly into a pair of Dockers and a cotton shirt. Slipping his feet into a pair of loafers, he yelled, "Rosemary! Let's go!"

He yanked a jacket from a hanger and was putting it on hurriedly, when the bathroom door opened and Rosemary came out. Frank stopped, one arm in the jacket, and stared at her.

Rosemary was wearing a bathrobe, and when she spoke, her voice was slurred. "Be—a few minutes, Honey."

She was so drunk, he saw, that she could barely walk. He stood there, filled with the hopeless feeling that always washed across him at times like these. He pulled on his coat slowly and walked over to her. Pulling her around to face him, he demanded harshly, "Did you *have* to get drunk today? Couldn't you at least have made it through Rachel's party?"

"I—only had a little, Frank—" Rosemary's lips trembled, and she tried to pull away. "It won't take but a minute—"

"You can't go like that, Rosemary!" Frank released her arm and suddenly could not bear the sight of her. She saw it in his face and began to tremble.

"Sorry!" she gasped. "So sorry!"

He stared at her and finally repeated the question he had asked many times before, "Why do you do it, Rosemary? You have everything! I don't understand it."

She wanted to tell him about the fear, black as midnight and thick as a wall, that closed around her, but the words would not come. Many times she had wanted to cry out for him to love her as he once had, but she always saw the disgust in his face. Now he would leave her, she knew, and the fear began to rise like a tide. She gripped his lapel, pleading, "Don't—leave me—please!"

Frank shook her hand off, stating bitterly, "What difference does it make if I'm here or not? You'll be dead to the world in half an hour." He turned and left the room, and by the time he got to the van he had control enough to announce, "Your mother's sick, Rachel. She won't be able to go with us." He knew from the look on her face—and every other face—that he was not deceiving them. *How long before even Pat knows his mother is a drunk?* he wondered. But he urged, "Well, let's go to the circus!"

When Frank threw himself into something, it was with all he had. As soon as Ben got to the city limits of Baton Rouge, he ordered, "Stop at that McDonald's on Seigen, Ben." When they unloaded and went inside, Rachel was enthralled to find a section set off, with a sign saying, HAPPY BIRTHDAY, RACHEL! and balloons everywhere. "Don't eat too much, now," Frank warned. "You'll all want peanuts and hot dogs at the circus!"

The circus itself was in the Centroplex, a large auditorium situated on the west side of Baton Rouge, close to the Mississippi River. Frank had tickets, center section, and soon they were all watching the acts.

Frank enjoyed some of the acts, but most of the time he watched Rachel's face. She was sitting next to him, pointing out all the exciting things. She was, he noted, too thin and had a complexion problem. *Why hasn't someone taken her to a doctor to get that cleared up?* he wondered. *Why haven't I done it myself?* Once he looked at Dani, seated on the other side of Rachel, and she gave him a conspiratorial smile. "This is nice, Frank!"she said, and her words had given him an unreasonable pleasure.

They took it all in, and Rachel loved every minute— especially the high trapeze act—the Flying Rudolphos. She had squealed and hidden her eyes, but looked back as the fliers defied gravity. When it was over, Ben came to ask, "Would you like to meet the Flying Rudolphos, Rachel?"

Rachel stared at him, her mouth an O. "Could I, Ben?"

"Sure." He smiled and looked at the others. "Come along."

"Will it be all right, Ben?" Frank asked.

"Why not? They're my parents."

Dani's head shot up instantly, and she thought at once of the time when he had told her of his early life, during their imprisonment by Maxwell Stone. She had not known Ben well, but she had always sensed that some tragedy had made him raise the wall he kept between himself and people. Finally he had told her how he had been reared by a circus couple who had made an aerialist out of him. He had fallen hopelessly in love with a girl named Florrie— one of the fliers. But there had been an accident during a performance. Ben had gone crashing into Hugo and Florrie. They had all fallen, and Hugo had been fatally injured. Guilt had ended Ben's circus career.

Dani said nothing, but held tightly to Pat's hand as Ben led them to the net. Almost at once, he called out, "Hey, you going to wait all night to check these traps?"

"Ben!" A man and a woman wearing robes to cover their spangled tights rushed forward, and Ben was swallowed by their embraces.

"Take it easy!" he protested, finally pulling free. He

looked them over and noted, "You look fine, both of you."

"Ben," the man cried, "it's so good to see you! He looks good, doesn't he, Anna?"

"He's too skinny," Anna Rudolpho objected. "We will put some meat on your bones! Come to the trailer."

"Mom, I can't tonight. When you get to New Orleans next month, I swear you'll be sick of the sight of me!" Ben warned. "But I have someone who wants to meet you—great fan of yours. This is Rachel, and it's her birthday. Rachel, Tony and Anna Rudolpho."

"Ah, what a lovely little lady!" Tony smiled and took her hand. "Did you enjoy the performance, Rachel?"

"Oh, it was wonderful!"

Anna reached down and hugged the girl. "That is nice to hear, Rachel—but you have not seen the best of the Flying Rudolphos."

"I haven't?" Rachel asked.

"No!" Anna pointed at Ben. "You should see this one! Oh, then you would see something!"

"Cut it out, Mom," Ben protested as the visitors stared at him.

"You used to do *that!*" Frank exclaimed, looking up at the trapeze bar high above. Then he looked at Savage with a new interest.

"Did he do it?" Tony asked with some indignation. "He did a *triple!* That's what he did! Oh, Ben, come back and do it again!"

"Too old and stiff, Tony," Ben protested with a laugh. "Maybe Rachel would be willing to go with you. She's just about the age I was when you took me in."

There was a great deal of talk, but finally it was time to go. "You call me as soon as you get to New Orleans," Ben ordered.

131

Then Anna asked, "Ben, have you heard from Florrie?"

Abby happened to be looking directly at Savage as the woman asked the question, and she didn't miss the expression that swept over his face. He masked it at once, saying tonelessly, "No, Anna."

"I'm afraid for her, Ben," Anna said. Then she saw that he was embarrassed. "We'll talk when we get to New Orleans."

They left, and as they headed toward the van, Abby kept close to Dani. "Did you see that look on Ben's face when the woman asked about that girl—what was her name?"

"Florrie."

"Yes. Boy, that answers a question for me!" Abby shook her head, adding, "I've been worried about myself, Dani. I've thrown myself at Ben, and he's been like a stone wall. Now I know why. He's in love with that Florrie, that's what his problem is."

Dani didn't answer. She had seen Ben's face and was shocked to see how the name had affected him. *I thought he was over that long ago*, she thought. She wanted to discover the truth, but knew she could never ask such a question. As they drove back to New Orleans, she kept glancing at Ben, wondering what was going on inside his head.

Ben let them out with a "Good night—and happy birthday, Rachel," then drove the van away.

"I guess these kids are ready for bed," Frank decided. A howl of protest arose from Matt and Rachel. Pat lay sound asleep in Dani's arms. Frank reached out and took the boy, saying, "No arguments!"

They mounted the stairs, and Abby went to her room at

once. "Matt, you and Rachel get ready for bed. I'll come in and say good night," Frank directed. He carried Pat to his room and watched as Dani undressed him and put his pajamas on him. When that was done, Frank offered, "I'll put him in bed." He picked up the sleepy child and laid him on the bed.

"Dani—" Pat mumbled in a sleep-drugged voice. "Say my prayer!"

Dani came to the bed, leaned over, and put her hand on Pat's head. "Lord, give Pat a good night's sleep. Let your angels protect him and keep him safe in the name of Jesus."

Pat muttered, "And bless Mommy and Daddy and Rachel and Matt. And Dani, too."

"You do that every night?" Frank asked as they stepped outside the room.

"Oh, yes." Dani nodded. "Now for Matt." She led the way to his room and found he was sitting on the side of the bed. "Have a good time, Son?" Frank asked.

"Yes. It was fun."

Frank tried to find something to say. He was not at ease and finally suggested, "Maybe you and I could knock a tennis ball around some day, all right?"

"Sure!" Matt's eyes lit up, and he proposed, "How about tomorrow?"

"Maybe so." Frank nodded. "Now go to sleep."

When they were on their way to Rachel's room, Dani hesitated. "Tell her how pretty she looks—and tell her you love her."

Frank looked uncomfortable. "Well, we're not too demonstrative, Dani—but I'll try." He went in, and Dani stood back. Rachel looked at her father with an odd ex-

133

pression. Dani guessed that Frank had not been in her room very often. She was aware that Lanza was stiff and awkward, but he uttered, "I enjoyed being with you. It was fun." He glanced at Dani, adding hastily, "You looked so pretty in your new dress—all grown up!"

"Did I really?"

"Sure you did." Then he put his hand on her head and blurted out, "Happy birthday—and—I love you very much."

Rachel's face tensed; then he put his arms out, and she buried her face against him. "It was—the best day of my whole life!" she declared, her voice muffled. "I love you, too, Daddy!"

Dani stepped out, and soon Frank joined her. She said nothing as they walked to the stairs, but when they got there, he offered in a strained voice, "Dani—thanks."

He said nothing else, but she knew what he meant. "I was so proud of you, Frank," she answered quietly. Then she grinned, her eyes gleaming with mischief. "I'd like to have heard what your father said to you!"

"I'm glad you *didn't!*" Frank managed a smile, then went on, "Well, I guess it's late. Good night."

Dani said, "Good night, Frank. I'm not going to bed, but thank you for a wonderful time."

He looked at her, then questioned, "Staying up for a while?"

"Oh, just to watch an old movie." She shrugged.

"What movie is that?"

"I'm a Dickens freak," she admitted ruefully. "There's an old film version of one of his books on at eleven. I'll hate myself in the morning, at six!"

"Mind if I watch a little of it?"

"It's your set," Dani commented. "You won't like it. Dickens is an acquired taste—like olives and snails."

"You can explain it to me," Frank suggested.

They went into the den, and Dani found the channel. Frank asked, "What's the name of it?"

"*Great Expectations*. It's about a young boy who wants to get rich so he can marry a rich girl he's fallen in love with," Dani explained.

"Sounds like a good idea." Frank grinned. "Does he make it?"

"I won't tell. Watch and find out."

They sat there, watching the black-and-white film flicker on the screen. Soon Dani became totally involved in the drama of Pip and his hopeless love for the beautiful Estella, with the mad Miss Haversham and her black beetles under the decaying wedding cake, with Magwitch and Jaggers and all the rest.

During an intermission, Dani made popcorn and fixed iced Cokes. They sat on in the murky darkness, watching the rest of the movie. At the point where Magwitch died, Dani pulled a handkerchief from her pocket and wiped the tears away. "I *always* cry when Magwitch dies," she whispered to Frank.

When it was over, they sat silently. Finally Frank asked, "I don't get it, Dani. It's not real—just a story. Why cry over that, when there are so many *real* things to feel bad about?"

"That's what drama does—at least for me," she told him. The spell of the performance was still on her. She put her head back on the couch, closed her eyes, and finally described her thoughts. "I know Magwitch isn't real—but when I see him dying, it reminds me that we

135

all must die sooner or later. And he died happy, after all his suffering. That always gives me great joy." She opened her eyes and moved her body around so that she could face him. "I'm just a mutt, Frank." She smiled. "Crying like a baby."

Frank studied her, then shook his head. "I don't know anything about drama or art, but it made me sad, too, when the guy died." He hesitated, then nodded, adding briefly, "It made me think of Pop."

He appeared much like a little boy who was hurt—like Pat—Dani thought. She suddenly put her hand on his. "I know. I thought of that, too."

He felt the warmth of her hand. "This is—it's like we— well, like we were an old married couple, isn't it?"

Then he raised his head and pulled her into his arms. Dani was taken by surprise, and when he kissed her, she did not protest. Once he pulled his lips from hers, she drew back. "That was my fault, Frank," she remarked gently. "We can pretend it didn't happen." Quickly she got to her feet. "It's been a wonderful time, hasn't it? But—you have a wife, Frank. And I'm praying that someday you two will be together—as you should be."

Frank stood up, his face a mask. He had been shocked by the feelings that raced through him at the touch of her lips. "She's not a wife," he accused bitterly. "Hasn't been for a long time!"

"Do you love her, Frank?"

"I don't know," he said. "I did once."

Dani stared at him, then replied, "Real love never changes."

"You don't really believe that!"

"Yes—I really do." Dani knew it was time to bring the

thing to a halt. "Good night, Frank." She moved, but stopped at the door, turning to continue, "Yes, I really do believe it. If it's real love, it never changes."

Then she was gone, leaving him alone in the room.

9
Vince

Dominic called a meeting for Sunday morning at nine o'clock. At that hour Max Darrow sat at the long walnut table in the large room used for such affairs, wondering if his father-in-law had selected that time just to be difficult. Not that it worked any hardship on Darrow himself, or his wife, Helen, for neither of them went to church—but for that matter neither did any of the others sitting at the table.

Darrow shifted nervously as his wife spoke in her high-pitched, rather shrill voice, and he wished she had not chosen to attend the meeting. Helen must have been softer spoken when she was younger, Darrow thought, but over the years as her weight had edged upward, her voice had risen as well. He looked across the long walnut table to where Frank and Eddy sat, then shifted his gaze to Dominic, who was attentively listening to his daughter.

More attentively than he listens to me, Max thought bitterly.

But it had been like that ever since he had married Helen. She had been rather pretty in those days, smart even then—as smart as Dom, some said and others added snidely, *And as mean as Phil!* He had been a penniless young lawyer, at the head of his class, but with no connections. When Helen Lanza had chosen him over a dozen other candidates, no one had been more surprised than Max Darrow himself.

But his visions of rising in the Lanza empire had faded quickly, and within a year, he had been relegated a glorified errand boy. Helen had made it clear that their sons would take over the empire in the future. When they had discovered that there would be no sons, Helen had grown harder. Often Darrow had wondered what she would have done, if it had been he instead of she who proved totally infertile. *She'd have had me out of the way in a minute,* he had told himself.

Darrow puffed nervously on a cigarette, wishing that it were over. Since Phil died, there had been immense pressure on him. Not that he wasn't a good lawyer, but none of them sitting at the table realized how hard it was to run an empire based on illegal activities and make it look good to the police and the tax people. Eddy was always ready to blame Max for anything that went wrong, but he wouldn't have the faintest idea of how to launder money.

We'd be in the pen or the poorhouse in six months, if Eddy were in charge, Darrow thought.

He snuffed out the cigarette and tried to listen to what was going on.

He had noted that Faye was at the meeting, as well as Vince Canelli. Faye, he knew, had lusted after entrance into the inner circle as most men lust after money or women. But Canelli was a newcomer, and Darrow couldn't remember a time when an outsider had been permitted to attend one of these meetings.

". . . Profits have been down for the last two months, " he heard Helen saying and wished she would sit down and be quiet. But she went on in her strident tone, as though everyone needed a hearing aid, "It doesn't take much of an analyst to figure out that, if something isn't done, we'll be broke in a year."

Dom nodded, yet took occasion to speak before she could continue: "You're right, Helen, but every business has to go through these low points. Things will change, and we'll see those profits flowing in again."

Eddy chimed in, "Not until we get Martino and Ring off our back, Pop. Helen can make charts, but we all know it's those two who've cut into our territory. If we don't do something, we may as well sell out and retire."

"That's what I've been saying, Mr. Lanza," Faye agreed. Then he added, "I admit I was a little hasty—I couldn't stand the thought of Ring pushing us around and handing nothing back."

Dom stared at him. "We've talked about that, Faye. It was a bad move."

"We ain't heard the last of it, either," Vince Canelli spoke up. "I been picking things up on the street, and the word is that Ring is hot enough to spit bullets!"

"Then hit him before he can hit us!" Faye argued. He looked at Dominic, and reminded him, "That's what Phil would have done, Mr. Lanza. It's what you did when you were fighting for your life in the old days. I've heard you say so many a time."

Dom Lanza, Darrow thought, didn't look as if he could

sit in his chair for five minutes. His illness was draining him of strength, and his vitality, once almost legendary, had become a pale shadow. Then Darrow looked at Frank, who objected, "These are new times, Faye. Those days were wide open, but we got all sorts of people now just waiting to hang us. Just ask Max."

Darrow felt Faye's eyes on him, and insisted, "Frank's right. We're just one step ahead of an IRS audit right now. They've assigned a crack team to us, and they talk about an examination—but they've really been told to nail our hides to the wall. If we get into a shooting war, it'll be just what they want!"

The argument continued for twenty minutes, always circling around the issue of the Martino threat. Dominic Lanza let none of the gnawing pain that tore at him show in his face. It seemed that he could feel the life slowly leaking out of his disease-ravaged body, moment by moment a part of his vitality lost—never to be replaced. He was like a man on a lonely, forsaken highway, with the needle on the gas gauge resting on *empty* and no welcome islands ahead; it was as if he sat tensely in the seat, waiting for the sudden cough that announced that the last drop of gasoline was gone. A matter of time. And no hope that some miracle would intervene.

Looking around the table, Dom studied the familiar faces as a gambler studies his cards. Being a man of intense practicality, he realized that if any part of his life survived, it would have to be in the lives of these. His eyes moved around the table as he cataloged each one.

Frank. Intelligent, more so than I ever was, he thought. *Plenty of courage, but he doesn't have the killer instinct that I developed. Phil had it. Frank's preoccupied with his family prob-*

lems. *That will make him careless. The man who holds this business together can't be thinking of anything but survival.*

Eddy. I have failed with him. He needed me more than the others, and I gave him less. Too late now! He would go down under pressure.

Irene. Cold and ambitious. She would love to control the business, but knows that Eddy will never be more than a minor figure.

Helen. She should have been a man! She's always been smart, almost as smart as Frank—and she's as tough as Phil. Too bad! If she had been able to have sons, she could have lived her life through them, but with a weak husband and no sons, she's trapped. A bitterness in Helen—I wish it were not so.

Max. A weak man. If he had exerted power over Helen when they first married, they could have been happy. She needs a strong man, but Max doesn't have it in him. Will do all he can, but like Eddy, he will cave in when the pinch comes.

Vince Canelli. Tough enough and shrewd. But he is not of my blood. He will be useful, and I think he has a loyal quality— something not found in most men of his type. Greedy for power, of course, but which of us around this table is not?

Faye. The most dangerous man at this table, Dom thought. *Cruel, violent, ruthless. As I have been. Will let nothing stand in his way. It would be nice if Frank had some of this in him, but I would not want Faye for a son. Phil was much the same—but he had a heart, at least for the family. Faye will try to marry Abby and make himself a part of this family. I see through that, but she does not. That will put Faye up against Frank. There must be one, single voice to control the rest—and when I am dead, it will be those two. And Frank will go down, for Faye is an animal with no thought except his own survival.*

A sense of heavy despair touched the old man, and he

interrupted, "We've done all that can be done today." Getting to his feet, he moved away from the table and went at once to his room.

Thomas Rossi took one look at Lanza's face and went to the medicine cabinet; he returned with two pills and a tumbler of water. "Take two instead of one," he ordered.

Lanza took the tablets, stared at them, then shrugged his shoulders. He swallowed them and leaned back in his chair, drained and empty.

"Not a good meeting?" Rossi asked as he knelt and untied the old man's shoes, slipping on a pair of soft carpet slippers. He had been with Lanza so long he could read his thoughts.

"No. Not good." Lanza sighed. He closed his eyes, laid his head back on the chair, and murmured, "It is bad to be old, Thomas. Very bad!"

Faye was slow leaving the house, and Vince knew he was waiting to catch a glimpse of Abby. But Frank dismissed the two of them curtly, and they made their way out through the foyer. As they came down the steps, Faye protested, "Just another meeting! When is Dom going to wake up, Vince?" His cold eyes were rash with an impatience that was ready to boil over, and he shook his head with an angry motion. "We're doing exactly what Johnny Ring wants—just waiting for him to pick us off like ducks in a shooting gallery!"

"Maybe's Dom's got something planned," Vince suggested. "He's a pretty shrewd guy." As he spoke, a movement caught his eye, and he saw Dani leave the side entrance, headed for the garage. "See you later, Faye," he ended their conversation and hurried to catch up with her.

"Hello, Dani," he greeted her. "This must be your day off."

Dani turned to him with a smile. "Yep. Ben's watching the store this morning." She was wearing a black skirt of buffed napa leather with an oversized trench coat of the same material. The coat had a padded shoulderline and two deep front pockets. The solid black was set off by a quilted jacket of purple and gold with a cowl-neck top. A pair of shiny black crocodile boots set off the outfit, along with a white wool felt fedora she wore at a rakish angle.

"I don't know much about fashions." Vince grinned. "But you look good in that outfit. Where you headed, all dressed up?"

"Going to church, Vince," Dani told him cheerfully. A thought came to her, and her full lips lifted in a smile. "Remember how you got mad when I had church in the silo? I told you then I'd let you take me to church someday. So how about it?" She saw that her invitation had caught him off guard and needled him: "You're not afraid of a preacher, are you, Vince?"

Canelli blinked, then broke into a smile. "No. I heard enough preaching from you when we were in that silo to get me used to it." He made a quick decision, nodded, and agreed, "I'll take you up, Dani. Hope the roof don't fall in."

"It won't," Dani asserted. "Come on, we can take my car." They walked rapidly to the garage, got into the Marquis, and left the property. Louie was on duty at the gate and grinned at them as they left, warning, "Watch out for that one, Dani!"

As they drove along the road, Dani asked, "How was the meeting, Vince?"

"Just a meeting. Nothing decided." Canelli looked at her, admiring the texture of her smooth cheek and the fresh color of her lips. He had known many women, but something about this one intrigued him. He had never forgotten the time when he lay almost dying in Maxwell's prison. Dani had sat beside him and encouraged him during his sickness. Thinking of that, he questioned suddenly, "Remember when I nearly kicked the bucket in the silo, Dani?"

She gave him a sober nod. "I can't ever forget that, Vince."

"I think of it a lot. But I never told you one thing about it."

"What was that, Vince?"

"Well, I thought I was going to die—and I guess you did, too. And I kept waiting for you to jump on me with a lot of preaching."

"Did you?"

"Yeah, I did." His heavy brows knitted together, and he shook his head in a gesture of wonder. "Most preachers would have, I guess. I sure couldn't get up and walk away!" Then he put his hand on her shoulder and abruptly demanded, "Why didn't you try to convert me, Dani? You didn't hold back on Candi or on any of the others. Was I just too rough a case?"

Dani removed the fedora, allowing her rich auburn curls to fall free. She didn't answer at first, but let the silence run on. Finally she shook her head and explained, "No, that wasn't the reason. I wanted to 'preach' to you very much—or at least to share what Jesus has done for me. But you weren't ready, Vince."

"Not ready?"

"No. You were dying—but you were still not ready to let God into your life. Until a person is ready, all the preaching in the world won't do much good. I prayed for you a lot, but the time never came for me to speak."

Vince sat there silently, watching the cypress trees reel by as the car hugged the edge of a small swamp. "Well, you were right," he admitted. "I was all tensed up. Had my speech ready for you, but it kinda set me back when you didn't say anything to me."

Dani spoke quietly, "Vince, it's time now."

He gave her a startled look, and she laughed at his expression. "Now don't jump out of the car! I just want to tell you about myself. I'm not going to drag you to a creek and baptize you—not unless you insist on it."

Vince grinned, nodded, and conceded, "Go ahead, Dani. I'd like to hear it. You bother me a lot—I mean, you've got it all, everything a dame ought to have. You're a real dish, and you're smart. So why aren't you out with the rest of the crowd, looking for a good time?"

Dani began to relate her experience in a steady voice—how she'd been raised in a Christian home, had been saved when she was fourteen, then gotten away from God. She explained how she'd been in love with a young man who was planning to be a missionary and how he had died in a car accident. "I thought it was my fault, Vince," she told him in a subdued voice. "So I decided to be a missionary—to take his place. But I had to find out that God had other plans. So for now I'm a private detective. But if Jesus wants me to be something else, then I'll be that."

Vince asked in a puzzled tone, "How do you know what Jesus wants you to do? He don't actually *talk* to you, does He?"

"No, but with people you love, you don't have to actually hear them say the words. With my father, for example." She smiled, and a thoughtful light touched her greenish eyes. "We know each other so well, most of the time I just *know* what he wants before he says it. It's a little different with Jesus, of course. But some things He commands are in the Bible. When I read what He's said, I know I'm supposed to obey. Then there's another thing that I can't explain. Jesus said that He would never leave His followers *alone*. Now, I'm His follower, but you don't see *Him* in this car. But He is here, Vince!" She gave him a brilliant smile, adding, "To me Jesus is just as real as *you* are!" Then she looked up and exclaimed, "Here's the church!"

He looked out at the small white frame building with the steeple and asked, "What kind of church is it?"

"Oh, nondenominational," she replied. The parking lot was crowded, but she found an empty spot and turned off the switch. "Not any particular brand. Come on." She got out of the car and walked around to his side. Looking up at his tense expression, she laughed and took his arm. "It's not going to hurt a bit, Vince. You'll like the preacher. He was a fighter pilot in Nam. Spent two years in the Hanoi Hilton."

Vince nodded. "I read about it. That was a rough place."

They made their way to the front of the church, and she led him inside. It was a small building, seating no more than two hundred. Dani led Vince to a row close to the front, and they sat down. A young man with a longish haircut was sitting at the organ, a middle-aged woman at the piano. They began playing at once. Five minutes later a choir marched in, clad in blue robes, and filled the small choir loft behind the rostrum. Then an older man with pure white hair and a deep tan came to the front, declaring, "This is the day the Lord has made. We will be glad and rejoice in it! Let us praise the Lord for his benefits!" For the next twenty minutes the sound of praise and worship filled the small building. It was a singing church, and this was what had drawn Dani to it in the first place. She loved singing, and the enthusiasm and obvious joy of the congregation had thrilled her the first time she had ventured in.

Vince looked at her strangely, whispering, "They sure are a noisy bunch! I never saw people *enjoy* singing so much!"

Dani smiled up at him. "I spent many years in a church that was nothing but ritual, Vince. But this is the real thing!"

The song service went on for nearly forty minutes, and then the preacher rose. Vince blinked and whispered, "Why—he's *blind*!"

Dani nodded, reporting tersely, "That's what the Viet Cong did to him."

"I don't think I could handle that." Vince shook his head.

"Reverend Taylor has gone back many times to Vietnam to preach. Three years ago he won the man who tortured him to Christ. Now, that's real forgiveness, Vince—and real love," Dani told him intently. "The kind only God can give a person."

Vince sat there for the next hour, lost in the sermon. He'd never heard a sermon in his life and had made up his mind that all preaching was dull. But the man with the dark glasses wasn't dull! He didn't shout and scream, but the excitement and freshness in his voice were contagious.

He had the gift of the storyteller, and woven into his message were little dramas that kept his congregation's attention riveted on his message.

His sermon was on the new birth, and the topic was familiar to Vince—for he had heard Dani speak of it often in their days together. But he'd managed to get around her by saying, *Well, she's just a woman. They're all emotional!*

But Ron Taylor was no woman. Congress had awarded him the Medal of Honor—and Vince knew what *that* meant! He sat there lost in the message. When it came to an end, he heard Reverend Taylor explain, "This is the part of the service when we give those who want to follow Jesus Christ an opportunity to do so." He hesitated and stopped dead still. The building was absolutely quiet. Vince began to perspire, and his hands trembled. Something about the sermon had shaken him, made him think of himself in a deeply troubling way. He wanted to run out of the church, but then Reverend Taylor spoke quietly, "I have the impression that there is one among us who is being dealt with by God in a powerful way. One who for the first time is finding out his need for God's love. Oh, I would love to tell you how wonderful that love is!"

Vince stood there, head down, and his hands locked on the bench in front of him so tightly that the knuckles ached. The preacher continued, "If you will allow Jesus Christ to come in and take over your life, step out of your seat. We will pray with you, whoever you are, and you will find peace."

The congregation began to sing, and Vince's jaw ached as he kept his teeth clenched. He lifted his eyes to see that two people—a young boy no more than fourteen and a young woman with a baby—had gone to the front. The

149

preacher prayed with them, and then one of the men led them away.

"We rejoice that these two have come, but I feel that there is another. All of us in this church will pray that God will find you—and that you will find Him!"

He asked one of the men to pray, and when Dani and Vince got to the door, he was waiting. "Reverend Taylor, I'd like you to meet a very dear friend of mine—Vincent Canelli."

Canelli put his hand out and found it grasped in a strong grip. "I—I enjoyed the sermon, Reverend," he confessed haltingly. The dark glasses were disconcerting, and he blurted out, "I guess it was the first sermon I ever heard, except for Dani's."

Reverend Taylor listened to Vincent carefully, seeming to search for something behind the words. He kept a firm grip on Vince's hand and then carefully replied, "I'm glad you came this morning." He paused again and seemed to be listening to something before continuing, "God is dealing with you, Vince. Don't run away from Him."

Canelli stood there, sweat on his upper lip, his eyes fixed on the preacher's face. He felt something that was like fear—yet it was not. Then Taylor very simply bowed his head and prayed, "Lord, this man is the object of your quest. I ask that you take him for your own the very instant he's ready." A smile came to his lips. "I'll be praying for you, Vince."

When they got back to the car, Vince sat down, pulled out a handkerchief, and wiped his face with an unsteady hand. Taking a deep breath, he put the handkerchief back in his pocket and then looked at Dani. "That's—that's quite a preacher," he muttered. Then he looked back at the church, at the people coming out, and finally brought his gaze back to her. "The reverend, he thinks I'm the one God's after."

"Yes. That's what he thinks, Vince," Dani admitted gently.

Canelli shook his head. "Let's go. I'm not feeling too well."

Dani started the car, drove out of the parking lot, and turned toward the city. "Let's go have something to eat," she suggested. She drove to Algiers' Point, and they went into Algiers, a restaurant perched on piers in a turn of the Mississippi. Sitting at a booth that overlooked the river, they ate slowly. Vince was off in a world of his own, more thoughtful than Dani had ever seen him.

Finally he looked at her and remarked, "I just don't know, Dani. You know what a mug I am. I been on the streets since I was twelve years old. Done it all." He watched the roiling waters of the big river, then spread his hand out in a helpless gesture. "What would I do for a living? I don't know how to do anything honest."

"Vince, you can do a great many things," Dani responded. "You could be a private investigator, for example."

He stared at her, then asked, "Would you hire me, Dani?"

"Of course!"

He smiled at that, but there was doubt in his dark eyes. Finally he demanded, "It's a big thing, this Jesus business, ain't it, Dani?"

"The biggest thing there is in life, Vince!"

He got to his feet and helped her on with her coat. When they got back to the car, he said, "Guess I'll walk around a little bit, Dani. You be all right?"

"Yes, I'll be all right." Dani smiled.

He smiled back, a glint of humor in his eyes. "You set me up, didn't you?"

"I did the best I could, Vince." Dani nodded.

"Well, I been wanted by the cops lots of times," he admitted slowly. "But this is the first time I've ever been on *God's* wanted list!" He turned and walked away, his heavy shoulders stooped and his head down.

10
The Witness

"Look at that, Miss Dani!" Eva Larson, the cook, was staring out the window of the kitchen. Shaking her head in disbelief, she turned to Dani, who was sitting at the counter. "Day of miracles is here!"

"What is it, Eva?" Dani got up and moved to the window. She saw Ben and Abby coming down the walk, dressed in tennis wear. "What's so strange about that?"

"Why, that girl never got up before noon in her life, Miss Dani!" Eva asserted. She turned the eggs sizzling in the skillet, adding, "Not till that good-looking Savage man got here." Pushing the bread down into the toaster, she grinned. "That Abby sure is man hungry!"

Abby burst through the door, towing Savage by the hand. "Eva! Fix us some breakfast—quick! I'm starving to death!" She was wearing the briefest of white shorts and a sheer, overpriced shirt with a small animal over the left breast. She was still holding Savage's hand, and there was a possessive quality in her manner as she turned to him and patted his cheek. "Go on, Ben," she commanded. "Tell them how I beat you!"

Savage was wearing a pair of ragged blue-jean cutoffs, not altered by a stylist, but by time and rough usage. His deep chest swelled beneath a thin blue windbreaker, and Dani saw the bulge made by the magnum on his left side. "Guess I had an off day," he remarked blandly.

Abby laughed with delight. "Like fun! You're just a male chauvinist, isn't he, Dani?"

"He always says that when he loses," Dani noted evenly, but there was a sardonic glint in her eye as she looked at the pair. She sat there while Abby walked around the kitchen, waiting for Eva to cook more eggs and bacon. There was a liveliness in the girl that had been lacking the first time Dani had seen her, and it was not hard to see that Savage's presence had made the difference. Ben said little, but leaned back in one of the kitchen chairs, drinking orange juice and smiling occasionally at Abby.

The breakfast was quickly cooked, and Abby suggested, "Let's go eat out on the terrace." The three of them carried their plates out, and Eva brought the whole pot of coffee to one of the modernistic glass-and-steel tables. The three of them sat down, and Abby did most of the talking. She finished first and got up with the words, "Don't forget, Ben, you promised to take me to the tennis tournament next Saturday."

"Hey!" Savage objected quickly. "I never said that!"

Abby laughed and shook her hair back. "You will, though," she demanded, reaching out with a possessive gesture to pull the thick hair that lay on his neck. "I'll tell Uncle Dom that I need a bodyguard. He'll make you do it,

Ben." She started to leave, but turned to give him an arch look. "I can make men do what I want them to, Ben! Haven't you noticed?"

Dani watched her leave and started to speak, but at that moment, Frank Lanza emerged from the house and started toward where she was sitting. His face was stiff, and she was not surprised when he said without preamble, "Dani, Rosemary isn't feeling too well this morning. Would you look in on her when you have time?"

All three of them knew that meant, *Rosemary has a hangover; look out for her until I get back.* But Dani said only, "Yes, of course."

Frank stood there, bitterness in his eyes, but he suddenly lowered his gaze and stated quietly, "You make a difference around here, Dani. I don't know what I did before you came."

Wheeling quickly, he walked away, his back rigid.

"You know," Ben offered in a casual tone, "I think that guy's got a yen for you, Boss."

Dani stared at him speechlessly, and then snapped, "Don't be silly! It's you and that teenybopper I'm worried about."

Savage tilted his head back, closed his eyes, and soaked up the sun. He had the gift of going loose at any time, and now he sat there bonelessly. "I'm just an uncle to her. She's only a child, you know."

"Oh, right!" Dani grated. "Anyone can see she's a sweet, innocent young girl! Rebecca of Sunnybrook Farm!"

Slowly Ben opened one eye and regarded her. His broad mouth turned upward slightly, and he shrugged. "Remember what the Good Book says, Boss—'Jealousy is cruel as the grave. . . .' That's in the Song of Solomon, if you want to look it up."

"Jealous!" Dani shrieked, outraged. "You think I'm jealous of you and that—that—"

When she found no word, Ben suggested, "Child. . . ?"

"You just keep your mind on your job, Benjamin Davis Savage!"

He grinned fully then and pulled himself up. "Hey, now I know you're sore. You only use all my names when I've been naughty. My mom was the same way."

Dani glared at him, then sniffed and told him, "Just mind your manners, that's all!"

"Sure." He sat there, watching the cirrus clouds drift across the azure sky, refusing to argue. Finally he asked, "What's going on with Vince? Ever since you took him to church, he's been wandering around like a lost soul."

Dani moved uncertainly in her chair. She was never sure how serious Ben was about those things that concerned her most, and now she responded cautiously, "He's a lonely man. And sooner or later the kind of life he's led will catch up with him." She rubbed the top of the glass table with her forefinger, thinking of Vince, troubled by the way he'd kept clear of her since the previous Sunday. Without meaning to, she spoke her mind. "Ben, sometimes I think I do more harm than good—trying to preach to people who don't want to hear it."

Her sudden outburst caught his attention, and he turned to face her. A quizzical light brightened his hazel eyes, and memories stirred as he considered her, touching the scar over his left eyebrow with a forefinger. Finally he shook his head. "Remember what John Wayne used to say? 'A man does what he has to do!' He said that in about ninety movies, didn't he? And I guess a woman has to do what she has to do."

Dani looked up at him quickly, for it was as close as Savage had ever come to expressing his opinion about her Christian faith. The sun washed over her face, bringing out the fine bone structure, and a fresh burst of yellow sunlight fired golden glints in her auburn hair. There was, Savage decided, some sort of inner strength or peace that revealed itself in her features. She was looking down at her hands, but suddenly she lifted her head, a serious expression in her eyes. "Is that some sort of compliment, Ben? I know the Duke is your hero and all—but are you telling me that you don't think I'm a complete nut?"

Savage usually kept his deeper feelings covered with a pair of expressionless eyes, just as he hid behind light words, but the moment caught him, and he told her, "I never thought that, Dani. You've got more nerve than any woman I've ever known."

The sudden compliment made Dani blink, and she was irritated at the absurd happiness his words gave to her. "Well, I guess I'd better quit while I'm ahead." She laughed and got up from her chair. "I'll take the dishes back. The kids will swarm you this morning. Try to wring them dry so I can get them still long enough to pound some math into their skulls!"

"Yeah. What's going down today?"

"Oh, Frank asked me to eat with the family tonight." She shrugged. "They'll all be there, and I think he wants me just to keep a tight rein on Pat."

"No, that's not why he wants you, Boss," Ben remarked. Wordlessly he got up and sauntered toward the gym.

Dani stared after him, but finally shrugged and carried the dishes back into the kitchen. Eva looked up as she came in and cautioned, "You tell that Ben Savage to keep clear of Abby. Mister Dom thinks a lot of her. Guess he'd shoot any man who messed around with her." She looked at a piece of paper tacked over the sink, and added, "They want seafood tonight. Maybe I'll give them some of that étoufée you gave me a recipe for, Miss Dani. Sure is good!"

The day passed quickly, and when Dani went into the dining room, accompanied by her three charges, she saw that everyone was there—even Rosemary. "Sorry to be late," she murmured to Frank. "I had to scrub them all down."

"You didn't scrub *me* down!" Matt pointed out quickly.

"Maybe she should have." Frank laughed. "You probably left enough dirt behind your ears to start a garden!"

"Aw, Dad, come on!" Matt scowled, but Dani saw that he was glad, as always, for any attention Frank paid to him. "Dani don't have to make me clean up like she does Pat!"

Frank looked at Dani, and his eyes glinted with humor. "I didn't do too well in English in school, but wasn't there some sort of grammatical error in that, Dani?"

Dani smiled at him, but patted Matt's arm. "I don't correct errors after six o'clock, Mr. Lanza. Do I, Matthew? Anyway, he doesn't make many."

Matt tried to look indifferent to the praise, but failed. He took his seat across from Frank, and Dani sat beside him. "Bring on the food, Mary," Frank instructed. "I could eat a horse."

"Got something better than *that*, Mr. Frank!" the red-haired maid answered with a smile. "Blackened redfish and fresh lobster."

The two maids started bringing in the food, and soon

the table was buzzing with talk. The family was, Dani saw, grouped into definite categories. Dom sat at the end, eating almost nothing, but listening and watching. At his right were Frank and Rosemary. On his left, Eddy and Irene. The children sat in a row, along with Dani, and across from them sat Max and Helen. Dani felt slightly out of place—yet she saw that even some of the others were not completely at ease. Helen Darrow spoke often and in a strident voice, and Dani saw that Irene frequently raised an eyebrow at some of her sister-in-law's comments. There was little love lost, Dani felt, between the two women. Dani had seen almost at once that Irene longed for her husband, Eddy, to move up in the structure, while Helen was just as determined that Max would do the same. Both women, Dani understood, were stronger than their husbands. Only Abby was missing, and when Dani asked Eddy, he replied that she was out on a date.

Rosemary Lanza looked beautiful. Dani could see no sign of the heavy drinking that had been going on for a long time. That would come, Dani knew, but now nothing marred the smooth cheeks, slightly flushed with interest as Frank spoke to her about a cruise vacation he was planning. Rosemary didn't take her eyes off him, but her obvious devotion was lost on Frank. *I wonder if she could get his love back if she tried?* Dani mused. But that was not likely, she knew, for Frank Lanza was a strong character and would demand that same strength in a wife.

As Dani thought of that, suddenly Pat broke out loudly, "Daddy, you and Mama have to come to see us tomorrow! Pleeze!"

"See you do what, Pat?" Frank asked.

"See us do our *act!*" Pat nodded. He had a mustache of

gravy on his mouth, and Dani reached over and wiped it off as he added, "It's a *show!*"

Frank looked at Dani, and she chimed in, "It really is a show." A smiled curved her lips upward, and she added, "Ben Savage has been working with them, and he says they're ready to show what they've learned. He asked me to invite you all to the performance at two o'clock."

Rosemary agreed at once. "Oh, that will be nice, won't it, Frank?"

Frank had opened his mouth to say that he could not come, until he saw the eager look on Rachel's face. Quickly he glanced at Matt and Pat, and seeing the same expectation, quickly changed his mind. "Sure! I'll be expecting great things from you all."

Dani confessed, "I wish all of you could come. It would be nice for the children to have an audience."

Irene excused herself, "Oh, I can't possibly make it! I have an appointment with the hairdresser at one."

"Aw, come on, Aunt Irene!" Matt begged. "Abby's going to be there, too!"

"I think we can make it, Irene," Eddy insisted, ignoring the quick, angry expression that touched his wife's face. "You can get another appointment," he urged.

"Oh, I think you should keep the appointment, Irene!" Helen interjected. "Your hair *does* need something done to it!"

Helen's words angered Irene. Her eyes flashed, and she spoke in a hard-edged tone, "I believe I will come to see the children. After all, it's the *children* who make life worthwhile, isn't it, Helen?"

Helen Darrow flushed, then turned pale, for she resented any reference to the fact that she had produced no children.

Max jumped in, "We may be a little late. I ordered that new rice bed Helen's been wanting. They're supposed to deliver it at two."

Helen looked at him with pleased surprise. "Why, Max!" she cried out with warmth. "You never told me you'd done that!"

"Sort of a prebirthday present." Darrow smiled. Then he looked down the table at the children. "But we'll be there as soon as we get the bed in place."

The meal ended, and as the party broke up Dani approached Dom Lanza. "You'll be there tomorrow, won't you, Mr. Lanza?"

"Yes." He nodded slightly and continued quietly, "I find myself wanting to take in everything. Not wanting to miss even a sunset."

Max Darrow was passing by, and upon hearing this, he paused and commented, "You'll enjoy it, Dom. Afterwards, maybe we can play chess."

He left, and Dom looked up at Dani. "Are you busy?"

"Right now?" she asked in surprise. "No. I was going to read a while and get to bed early."

"I'd like a little company—if you don't mind?"

"I'd like it very much." Dani smiled. "Where shall we go?"

"I want to show you some photographs. Let's go to my room." He got up slowly, and as he turned, a pain caught him. It was violent enough to twist him around and cause him to miss a step.

Dani almost reached out to help him, but caught herself just in time. Glancing around, she saw that no one else had noticed and quickly moved to stand beside him, admitting, "I like pictures, but I could never take good ones myself." She kept up the conversation, and his pain-filled eyes touched her with gratitude. He had not missed her impulsive move to help him or the tact that made her suddenly withhold it. He said nothing, but when they were in his room, he sat down slowly and requested in a tight voice, "Dani, will you get those albums in that chest?" He leaned back and shook his head sadly. "A terrible thing—to have to be waited on all the time!"

Dani found no answer. It was painful to have to watch the strength drain out of the old man day by day. She suspected that he was heavily sedated most of the time, and somewhere down the line was the moment when even drugs would be inadequate to stem the pain that lined his face. As she brought the three thick leather albums back and sat down in a chair beside him, she wondered again how she could ever bring herself to speak of God to Dom Lanza. The man's pride had not been destroyed by the disease that was ravaging his body—and that pride revealed itself in the fierce light in his old eyes and the defiant set of his thin lips. He had lived by a savage code all his life, using his superior strength to beat down those who contended with him. Now that the end was come, he was seeing the family and the empire he had built begin to crumble—and he had no power to defend it. Dani could not imagine what went on in his mind, but she knew he had to be experiencing doubt and despair as he came to the end of life.

"Nothing is more boring than to look at someone else's snapshots." Dom shrugged. "But there are a few in here that you might like to see." He began leafing through the thick album, but Dani put out a hand and interrupted him. "Oh! Isn't that George Raft?"

"Yes, it is." Dom smiled at her. "We were very good friends. I'm surprised you even know who he is, Dani. He was way before your time."

"Oh, I'm crazy about old movies. And I always liked those old gangster movies—" She bit her lip suddenly, adding hurriedly, "Tell me, did you know any more movie stars—James Cagney?"

"I met Cagney twice. He was a fine man. . . ."

For the next half hour Lanza leafed through the album, and Dani was fascinated. Lanza had been on the dark edge of respectability, but many people, she knew, felt drawn to criminal figures. As he showed her the pictures of politicians, movie stars, and writers he had known, he seemed to grow milder. The pain was not so bad, and he relaxed in the chair. Time ran on, and they finished the album. Closing it, he told her, "That takes me back. I haven't looked at it for a long time." Then he laid it on his lap and ran a thin hand over the embossed cover. "Most of them are dead now."

The silence deepened in the room, broken only by the ticking of the clock and the high-pitched chirps of the purple martins that were nesting just outside the window of Lanza's room. The room was dark, almost gloomy. *It's like a mausoleum!* Dani decided. She wanted to be all the help she could to the old man, but at the unpleasant thought, an impulse came to leave.

Then a second impulse overtook her, and she knew at once that it was time to speak to her employer about the thing that mattered most to her. As always, she wished that she had more boldness, for she knew that if she did speak of what was on her heart, Lanza might order her out of his house. She had heard stories of his quick and deadly temper and feared that she might be subject to it.

163

He sat there, his eyes closed, his breathing shallow, and she asked breathlessly, "Mr. Lanza—may I say something to you?"

The eyes opened quickly, and there was something predatory in them. Dom Lanza had endured in a jungle by being watchful. He looked at her silently, then slowly nodded. "Yes." It was not a cordial invitation, but Dani plunged ahead.

"Well, you may be embarrassed, Mr. Lanza," she warned evenly. "But since I've been here, I've become very fond of your family—and of you." The color in her cheeks rose, and she laughed shortly, shaking her head. "I suppose you must hear that a lot, a famous man like you."

Lanza stared at her. "No," he replied slowly. "I have not heard it a lot. I am not a man who inspires that sort of thing." A light of surprise touched his eyes, and he spoke in a wry tone, "It surprises me that you say such a thing— but not very much. You are an unusual young woman. I've never seen anyone like you. You understand, many people have tried to gain my confidence—most of them for their own ends. But you are different. I have watched you carefully, Dani." He raised one hand and rubbed his forehead thoughtfully. "If you are a fraud, you are the best I have ever seen!"

"Oh, I'm not so unusual," Dani denied his words quickly. Then she took her courage in both hands and almost blurted out, "If you've seen anything good in me, Mr. Lanza, it's because the Lord Jesus Christ put it there!" She waited for him to raise a hand, to cut her off abruptly— but he only watched her intently, so she went on, "I came from a Christian home, but it was only a few years ago that I discovered that Jesus Christ is really alive—that He can live inside a person. . . ."

Dani never raised her voice, but for the next ten minutes she told Dom Lanza how she had found Christ. It was a simple testimony with many Scriptures. Finally, "It's hard for me to speak to you like this," she told him, "because I know you don't believe as I do about God. But for me, Jesus has meant so much—and I want everyone to know the peace that He brought to me."

Lanza had not moved for a long time, but now he stirred slightly. "Peace! I've known little of that!" Then he shook his head. "I have thought of Jesus Christ," he admitted. "What man hasn't? But if what I have heard of Him is true, how could He help a man like me? You know what I've been—the kind of life I've led." A thought struck him, and he asked, "You've said these things to Vince, haven't you?"

"Yes." Dani nodded. "I think a lot of Vince. We went through a hard time together. Did he say something to you about me?"

"Not a lot," Lanza answered. "But he's been going around like a man in a dream. When I asked him what was wrong with him, he just muttered, 'Oh, it's that preacher woman! She's been at me!' So now I know what's eating at him. But what can you hope for? Men like Canelli and myself, our hands are red with blood."

Dani sat there, not knowing what to say. Finally she shook her head. "You and Vince are not different from other men, Mr. Lanza. The Bible says that all men and women are sinners—that every one of us is cut off from God. Some may have committed what seem to be *worse* sins—but may I read you a few verses from my New Testament?"

He smiled slightly as she took a thin book from her side pocket. "I notice you always have two things on you, Dani—your Bible and your thirty-eight! I am glad for the gun—so now I must pay heed to the other. What does it say?"

"In James chapter two, there is a verse that says, 'For whosoever shall keep the whole law, yet offend in one point, he is guilty of all.' Do you see what that means? No matter which *particular* sin we might commit, we are equally guilty before God."

"But murder is worse than stealing!"

"In the eyes of men—but the next verse says, 'He that said, Do not commit adultery, said also, Do not kill. Now if thou commit no adultery, yet if thou kill, thou art become a transgressor of the law.' Don't you see? If you hired a man, there are many ways he might betray you. But no matter which one he chose—that wouldn't matter, would it? He would be a traitor."

Lanza stared at her with fresh interest. "I never thought of that—but it is true." With a puzzled look, he pondered, "I know little of these things, but surely it matters what a man does? I mean, is Adolf Hitler no worse than your ordinary person? He butchered millions of Jews! Surely God doesn't look on him as He looks on *you*, for example?"

"Hitler was a sinner," Dani agreed quickly, "and a terrible human being. But the point of the whole Bible is that all of us are sinners! And it is God's purpose to save us all from what we have become. My sins were not as terrible in your sight as those of Hitler, but in God's sight I was a traitor. That's why I had to be saved. Jesus said in John 3, speaking to a very religious man, '. . . Ye must be born again.' If keeping the law had been all that was necessary, that man would have been in good shape—for he was very religious, keeping all the outward laws. But in his heart he was wrong! Jesus really meant, 'Nicodemus, you look very good on the outside, but your heart is wrong. I must change *that* before you can be acceptable to God!' "

Dom sat there, studying her. "This is very different from what I have believed," he finally pronounced. "I have thought of God, but long ago I became so hard that I put Him out of my life and out of my mind. Now that I am going to die, I find myself thinking more of these things. But it is too late."

"No, it's not too late," Dani corrected him. "Jesus came to make men and women what God wants them to be. I know there are many who profess to be Christians who are not what they should be, but that's true of any movement, isn't it? Not all soldiers are patriots. Some are vicious or even traitors—but that doesn't mean that America is evil! Sometimes Christians make very bad errors. I certainly have! But you see, Mr. Lanza, when God comes into a person's life, it's a *beginning*, not an end. We won't be perfect in this world, but the Bible says that we will be resurrected someday—and then we will be like Jesus. Not tied to these frail, sinful bodies, but as God intended for us to be all along."

Once again the room fell silent. Dani knew intuitively that she had said what God wanted her to say. She sat there waiting, and finally Dom told her heavily, "I cannot explain what I think. I am old and dying—and my family that I have lived for is in terrible danger. I am too weak to protect them, and it seems that my life is a failure. I have lived for my family, and now I can do nothing." He lifted his head, and a terrible look of despair filled his old eyes. "But I will think on what you have said."

Dani saw that the pain was back, and she asked, "Can I get you something?"

"Yes. Some water, if you will." He waited until she returned with a glass of water, shook two pills from a bottle, and swallowed them. "I am tired," he excused himself. "I think I will lie down."

"Thank you for listening to me, Mr. Lanza. I meant what I said—about becoming fond of you and your family." Dani left the room, closing the door quietly. As she moved down the hall, a sense of failure closed in on her, and she prayed, *I didn't say it well, Lord—but take what was good, and let Dom Lanza find his peace with You!*

11
The Hit

"You couldn't lay off the stuff for one day?" Frank glared down at Rosemary.

Rosemary was trying to tie the bow of her sash, but her fingers were numbed by too many sips from the bottle of Scotch. She looked up at Frank and tried to smile. "I—I only had one or two, Frank," she excused herself.

He walked over and opened the drawer of her vanity. Pulling out the fifth of whiskey, he stared at it, then exclaimed, "You've had more than that!" In a sudden explosion of anger, he threw the bottle across the room. It shattered and left an ugly blotch on the pale ivory wall, but he paid it no heed. "The kids have been looking forward to this," he barked bitterly, turning to face her. He had no idea how he looked to her at that moment, with his face iron hard and his voice cutting like a razor. Until her marriage to him, this gentle woman had been shielded by loving parents. She could not remember the day or the month when fear had come to take her by force. Her romantic ideas of marriage had not lasted long, and though she had never been a drinker, within six months of her wedding she had started seeking a refuge from fear in the bottles of liquor so readily available in the Lanza home.

As she looked up at her husband, Rosemary remembered how gentle he had been when her drinking problem had first started. She lifted her hand and whispered, "Frank—don't hate me! I—I don't want to drink—!"

He avoided her hand, thinking of all the promises she had made and broken. He was a drinking man himself, but it held no compulsion for him. There was something shameful in the way she clung to the bottle, and he could not understand it. "You keep saying that, but you always go back to it. Do you want the kids to grow up knowing their mother is a drunk?"

She began to cry, shaking her head. "No! No!"

Then Frank made a mistake. Without thought, he burst out, "Why, Dani is a better mother than you are to the kids!"

The words shook Rosemary's nerves, and she raised her tear-stained face to stare at him. "And I suppose she's a better wife to you than I am? Is that what you're thinking, Frank? Do you think I haven't seen the way you look at her?"

Frank blinked at her words, for they stung him. "Nobody would blame me for looking at another woman!" he shouted. "You're no wife—and no mother!" He whirled and left the room, slamming the door.

Rosemary got up, ran to the bed, and collapsed on it. She lay there, sobbing, for a long time. Finally, she sat up, took a deep breath, and got to her feet. The scene had sobered her to a great extent, and she walked to the mirror to examine her face. As always she hated to see her own reflection. But she set her jaw, went to the bathroom, and began to wash her face in cold water.

Downstairs, Eddy and Irene were talking to Dom as Frank came in. Dom saw the expression on Frank's face, and when he announced shortly, "Rosemary won't be able to make it," he knew at once what was wrong. But he said nothing. He had welcomed Rosemary as a daughter-in-law, for she had been of a good, respectable family, and he had known her to be a virtuous girl. Nothing had hurt him more than to watch her decline, and he had never ceased to long for her to gain control over the demon that drove her to drink.

Eddy was less sensitive to such things. He nodded to Frank and asked, "Well, ready for the big production? All I've heard from Abby is about this guy Savage! She's got a king-sized crush on him."

Irene gave him an angry look. "You wouldn't be so happy if she decided to marry him, Eddy."

Eddy stared at her, nonplussed. "Marry him? Don't be crazy, Irene! She's got more sense than that!"

"I don't know why you think that," Irene countered. "She was all set to marry that guitar player."

"Well, sure." Eddy shrugged. "But I discouraged him."

"You had Faye beat him up," Irene snapped. "I don't think that would work with Savage."

Eddy started to argue, but at that moment Max and Helen came in. With interest Dom saw that Helen was angry. Except for Phil, she was the child who was most like him, Dom had often thought. His daughter had gotten much of her makeup from him—his quick ability to make decisions, his crafty ways, and his ruthless determination. *She should have been a man*, Dom thought as he studied her. He was aware, as well, that she had decided that Max should take his place at the head of the family—which meant, he knew, that *she* would rule the empire he had built up. That might be the way it would work out, Dom had often thought.

Helen stiffly objected, "I don't see why I can't go watch the children do their show."

"Helen, we've been over that," Max responded patiently. He removed his glasses and wiped them carefully with a spotless white handkerchief. "I had that bed shipped from Pennsylvania. If it has one scratch on it, you'll send it right back." He put his glasses back on, replaced the handkerchief, after folding it carefully, then spoke with rare firmness, "We can go see the children as soon as the bed comes. I want you to check it and be sure it's what you want."

Helen sighed. "All right. But you were never so careful about furniture before."

Max smiled slightly. "I am now—because you sent all that antique furniture back last year, when you didn't like it."

Frank broke in impatiently, "It's nearly two. Helen, you and Max come on down, if you can. Let's go!"

As the small group passed through the front door, Faye and Vince ascended the front steps. Frank paused, ordering, "Faye, you and Vince get downtown." A frown creased his brow, and he shook his head with a trace of anger. "Fats Marone has been getting out of hand. Go down and shake him up."

Faye grinned, for this had been his idea. "I'll take care of it, Frank. But I won't need Vince for a little job like that."

He turned to Canelli and instructed him, "You keep an eye on things here."

"Sure, Faye." Vince nodded absently.

Dominic Lanza's lifetime of watching men made him catch something out of the ordinary here. When he had first come to the organization, Vince had been a pusher, aggressive as any man Dom had seen. Then the big man had not been the sort of man to take the slight Faye had just administered. In Dom's eyes Canelli's lack of fear of Faye Dietrich made him valuable, for Dom liked and needed strong, aggressive men.

Something's working on Vince Canelli, Dom decided. *Perhaps his encounter with Danielle Ross?* The thought caught at Dom, for he had been considering the young woman's words more than he would have thought possible. Though he had tried to shrug it off, the woman's genuine honesty made her words echo in his mind. He had tried to tell himself it was just because he was old and sick, but here was Vince—a strong man in the prime of life—and he seemed vulnerable to the same thoughts.

As Vince and Faye turned and walked away, Frank called out, "Let's go." He led the family down the path toward the swimming pool, adjusting his steps to allow his father to keep up with them.

Dani held the children to their academic schedule all morning, but after a light lunch, she accompanied them to the gym. Ben had met them, dressed in trunks and wearing a finger-tip-length, white terry-cloth jacket. He was doing some work on the trampoline when they entered, and as he swung to meet them, Dani noted that the magnum was in a side pocket rather than in the customary shoulder holster.

173

"Hey, you guys ready for the big number?" he called out as the group approached.

"Pat's going to sink like a rock," Rachel objected in disgust. "He ate like a pig at lunch."

"No, I won't," Pat argued loudly. "I ate a lot so it'll help me swim underwater. Make me sink more better."

Ben grinned and shook his head. "Never thought of it that way, Pat. I may have to jump in and pull you up. Okay, you guys warm up a little bit, while I talk to teacher."

Dani waited until they scattered, Abby and Rachel to the trampoline, Matthew and Pat to the pool. "I talked to Dad this morning. He says the work is piling up. Wants to know when we're going to be able to get back to business as usual."

"Been wondering that myself," Savage told her. "What's it look like to you?"

"Oh, I don't know, Ben," Dani voiced a trace of irritation. "On the one hand, Lanza's paying us a bundle. But we're not creating any new accounts. When this is over, we'll have a good bank balance, but fewer jobs. And Dad's working too hard."

"Want some advice?"

"I need some. What's your idea on all of this?"

"I think we ought to give Lanza some notice and pull out." Savage looked at the young people, then brought his gaze back to meet hers. "You're getting too emotionally involved in the Lanza family, Boss. And they're using you as a crutch—especially the kids."

"Even if you're right about that, Ben, it won't stop me from doing a good job."

"No, but there's no end in sight." He shifted his weight

and considered her carefully. "Martino's outfit isn't going to give up, not with a hardcase like Johnny Ring running it. And Dom Lanza will have to die before he gives up. We're all sitting on a bomb, and sooner or later it's going to go off."

"Just walk off and leave the children?" Dani shook her head stubbornly. "I can't do that."

Savage gave her an odd look, but there was no time for him to answer. Looking over his shoulder he warned, "Here they come."

Dani followed his glance and turned to walk toward the front of the building, where Frank led the others. She called brightly, "Come in, everyone. The show's about to start. Plenty of seats for everyone." She noted at once that Rosemary wasn't in the group, but said nothing about it. "This is Ben's show today. Sometime we'll have an academic performance, but I'll let him tell you what's on the program." She walked over and took a seat next to Dom, who touched Dani's arm and smiled at her.

Savage stood beside the kids, who grinned nervously. At the moment he started to speak Rosemary came in. She erupted through the entrance, but hesitated before taking a seat beside Frank. She said nothing, and her face was pale, but she managed to wave to the children and give them a faint smile.

Savage announced, "I'm not much of an emcee, folks. But I do want to say that all of our performers have worked hard for this. First we have Mr. Patrick Lanza. Let's hear a little applause as he does his thing. Go to it, Pat!"

Shrugging out of his short coat, Ben dropped it on the tile as Pat ran to the side of the pool. The gun in the pocket rang as it struck the surface, and Dom smiled and whispered to Dani, "I'll bet that's the first time he's been without that iron since he came here!"

Pat jumped into the pool and dog-paddled vigorously across. When he got to the far side, he cried out, "Now watch, Daddy! You just watch!" He ducked and came across the pool underwater, surfacing when his head banged on the side of the pool. He came up spouting and gasping, but as Ben reached down and pulled him out, he waved frantically, calling, "Did you see me, Daddy?"

"I saw you, Pat," Frank answered. "That was great swimming!"

Everyone applauded, and then Ben cried out, "Now, an exhibition of precision diving by Matt Lanza." He walked down the pool to stand beside Matt, who was nervously looking up at the diving board. Ben slapped him on the shoulder, saying quietly, "Break a leg, Matt! Just like we did it in practice. It's no different now."

Matt swallowed, but went to the one-meter board, and without a pause executed a perfect jackknife.

"Let's hear it, folks," Ben encouraged. "Matt's put in a lot of hours working on that one."

Dani whispered to Dom, "He's right about that, Mr. Lanza. When they started, Matt was afraid to jump in from the side of the pool, but Ben just kept encouraging him."

They all applauded as Matt did several dives from the low board. "Now, I'm going to do a one and a half from the high board," Matt proclaimed.

Ben gave him a quick look and warned, "You haven't got that down, Matt." But Matt ignored him and climbed to the top of the three-meter board. His face was pale, and everyone saw that he was afraid.

"That's too much for him," Dom stated quietly. "He could get hurt."

Matt made his approach and seemed to be all right, but at the last moment, just as he left the board, he lost his courage. He tried to correct, but it was too late. He made a half turn, arms waving and legs kicking, and hit the water facedown. Rosemary cried out and rose, but Frank pulled her into her seat again.

Matt came up, his face red with the force of the impact and with shame. He pulled himself out of the pool and was about to run, but Ben caught him by the arm. "That wasn't your best shot, Matt. Go back, and this time forget about everything except the dive." Matt hesitated, but Ben continued in a low voice, "You've got to do it, kid! If you don't, you'll never dive from that board again. You can do it!"

Matt stared at Savage's hard face, and something in the steady hazel eyes seemed to reassure him. He nodded, and as he went back up the tower, Ben called out, "Watch this, folks!"

Matt took a deep breath and closed his mind to everything. He seemed to be praying, and when he made his approach, he made a perfect spring and went into a ball, coming out just in time to cleave the water.

"Hey, that was a perfect ten!" Savage yelled. He started to run over, but Frank Lanza had leaped from his seat and rushed to pull the boy out.

"That was great, Matt!" Frank exclaimed. He had been afraid that the boy would run away, and when Matt had gone back and tried again, it gave him a thrill. "You're going to be a champion!"

That was the first time he had said such a thing to Matt,

and the boy stood there, dripping, his face shining with perfect happiness. Dom said, "He should have done that a long time ago, Dani! Look at the boy."

"Yes. Matt needs encouragement. Especially from Frank."

Finally Frank returned to his seat, a broad smile on his face and his clothes wet from Matt's dripping form. Ben directed, "Now let's move over to the trampoline."

As they changed seats, Dani applauded Ben's efforts, "He's done a wonderful job, hasn't he, Mr. Lanza?"

"Yes, he has." Dom nodded. His face was lined with pain, and she knew that he was hurting. But he seemed pleased. "It was a good thing for my house when you and Savage came to it," he told her.

Dani glanced at him, thinking of Ben's warning that she was getting too close to the family. Was he right? They all took their seats, and Ben announced, "For our next act, we have Miss Rachel Lanza. Come on, Rachel."

Rachel looked frail in her pink workout suit, but Ben's careful coaching had developed her strength. She mounted the trampoline and began to bounce. Ben had told Dani, "She's got a knack for it. Balance and nerve." When she rose to the air and did a perfect somersault, she exhibited a natural grace that made Dani see what he meant.

Eddy crowed, "Why, the kid's good enough for the circus!"

Rosemary cried out in delight and clapped her hands as she watched, grabbing Frank's arm with fear as Rachel did one especially difficult number. Finally, when her daughter finished, Rosemary went to her and gave her a hug. "That was *wonderful*, honey! I never knew you were so good!"

Frank had crossed over to her as well, and when he picked her up and kissed her, Rachel's delicate face glowed. Dani saw Dom nod, and she squeezed his arm, saying, "Nothing but stars in the Lanza family!"

Then Savage called out, "For our final act, we have Miss Abby Lanza."

Wearing a more discreet workout suit than usual, Abby looked slim and beautiful as she got on the trampoline. She went through the routine that she had worked hard on, and her parents glowed with pleasure.

When the applause was over, Abby suggested, "Come on, Ben. Give us a real performance!"

Ben shook his head. "This is a family show, Abby." But she begged him, and soon Pat and Matthew were urging him. Finally Frank chimed in, "Come on, Ben, let's see your act."

Ben didn't want to do it, Dani saw, but shrugged his shoulders and took Abby's place on the trampoline. He began bouncing and soon was amazing them with somersaults and flying rolls. "That is marvelous!" Dom exclaimed to Dani. "I had no idea!"

"Ben was one of the greatest aerialists in the circus," Dani replied warmly. "He did a triple—and not many can do that one."

Finally Ben was springing up and down, preparing for another trick. Dani, watching him, saw when something took his eye. He had told her once that the secret to being a good gymnast was never to take your mind off the work—but something had. He was at the top of a jump, when she saw his head move slightly.

Then he plummeted down, collapsing to break his fall, the way acrobats do when they want to stop the force of a trampoline leap. At the same time he shouted, "Dani!"

She leaped out of her chair and whirled toward the door.

Two men wearing dark stocking caps and stocking masks that blurred their features had entered the building. Each carried an automatic weapon, and even as Dani saw them, one lifted the muzzle toward the group.

Something like a cold electric shock went through Dani. Simultaneously she knew that Ben's gun was in his coat by the pool and that though he had killed his jump and was starting to move toward the coat, he had no chance to get to it before the two men could open fire.

With one motion she drew the .38. Dani had practiced it often enough, but had never really believed that the time would come when she would have to use it. Now that the thing was happening, as she swung the weapon up to clasp it with both hands, she thought, *I can't do it! I can't kill a man!*

The muzzle of the automatic weapon in the closest man's grip centered on Dom Lanza, and she moved at once to stand in front of him, squarely facing the gunman, her body protecting the old man. But she knew that the burst of fire from the weapon would not only cut her down, but would get Dom as well—and perhaps some of the others.

The man's face leaped into focus; distorted as it was by the stocking, it appeared to belong to a demon from hell. No humanity showed in the features—just a blurred blob of flesh.

"Shoot, Dani!"

Ben was desperately darting across the floor, but Dani saw he had no chance at all.

Perhaps his charge into certain death made Dani decide,

180

or perhaps it was the sight of the muzzle and the man's grasp on the trigger. She knew all at once that, if he touched that trigger, some of them would die.

So she pulled the trigger of the .38.

The explosion echoed in the high-ceilinged room, and the weapon kicked back in her hand.

By keeping her eyes open, as Ben had taught her, she saw the gunman driven backward as though he had been struck by a massive and invisible fist! He sprawled on the floor, his weapon falling with a clatter to the floor. Perhaps because he never moved, Dani knew somehow that he was dead as he fell.

A sickness grasped her, but she became aware that the other gunman was leveling his rifle at Ben. Without conscious thought, she whirled and threw a shot at the man. It saved Savage's life, for her slug raked the arm of the attacker just as he pulled the trigger. Savage had anticipated the burst, for he charged to one side. The slugs went wild as Dani's bullet knocked the man off balance.

Dani pulled the .38 down and began throwing shots as quickly as they could leave the weapon. None of them struck, but their nearness rattled the gunman. He returned a burst of fire toward Dani, then wheeled and raced for the door, dodging wildly so that Dani could not hit him.

As he disappeared, Savage got to his coat, ripped the magnum free, and raced outside.

Dani lowered her gun; then it slipped through her fingers, striking the floor with a loud noise. She felt Dom's hands on her as she began to tremble uncontrollably. Heartsick, she could not bear to look at the bundle of flesh that lay terribly still, across the room.

Dom comforted her, "You had to do it, my dear!"

181

The stunning thought, *You have killed*, kept echoing through Dani's mind.

Becoming aware of cries coming from behind her, Dani forced herself to turn and found that Rosemary was on the floor, facedown, with scarlet blood soaking the small of her back. Frank bent over her, while the children stood in shock.

Quickly Dani went to them. Her own feelings she forced down deep, knowing that they would return. "Abby, take Pat!" she commanded. When Abby picked up the boy, Dani ordered, "Eddy, you and Irene take Matt and Rachel out of here. Call the police and the ambulance!"

She got them all moving, but at that moment the sound of gunfire reached them from outside. "Don't go that way," Dani directed. "Take them out the side door."

As the others obeyed her instructions, Dani kneeled beside Frank, who stared at Rosemary with horror. He started to touch his wife, but Dani caught his hand. "Let's not move her, Frank," she advised quickly. "She might have a spinal injury."

The two kneeled there, Frank in total shock and Dani shaking with reaction. She put her hand gently on Rosemary's head, praying in an agonized voice, "Lord—don't let her die! Save her, Lord Jesus!"

How long she kneeled there, she never knew. But she heard Ben's voice call, "Dani—come with me!"

His tone was urgent, and she got up to see him standing there, gun in his hand and a tense look on his face. "Is she all right?" he asked, looking at Rosemary.

"She's alive," Dani croaked through dry lips. "What was that gunfire I heard?"

"They were in the furniture van," Ben explained. "I

guess Vince heard the shooting. He was running to get here and help—but they caught him."

"Is he—dead?"

Savage's lips became thin lines. "I think he's had it," he bit the words off in a hard-edged tone. "He's calling for you." He glanced at Dom and Frank, adding, "Eddy said the medics are coming. Don't move her."

Dani followed him, and as they passed the body of the gunman she averted her head. Outside, the bright sunshine hit her like a blow, and she saw Vince's body lying on the grass, twenty yards from the drive. She ran to him and fell to her knees. Slowly he opened his eyes. Blood covered his chest, and Dani didn't see how he could live with such terrible wounds.

"Hey—" he gasped, and the blood bubbled through his lips as he tried to speak. Dani pulled a handkerchief from her pocket and wiped his lips with a trembling hand. He blinked his eyes and whispered, "Not much—time— Dani!" He gasped, "Been thinking about—what you said—about Jesus!"

"Yes, Vince!" Dani's tears ran down her face and fell on his. "He loves you, Vince!"

Canelli tried to smile and shook his head slightly. "Don't see—why. But it's been eatin' on me—couldn't forget it!" He coughed, and the blood welled up. When Dani wiped it off, he asked, "What about it—? Looks like—I'll be seein'—Him—pretty soon."

Dani put her arm under him, fought back the tears, and said, "We all come the same to Him, Vince. All of us die, and I think God's got you ready. Do you believe in Jesus— that He's the Son of God?"

"Always—believed that," he breathed.

"All of us have done wrong, Vince," Dani explained. "God wants to make us right. He asks us to seek His forgiveness. Can you tell Him you've done wrong with your life?"

"No doubt—about that!"

"And one more thing, Vince—just one. Ask Him to come into your heart!" The eyes fixed on her were glazing, and she rushed on, "Let me pray with you, Vince—just think about Jesus dying on the cross for you!" She closed her eyes and prayed haltingly, "O Lord, Vince wants You to make him ready to meet You. You love him so much! Vince, just say, 'God, I believe that Jesus is Your Son. I have sinned against You, but I ask You to forgive me, and I ask in the name of Jesus Christ'!"

Dani heard Vince's voice, falling and faint, repeating her words. She opened her eyes and saw a look of wonder in his eyes. He gazed at her and whispered, "Dani—I did it! He's—real, isn't He?"

"Oh, yes, Vince!" Dani held him tightly.

The broken man cried out, "Good thing—I met you! Now I ain't—going to dread—" He faltered, and his eyes fluttered rapidly. Then he raised himself up, and a smile touched his lips. She leaned forward to catch his words, which faded off at the end.

"Finally—met—Jesus. 'Bye—Dani. . . !"

Then he was gone. Dani's hot tears fell on the still face, and she shook with grief—but joy interlaced her sorrow, for she knew that Vince Canelli was now the man God had always wanted him to be!

12
Rosemary

On Thursday somber skies closed down over New Orleans. Low-lying clouds seemed heavy and oppressive, and in a clinical tone that matched her sterile expression, the weatherperson on channel 4 announced that a tornado had touched down in Hammond, killing two people.

Savage considered her and wondered where they managed to find people who seemed so far removed from the triumphs and tragedies they chronicled. Most seemed like plastic mannequins frozen in department-store windows: attractive, well-dressed, and totally artificial.

"Turn that thing off," Frank Lanza snapped, his tone edged with irritation. He waited while Faye got up, walked to the TV, and shut it off. Then Frank turned to Luke Sixkiller, who was sitting across the walnut table, and asked, "What does it look like to you, Lieutenant?"

Sixkiller was wearing a pair of gray slacks and a charcoal sports coat that was set off by a flowered, black-silk tie. He looked too dapper to be a cop from homicide division, but when he raised his hand to rub his coal-black eyebrow, his bicep swelled, straining the fabric of his coat sleeve. Without effort he exuded a sense of physical power, and the sheer strength in his solid body somehow made the other four men in the room seem a little unsubstantial.

"The gunny Dani put down is a small timer from Detroit, Roy Dusenberg. Got a record long as a piece of rope. Done time in Angola for manslaughter." His smooth, coppery face showed little, but a glint in his ebony eyes revealed a trace of anger. "Should have been fried, but the judge was bought off."

"He's not one of Martino's guys," Faye reported quickly.

Dominic Lanza had said little during the interview with the policeman. Now he nodded, commenting briefly, "Even Johnny Ring's not that stupid. He can hire punks like Dusenberg by the dozen. If they get hit, who can tie them to Martino?" His gaze moved to Sixkiller. "Nothing you can do, is there, Lieutenant?" he prodded.

"If we can make any of the other guys, maybe." He leaned back in his chair and studied Dom carefully. "It was timed perfectly. They were waiting for the delivery truck from the furniture store, and the driver and his helper never got a glimpse of a face."

"How'd they stop the truck?" Savage asked.

"Parked in the middle of the private road, with the hood up," Sixkiller answered. "The driver of the truck said two guys had their heads under the hood, as if they were looking at the engine. When he went up to help, they laid a gun on him and made him wave his helper to come up. Both gunmen wore stocking masks, so neither of the delivery men could pick them out of a lineup. The thugs tied them up and kept them in the back of the van while they made the hit."

"So they knew exactly when the delivery truck was coming," Dom noted quietly.

Sixkiller nodded. "Wouldn't have been too hard to find out, I guess. But the people at the furniture store look clean. No connection at all with Martino. The owner did tell us that somebody called and asked what time the delivery would be made. Didn't give a name."

"Max said it would be coming about one o'clock," Frank informed him slowly. "That's why he and Helen couldn't come to see the kids perform."

"How many people knew about the delivery?" Sixkiller asked.

"We all knew it," Frank said. "And the men at the gate were notified so they would admit the truck." He added disgustedly, "We might as well have had Snow White guarding the gate. Frenchie went out to the truck, and one of the guys stepped out and pushed a gun in his face. They tied him and Legs up like trussed chickens! One guy stayed with them at the gate until the truck came back."

Dom interrupted, "Is that all the questions, Lieutenant? Frank can take care of any details." He got up and left the room, looking tired and sick.

Sixkiller rose, warning, "Don't hold your breath until we get a suspect on this one, Lanza. It was a slick job." Frank nodded, and then the policeman demanded, "I want to talk to Miss Ross."

"She's with the children. Savage, show the lieutenant, will you?"

As soon as the two men left the room, Faye burst out, "Frank, *now* will you listen to me? This is twice they've

187

tried to wipe us out. We gotta hit Martino and do it quick!"

Frank stared at Dietrich, but shook his head. "Maybe that will come, Faye, but not today. You know what my father says. If we hit back, it'll start a full-sized war."

"He's sick, Frank," Faye protested. "He's not the man he used to be—and you know it!"

Faye Dietrich's words struck hard at Lanza. Indeed, he had been wrestling with the problem since the shooting had taken place. He knew that Faye compared him unfavorably with his brother Phil, and it cut him. Though he wanted to lash out at Faye, doubt had slowed his decision-making processes to a crawl. Phil would have taken some action, he decided. His father had not mentioned the older brother's name, yet Frank knew Dominic had looked to Phil to keep things together. Despite the temptation to give in to Faye's insistent demand to move quickly, to hit Martino with all he had, Frank did not let his thoughts show in his face.

"I've got to see to Rosemary, Faye. And the kids. If trouble starts, they'll be right in the middle of it." He saw the stubborn anger in Faye's cold, blue eyes, but before the man could speak, he snapped, "You've got plenty to do! Whip those clowns you call guards into shape! If they'd been on their toes, we wouldn't have lost Vince. He was worth the whole bunch of bums you've hired—so get them on the ball or get rid of them!"

With Savage, Sixkiller walked down the hall toward the study room. "How's Dani taking it, Ben? Icing that punk down, I mean?"

"Hasn't had time to think about it much," Savage answered. "She's been too busy keeping the kids from folding." He paused outside the door and turned his eyes on the policeman. "But you can bet it'll fall on her like an anvil when she gets alone."

"I figured. Any new word on Mrs. Lanza?"

"She's going to make it, I guess. Frank is visiting her a lot in intensive care. He's only here now because you are." Ben added slowly, "This may open the ball, Luke. Dom's been sitting on Faye for a long time. Now I think he'll have to do something—and there's only one thing a guy like him knows to do."

"He didn't get where he is by turning the other cheek," Sixkiller agreed. "Well, let's see the teacher."

They entered the room and found Dani sitting in a chair reading to the children. Sixkiller saw at a glance that the girl was in the worst state of the three. Her thin face was almost colorless, and her eyes held the same expression he'd seen many times in the faces of survivors of a very bad wreck. The older boy, he noted, was pale, but trying to tough it out. The smaller boy listened to the story as if nothing had happened. Sixkiller thought, *Kids can throw things off—but it's just buried. It'll catch up to him, especially if his mother dies.*

Then he spoke, "Hello, Dani. Sorry to interrupt your class."

Dani rose. She moved carefully, and Sixkiller saw that she was keeping a tight control over herself. There was a "stretched" quality in her face, such as one sees in the expressions of men who are about to go into battle. "Hello, Lieutenant," she answered quietly.

"Got time for a talk?" he asked.

"Of course. Ben, would you take the children out for some exercise? I've kept them at their studies pretty hard."

"How about a swim, you guys?" Ben suggested. He

189

spoke easily, as if nothing had happened, and no sign of strain showed in his face. Pat cried, "Yes!" at once. Matthew was slow to respond. He was thinking of the shooting and wanted to refuse. But Ben came over and put his hand on the boy's shoulder. "Be better to go now," he observed quietly. "When you take a fall, go back and try it again right then. Easier that way." He reached out his hand and invited, "How about it, Rachel?"

The girl looked up at him, her eyes enormous, but something in Savage's face gave her what she needed. "All right, Mr. Ben," she uttered. She took his hand, and the three of them left the room, Savage talking cheerfully as the door closed.

"Is that the way?" Sixkiller raised one heavy black eyebrow. "Those kids had a rough deal. Pretty soon to take them back in there."

"Ben thinks it's best," Dani pointed out. "He had some bad falls when he was with the circus. He says the longer you stay away from what hurt you, the harder it is to go back to it." She shook her head and added, "I don't know, Luke. I guess he's right. Ben's pretty smart about things like that."

Sixkiller considered her, then suddenly demanded, "You been back in there, Dani?"

His question startled her. "Why—no, I haven't."

"Let's go have a look," he advised.

He saw, then, what he expected to see. Dani stiffened her back, and her lips drew into a thin line. Her eyes suddenly widened with what looked like fear. "Why— why do you want to do that? We can talk here."

"Same reason Savage wanted the kids to go. You've been ducking this thing, Dani. Time to take a look at it."

Dani licked her suddenly dry lips. "Are you taking up psychiatry as a hobby, Lieutenant?" she snapped. She turned and walked over to the wide window, her back straight and tense. "I don't need any amateur shrink working on me!" she exclaimed, staring into the yard.

He came over and stood beside her. Keen gusts of March wind bent the tall oaks and sent ripples through the green hedges that outlined the house. Overhead the sky was busy, large thunderheads rolling along high in the sky, their edges tinted amber. Even as he watched, a sudden flash caught his eye—far away a forked tongue of white light licked at the earth. He counted the seconds until the faint rumble came to his ears, noting that it was at least ten miles away.

Then he shared, "The first time I saw action in Nam, my buddy got it. He was no more than five feet from me when he went down. After the fight, I wanted to run away and cry. But my officer wouldn't let me. He said, 'Go back and help with Tom.' I told him what he could do with his army, and he explained, 'Luke, if you don't go back, he'll never be dead to you.' " Sixkiller was quiet, and Dani turned slightly to see that his stolid face was softened. "It took all I had, Dani, but I went back. Helped put him in a body bag."

He said no more, but Dani suddenly knew what he was trying to tell her: *Face up to the problem.* She suddenly breathed, "All right, Luke. Let's go to the pool."

A smile lifted the corners of his lips, and he put his hand on her shoulder. "That's a good soldier," he encouraged her.

Dani led the way out of the house and down the back walk toward the domed pool. It took all the courage she could muster to open the door and enter, but she tried to let none of the sudden fear that stirred her nerves show in her face. It helped some that Savage had the kids in the shallow part of the pool, teaching them a butterfly stroke. Pat was yelling as usual, and the other two were functioning, at least. "Hey, look at me!" Pat cried and thrashed awkwardly in the water.

"Good, Pat!" Dani called out.

She turned to Sixkiller. "Well, this is it." She glanced involuntarily at the spot where the body of the gunman had fallen. The people from the crime lab had come and done their thing, so no trace of the shooting appeared. Or so she thought.

"I was standing over here, Luke." She took him to the spot and was about to continue, when he looked down at the tiles. Two of them were broken, not five feet away from where she had stood.

Sixkiller stared at the broken tiles. "He came pretty close, Dani. If you hadn't gotten him, he'd have wiped out the whole family—and you in the bargain." He watched her as she studied the scarred tiles. He had been around violence in many forms and well knew that some individuals were incapable of handling it—just as others loved it. Finally he remarked, "Savage told me how you jumped in front of Dom. He thought that was pretty good."

Without lifting her eyes, she commented, "I didn't think about it, Luke." She paused, then lifted her head, and he saw the anguish in her eyes. "It was—the other thing that I can't get over."

He stood there, considering her with a pair of steady black eyes, and shook his head. "Do no good to tell you this, but the guy you put down was a bad one. Been in jail most of his life and had no future. He'd killed three men and one woman, and he'd kill more, if he was alive." Then he stopped and shrugged. "But you can't see it like that."

"He was a human being, Luke," Dani whispered. "And I killed him."

"You'd rather see those kids dead?" Sixkiller demanded. "Forget about Dom and Frank. They know what they're doing, but Rosemary Lanza and those kids, you'd swap them for that two-bit hood?"

Dani blinked at his blunt attack, but only shook her head. Ever since the shooting, she had thrown herself into the task of keeping the horror of the affair from scarring the children. She had closed off the blinding memory of the moment when she had centered the muzzle of the .38 on the masked figure and had pulled the trigger. But the details were not obliterated. She had already discovered that if she allowed a break from the activities, the scene would begin to unroll like a video. More than once, when she had let the barriers of thought down, she found herself looking across the swimming pool at the gunman, hooded like a ghastly specter. And she touched the cold metal of the gun as she drew it from the holster, felt the kick as she pulled the trigger, and smelled the acrid odor of cordite. She saw the slug strike the man, driving him backward.

Her hands began to tremble as the scene rose before her, and she shook her head jerkily. "I can't answer that, Luke. I just can't!"

For a moment he stood there silently, wanting to help, but knowing nobody could do that. "Dani, get out of this thing," he advised finally. "Some people are tough enough for this game, but I don't think you're one of them. Leave it to hardcases like Ben and me."

Dani stared at him, her gray-green eyes as serious as he had ever seen them. "I may have to do just that, Luke," she agreed finally. "There may be another thing like this, and I'm not sure if I could—do it again."

"Be best if you got out," he told her gently. Then he shrugged his heavy shoulders. "Well, I got to go catch some criminals. If it gets bad, I keep a shoulder available."

"May take you up on that, Lieutenant." She smiled wanly.

They walked out of the pool area, Dani waving to the children.

When Sixkiller left, she found Rossi waiting for her. "Mr. Lanza would like to see you."

"How is he, Thomas?"

"No better." Thomas shrugged with an air of fatalism. "All this hasn't helped him any."

"No." Dani left and went to Lanza's room. He answered her knock, and she went in at once. He lay in bed with a book. A reading lamp over his shoulder provided the only light in the room. She went over and drew a chair beside his bed. "How do you feel?" she asked.

Lanza's face was skull-like, more than usual, Dani thought. He shrugged, but made no comment. He was tired of the question, though he realized that Dani and others asked it out of concern. "How are the children?" he demanded. His voice was thick, for he was heavily sedated. "Are they all right?"

"Yes. Ben's got them in the swimming pool. We thought it might be best to get them back to a routine as soon as possible."

He nodded, then questioned suddenly, "How are you, Dani?"

"Me? Why—I'm fine," she said, surprised at the question. "I didn't get a scratch."

"Not all wounds are in the body," he pointed out, watching her eyes. "I think maybe you are hurting, yes?" She shook her head, not wanting to burden him with her problems, but the medicine had not dulled Dom's discernment. "I am sorry you had to shoot that man," he asserted slowly. "You put yourself in front of me—which I will tell you never to do again. Not that I am ungrateful, but it is futile. The children, the family—they are the ones."

Dani nodded. "I'm going to the hospital to see Rosemary. The doctors say she's holding her own, but she might need me."

Lanza considered her for a long moment, then shook his head. "I wish I had known someone like you when I was younger," he averred. "But I was convinced that there was no one who cared, outside of the family. It was one of my big mistakes. I know that now. But in the early days, I lived one day at a time. Just to live another week—that was a real victory, Dani! It was a jungle, I tell you! And in a jungle, you grow cunning—and cruel, of course." He paused and stared down at his hands, where they rested on the book. Then he lifted his eyes and continued, "I built a wall around myself and my family, and I allowed no trespassing. Now I meet you and find that there is love in the world, unselfish love. I never knew that."

"Is there anything you need? Can I tell Rosemary anything?"

"I have not been fair to my daughter-in-law," Lanza worried, shaking his head. "She's been afraid, and I've done little to help her. Tell her—tell her that I love her and that I long for her to come home."

"That's good." Dani smiled. "I'll come and see you tomorrow." On impulse she reached out and squeezed his hand, then, a little embarrassed at her action, asked, "What are you reading? Is it a good book?"

Dom Lanza gazed at her. "You'd say so, Dani." He held up the book, and she saw that it was a hardcover Bible. "I had Rossi sneak off and buy this for me." His lips drew back in a smile. "He was shocked. In all the years I've known him, I've never seen him so shook up! It did me good, seeing Thomas confused for once!" Then he stroked the cover of the Bible, and spoke thoughtfully, "I started in the New Testament, the book of John, as you suggested. It's not what I thought it would be, though."

"What did you expect?" Dani asked curiously. The sight of the dying mob boss with the Bible in his emaciated hands had done something to her.

"I can't say. I guess I was looking for a book of rules," Dom confessed. "But it's about a man. Jesus was a real man—that's what's really gotten to me. I had Him all fixed in my mind as a hazy figure with a halo, sort of like a stained-glass window in a church. But what I keep seeing is a man who got tired, who had to put up with followers who didn't really believe in Him. Lots of people shouted His name, but none of them seemed to understand Him."

"Yes, Jesus was like that," Dani agreed. "You've read it well."

Dom stirred restlessly, then looked up. "I read the story of the crucifixion just before you came in." He fell silent, his face set in a strange expression. She had never seen him exactly like this and sat there waiting. Finally he added softly, "I've been a hard man, but when I read that story, how Jesus died, I found myself weeping, Dani. That's strange, isn't it?"

"I don't think so," she argued. "I think when we discover that someone really loves us—not for what we've done, but in *spite* of that—it strikes home in the worst of us. I think you've just found out what the word *gospel* is about. It means 'good news,' the news that Jesus has died in our place, and now we don't have to be ashamed before God for all we've done that's wrong."

His dark eyes, hooded and enigmatic, were fixed on her. She could not read them, but he nodded suddenly. "Maybe it's so. I think it's too late for me. Too many bad things. Too many! But it's good to know that even a man like me can still weep over a good man."

Dani squeezed his hand. "It's not too late for you, Dom. It's never too late." Then she saw that he was almost asleep. "Keep on reading," she whispered. "I'll see you when I get back from the hospital."

She left the room and went at once to change. She donned a pair of light taupe slacks and an ivory blouse with antique buttons down the front, then paused. The .38 lay on top of her dresser, and she longed to leave it there. The sight of it started memories of the shooting, and she put her hands to her temples suddenly, trying to shut them off. "Help me, Lord!" she cried out in agony. For a few minutes, she stood there, hands pressed against her temples. Then she straightened up. Walking to the dresser, she picked up the belt and holster, fastened it around her waist, then put on the burgundy linen blazer. Fastening the single gold button in front, she turned to the mirror, noting that the loose-fitting garment concealed the bulge of the weapon. Then she picked up a small purse and left the room.

When she got to the hospital, she found Frank in the

waiting room. He got up at once, came to her, and held her hands. "How is she?" Dani asked.

"Better," he informed her. "She's going to make it. The nurses are doing something for her now." He held her hands tightly and shook his head. "Physically, that is."

Dani stared at him. "What does that mean, Frank?"

"She's not herself," Frank cried out. "She won't talk, Dani. Just lies there and stares at the ceiling."

"She's had a rough time, Frank."

"Sure, but—it's more than that. Even the doctors say so." He dropped her hands and lit a cigarette, puffing at it nervously. "One of them talked to me about an hour ago. He says she's not doing so good mentally. Says she could lose her mind. Oh, that's not the way he put it, of course! But it's what he meant."

"I don't believe it." Dani shook her head. "God didn't spare her life to let her lose her mind."

Frank's head came up, and he stared at her intently. "Good to hear you say that." He tried to smile and failed. "I've been here all this time, thinking about what a sorry deal I gave her. Rosemary's got her problems, but then who hasn't? I should have been more help to her."

"It's not too late for that."

He nodded slowly. "Yes, that's so. Say, only one person can go in. Would you take the next visit, Dani? I think it might help her to see you. And I need to get back home and see the kids. I'm worried about them."

Dani said, "I've stayed close to them all morning. Ben's got them now." She told him about Savage's idea to take them back to the pool area at once. "It worked, too. Now that place won't be filled with ghosts."

Frank was impressed. "That Ben, he's pretty sharp!

Well, I guess they ought to be finished by now." He led her out of the waiting room down the hall to number 1133. Stepping aside, he let Dani go first. Dani saw Rosemary lying on the bed, her eyes closed. She looked pale, but not as bad as Dani had imagined.

Frank walked to the bed, announcing, "Rosemary, Dani is here to see you." But Rosemary lay absolutely still and silent.

"Don't wake her up, Frank," Dani directed. "You go get some rest. I'll stay with her. Maybe you could come back about midnight."

"All right." He turned to go, then paused, a thoughtful expression in his dark eyes. "Dani, I don't see how the Lanzas could have made it without you. I saw how you jumped in front of my father. And the way you've held the kids together through all this—"

Dani didn't want a heavy scene. "It goes with the service," she told him lightly. "Ross Investigations—best in town!"

"It's not that way," Frank objected, but then turned and left.

Dani sat down beside Rosemary, looking into her face and praying silently. Time flowed by slowly, and finally Rosemary stirred.

Dani quietly called out, "Rosemary, it's Dani." At first there was no reaction, but then as Dani continued to speak, Rosemary opened her eyes. The eyes did not turn; they remained fixed on the ceiling, just as Frank had said. Perplexed, Dani continued to call Rosemary's name and even moved to where she could face the sick woman, but there was no response, none at all. After an hour, Dani felt defeated. Then a thought came to her. She put both hands

199

on the woman's head and began praying audibly. "Lord Jesus, thank You for Rosemary's life. Thank You that she is getting well! You, O Lord, are keeping her from death, and are putting Your health into her. . . ."

She prayed fervently but in a quiet voice for a long while, not conscious of time at all. Suddenly she came back to the sense of the room, for she had felt a movement in Rosemary's body. Looking down, she saw that the woman's eyes were open. "Rosemary? Are you awake?"

There was a slight flicker in Rosemary's eyes, but no more than that. The woman seemed to be in a coma of some sort, for though she stared at the ceiling, no recognition entered her eyes. Dani kept speaking to her very softly, calling her name and trying to awaken her. But there was no response. Finally Dani's back grew strained, and she got up and stretched. Rosemary didn't move, and there was something a little frightening about the way she stared blankly at the ceiling.

Dani walked over and got a glass of water, then moved back to the bed and once again began praying for Rosemary. This time she felt as if she were trying to swim against an overpowering tide. The words she tried to speak lodged in her throat, and she had to force them out. Her neck began to ache, and as time ran on an almost overwhelming urge to get up and leave the room pulled at her. Just to get away! But something in her rose up, and finally she cried aloud, "In the name of Jesus Christ of Nazareth, I rebuke you, powers of darkness!" As soon as she spoke, something like an overwhelming nausea came to her, and she felt that she was going to be sick. But she continued to pray, rebuking the devil and crying out for God to deliver Rosemary.

Finally she felt so exhausted she laid her head on the bed, eyes closed and almost panting for breath, so severe had been the struggle. It was so quiet all she could hear was the sound of her own ragged breathing. Then—something touched her head!

Quickly she lifted her head and found that Rosemary was looking at her. The injured woman had reached down and touched her, and there was life in her eyes.

"Rosemary!" Dani exclaimed, grasping her hand. "Are you all right?"

Rosemary licked her lips and stared around the room. "Dani? What is this place?"

"You've been hurt, Rosemary, but you're going to be all right."

Rosemary looked at her, then Dani saw her memory return. She tried to lift herself and cried out, "The children—!"

"They're fine," Dani assured her. "But how do you feel?"

"I don't know." She looked around. "I've been having awful dreams, Dani. Everything was dark, and I was being pulled down into some kind of terrible pit!" Then she grabbed Dani's hand and held it tightly. "And then I heard you praying—and it was as if you pulled me back out of it!"

"Don't think about it," Dani told her. She poured a glass of water and gave it to Rosemary. "The doctors say you're going to be all right, Frank told me."

"Where—where is Frank?"

"He's been here all the time." Dani smiled. "I just came a little while ago and made him get some rest. He'll be back soon."

Rosemary stared at her, then shook her head. "I let them down, Dani. The children and Frank, too. It would have been better if I had died."

Dani cried out at once, "No, don't say that, Rosemary! God has spared you, and now you have to use your life for His purpose."

Rosemary stared at her, and for the next hour Dani sat there, reading from the New Testament and giving what encouragement she could. Rosemary seemed to hang on her words. Finally a doctor came in and stopped abruptly. "Well!" He spoke in obvious amazement. "Look at this!" He came over and took Rosemary's hand, then looked into her pupils carefully. Finally he smiled and announced, "You're doing fine, Mrs. Lanza. We were getting a little worried about you."

Dani rose and reported, "I'll be going now, but Frank will be here as soon as he can."

"Will you come back, too, Dani?" Rosemary asked, holding out her hand.

"Of course I will!" Dani smiled. "I'll be a regular pest!"

She left and, driving home, began to thank God for what He had done. It was a miracle, in her mind, and when she got back to the house and told Frank, he was incredulous.

"You say she knew you?"

"Yes, and the doctor said she was fine. He was worried about her."

"Yes, I know." Frank hesitated, then demanded, "Dani, will you be staying?"

The question was direct, but Dani was exhausted. "Oh, Frank, I don't know!" She drew her hand across her forehead, then stared at him. "I'm too tired to think now. But

I've already found out that I'm not going to handle what happened." She could not even force herself to say that she had killed a man.

Frank took her arm and held her still. "Dani, you must stay!"

He would have said more, and Dani saw the impulse in his eyes to put his arms around her. She drew back at once. "Frank, I'll do what I can, but you have a fine wife with some big problems. Your first priority is to stand beside her like a rock. Don't let anything get in the way of that." She hesitated and added, "A lot of men can't handle it when their wives fail. They start looking for a newer model—and I've never seen that work out one time! Rosemary is all the woman any man needs, and you and your children are going to have to put it all together. It'll cost you something. But I believe those words in the ceremony, 'for better or for worse,' mean something!"

Frank flushed and pulled back his hand. "Sorry, Dani. It's just that—well, we need you bad right now." Then he turned and said, "I'll get to the hospital. Will you tell my father and the kids about Rosemary?"

"I'll tell them, Frank. But remember, she's on the razor's edge. It's no time to lecture her. What she needs is—what we all need, I think." She felt his inquiring gaze and smiled faintly. "A lot of *unconditional* love. Not 'I'll love you *if*,' but 'I'll love you *no matter what*'!"

13
Savage Pays a Call

"Aw, Dad, you're not going to make me pay the *whole* thing, are you?"

Frank Lanza grinned broadly at Matt, who had just landed on Boardwalk and was scowling fiercely. "This is the big time, Matt," he warned. "We're playing hardball here, not some kiddie game!"

"Oh, Frank," Rosemary objected, "that's mean!" She was sitting up, propped in an armchair, and there was more color in her face than usual. Ever since she had come home from the hospital she had been very quiet, but Dani had spent much time with her, building up her confidence. For the first time in years she was not drinking, and best of all, all the children had come to visit her often. She had been confined to her bed, but Dani maneuvered them so adroitly that much of their free time was spent in Rosemary's room. She had bought every game she could find, including one called Chutes and Ladders that Pat loved but the others hated. Scrabble was a battle, but the old standby, Monopoly, was the favorite, and every evening the children gathered for a game that ended with cries of protest as Dani had to drag them off to their bedrooms.

Just before time for the game to begin, Dani had sought Frank out in his office. He looked up with a smile as she came in. "Hello, Teacher. What's up?"

"Monopoly is up," Dani told him. "I want you to join us tonight for a little while, Frank."

A frown creased his brow, and he shook his head. "I'm not much good with games, Dani."

"I don't care about that," she objected sharply. "You need to spend some time with the children—and with Rosemary. They need you, Frank." She smiled and added, "It'll be good for you. You're looking washed out."

He tossed the papers down on the desk, which was littered with all sorts of reports and he sighed wearily. "I'm no bookkeeper, Dani. No matter how many times I go over this stuff, it doesn't make any sense."

"I thought Eddy did the accounting."

"Yeah, he does—him and Max. He was in here for three hours, trying to explain what's happening, but I just don't have the brain for it." He struck the papers with his fist and gave a frustrated look at the ceiling. "If this keeps up, we'll all be in the poorhouse!"

Dani hesitated, then offered, "I'll make you a deal, Frank. You go play Monopoly, and I'll look at the books."

He stared at her, then nodded. "Hey, I forgot about you being a CPA. That's a deal!" He got up and walked around the desk. "I'd dig ditches to get away from these books. Take over, Dani, and I hope you can make something out of this mess!"

He had gone to Rosemary's room and found her sitting up. "I put your teacher to work," he announced. "So I'm here to show you guys how this game should *really* be played!" All three children came to hug him, and he was ashamed when he realized how little time he'd spent with them. *Got to do better than I've been doing,* he thought. He hugged them all and sat down. Looking at Rosemary, he asked, "Isn't this too much for you?"

"No, Frank," she disclaimed quickly. "I—I like it!"

She was, he saw, more beautiful than ever. She had always been a beauty, but the wound had thinned her down, until her features became one sharp relief. Her dark-blue eyes looked enormous as she stared at him, and there was a softness in her lips that had been lacking for a long time. She wore a pink flowered silk robe and a new hairstyle.

"You look great," Frank interjected. "Done something new with your hair, haven't you?"

Rosemary's hand fluttered to her breast, and she nodded. It had been a long time since he had noticed her. "Yes. Dani helped me with it."

"It looks good on you." He hesitated, then suddenly reached over and took her hand. It felt like a fragile bird in his. "You gave us quite a scare, you know? I just about lost it when I thought you were—" He broke off suddenly and dropped her hand. "Well—I'm glad you're feeling okay."

"Dani said that God saved her, Dad," Pat pronounced loudly.

Frank looked at him; then a smile touched his tough lips. "Well, I'm no expert, Pat, so if she says it, it must be so." Then he felt awkward and brusquely asked, "Well, what about this game? I haven't played for a long time, but I gotta warn you, I play for keeps!"

The game had gone on, and soon Frank was immersed in the action. He found himself watching the children, finding in their style of play a revelation of their personalities. Timid Rachel tried to keep a large amount of cash rather than plunging into building houses and hotels. Matt, on the other hand, was reckless to a fault. He played intently, howling with agony when he had to pay a large sum and gloating when he had a victory. Pat was partners with Rosemary, and he insisted on moving his man around the board. Though he understood little about the game itself, he loved sitting close to his mother, and he joined in the cries that went up from time to time as players won or lost.

Rosemary, Frank saw, was incapable of playing a hard game. Any time one of the children got into trouble, she would try to get the others to show mercy. Hers was a gentle spirit, one that he suddenly remembered had drawn him to her in the first place. As the game went on, he watched her covertly, marveling at how the tragedy had transformed her. He had always admired her beauty, but he became aware that it was her gentleness that made her what she was. He was painfully aware that he had not taken that gentleness into account in days gone by. When she had first started drinking, he had spoken to her sharply, disciplining her as he would have a member of his organization. Because he had grown up in a hard school, Frank had no knowledge of how a gentle hand is sometimes best.

Should have treated her better, he thought. *She would have responded to kindness better than what I gave her.*

Just then Matt landed on Boardwalk and began pulling at his hair. It amused Frank, and he teased the boy, "This is the big time, Matt."

But Rosemary had looked at her son's face, and suddenly she reached out and laid her hand on Frank's arm. "Frank, let him off this one time!"

Frank smiled at her and looked at his son's face. "You'd want to let Jack the Ripper off, Rosemary. Okay, just this one time," he relented. "But the *next* time I land on one of those orange places, Matt, you better be nice to *me!*"

Rosemary's smile bloomed then, and she encouraged him, "That's nice, Frank!"

Her husband shook his head. "Good thing you don't run the business, Rosemary," he commented. "We'd be broke in a month!" He stopped then, for something had taken the sweet smile from Rosemary's face. Of course, he knew that it was her distaste for the business. She had always hated it, and that had been at the core of many of their misunderstandings. Frank had felt her displeasure and had hardened his manner toward her.

Once he had lashed out at her, "I notice you don't mind spending the money I make! You're not too good for that!"

But he never forgot her answer. With a quivering lip, she'd commented, "I don't care what we *have,* Frank. I just don't want to be ashamed of what we *are.*"

As the game went on, Frank was quieter, hopelessly wondering how he and Rosemary would ever reconcile their views.

Finally he noticed that Rosemary looked tired. "Hey, it's time to get some sleep," he announced. As usual there were cries of protest, but he stilled them all. "We'll call this game a tie. The next time, I'm wiping up all of you."

"Tomorrow, Daddy?" Rachel had come to take his hand and was looking up at him with a pleading expression.

"Why—sure, Baby," he responded. He picked her up,

then Pat came and leaped into his arms. "You're too big to haul, Matt," he said. "Come on, I'll throw you all in the sack."

He made a game out of it, throwing them into their beds time and time again as they squealed like small pigs. Finally he got them down and came back to Rosemary's room. She was still sitting in the chair, a happy look on her face. "They had such a good time, Frank!" she told him.

"Well, so did I," he admitted. "Have to do this more often."

"It was—like it used to be, wasn't it?"

He shifted uncomfortably, then nodded. "Yeah, I guess so. You need help to get back to bed?"

"If you wouldn't mind, Frank."

She got to her feet, and a spasm of pain crossed her lips, pulling them into a thin line. When he saw that it hurt her to walk, he suddenly reached down and picked her up. She turned pink and cried, "Oh, I can walk!"

He ignored her and carried his wife across the room, thinking how light she was. Reaching the bed he glanced at her. She raised her eyes, and met his. The vulnerability he saw there softened him. "I'm glad you're all right, Rosemary," he told her quietly. He struggled for words and could not seem to find them. Finally he put her gently on the bed and drew the covers up. It was an awkward moment for both of them as bitter words and harsh scenes tried to rise from the past.

Rosemary suddenly pled, "Frank, I'm sorry—for so many things. I've been awful!"

He shook his head, and there was a thickening in his throat. He cleared it and managed, "You've had a hard time." That was not what he meant to say, and he finally gasped out, "What I mean is—I'm sorry I wasn't a little easier with you, Pet."

His sudden and unplanned use of his old nickname for her suddenly brought tears into Rosemary's eyes. She turned her face away so that he would not see, but could not keep her body from the sobs that suddenly racked her.

He stood there, a big man filled with all the hardness of the life that had been his lot, his face twisted with an emotion that he had not known could touch him. Awkwardly, he put his hand on her shoulder. "Rosemary—don't cry!" He wanted to say more, for the sight of her weeping had broken something in him. His own eyes burned, something he'd felt so rarely that it shocked him. He patted her shoulder, then admitted, "I—I guess we're all having a hard time, Pet. But we're going to make it."

She turned her tear-stained face toward him and whispered, "I love you, Frank! I always have!"

Her words ran like a shock down his spine, and he could not answer. Though he wanted to say something, he could not find the words. Finally he bent down and kissed her lips, then walked stiffly out of the room. She lay there in the bed, and when the door closed, she wept as she had not for years. "Oh, God," she prayed, "give me back his love!"

Frank left the room and was shocked at the emotions that seemed to batter him. He was a private sort of man, not given to expressions of love, and the scene had left him drained. For some time he had been aware that the one thing that he prized above all things—his family—was slipping away, was, in fact, lost to him. The death of his brother Phil and the crisis with the Martino gang had consumed all his energies, but as he entered the den and sat down in the dim light, he struggled with the tidal wave of problems that had crashed in on him.

Moving over to one of the tall windows, he stood staring out at the moonlit terrace. The full moon was frozen in the sky, huge and silver. It was a peaceful scene—but none of it meant anything to Frank Lanza. Finally he turned and made his way to the study.

Opening the door, he found his father sitting across the desk from Dani. Both looked up as he came in. "Who won?" Dani asked with a smile.

"A tie," he answered and went over to pour himself a drink. "What are you doing up this time of night?" he demanded of his father.

Dom's old eyes glinted with a sudden gleam of humor. "I didn't want to waste time sleeping," he remarked. "Dani's found something that's interesting."

"In the books?" Frank asked in surprise. "They bore me to death."

"This won't," Dom promised. "There's a big hunk of money missing."

The statement brought Frank's head up instantly. "You mean—*stolen?*"

"I can't say that," Dani denied quickly. She waved at the papers on the desk, which she had arranged into neat little piles. "I don't have all the books here. And even if I had, it'd take longer than a couple of hours to make any sense out of them." She looked puzzled, then shook her head. "All I can say, Frank, is that something is *wrong*. It may be a very simple thing, but some funds have just disappeared. Maybe they've been transferred, and the record of transfer isn't here. But from what I see here, I'd say you need an outside audit."

Frank and his father exchanged a quick glance. Dani didn't realize that their particular business was not subject to *outside* auditors. Of course one level of accounting had to be open to the tax people, but there were other layers that were buried, stockpiled, and carefully concealed. Dom asserted, "I think we must find out about this 'transfer,' but not from an outsider."

"Couldn't you do it, Dani?" Frank asked. "I know you're busy, but I'd like to keep this in the family."

Dani was flustered. "I—I don't see how, Frank. After all, I'm not really family. And—"

"And you might learn more about the Lanza business than you want to know?" Smiling at her, Dom shook his head. "Well, I can understand that. But all we want is a bookkeeping answer. An overlook of all our enterprises. You'll be shocked to learn, Danielle, that we operate quite a few honorable businesses."

"I'll have to think about it, Dom," Dani fended him off. She rose, adding, "I have to go now. Remember, there may be a reasonable explanation about the books. Good night. And Frank, I think you'd better spend more time playing Monopoly."

When she left, Frank asked at once, "What do you think?"

Dom closed his eyes and thought hard. "Get Savage in here, Frank."

Frank stared at him, then shrugged his shoulders. He went to the desk, picked up the phone, and dialed. "Savage? This is Frank. My father would like to see you. Sure, that'll be fine." He put down the phone and asked, "What does Savage have to do with the books?"

"Nothing. This is something else." Dom lay back in the

212

chair, and Frank said no more. Finally, he did remark, "We'll have to get with Eddy and Max on this problem."

"No, get Sam Vino to do it."

"Sam? Sure, he could do it. But we'll have to let him know more than we've ever let an outsider know."

"Sam's all right."

Five minutes later the two men heard a tap on the door. "Come in," Frank invited. Savage entered and came to stand in front of the two men. "Sorry to keep you up, Ben," Frank apologized.

"No problem. What's up?"

Dom opened his eyes slowly. "Ben, I've been thinking about what you mentioned the other day—about throwing a scare into Martino. Do you think it can be done?"

"Maybe." Savage's squarish face and deep-set eyes picked up the shadows from the light overhead. He looked tough as he stood there with his short, broken nose and the shelf of bone over his eyes. The scar on his forehead traced its way into his left eyebrow, and there was an air of certainty in his manner as he considered the older Lanza. "I've done harder stunts."

"What's this about?" Frank asked.

"Tell him, Ben." Dom nodded.

"I think you've got a chance to stop the pressure," Savage explained. "Ring won't scare, but Joe Martino isn't the man old Sal was. Scare him bad enough, and he'll pull back."

"Scare him how?" Frank demanded. "He's protected like the president."

"Any security can be broken," Savage pointed out quietly. "You've discovered that. If somebody got to Joe and shoved a gun up his nose, I think he'd break."

Frank stared at him. "You're saying you can get at him? Faye says hit them with an army, that nobody can get at Joe Martino personally."

Savage shrugged. "Never know about things like that."

"Would you be willing to try, Ben?" Dom asked.

"If the boss lady says it's all right with her."

Dom nodded slowly. "We'll pay for the job."

Savage explained, "I'm not pulling a trigger on him, you understand? Dani wouldn't stand for that. And even if you did get Joe out of the way, you'd have Johnny Ring in charge. But if you can scare Joe enough, he'll dump Ring, and then you won't have to worry about any more calls from Martino's goons."

"How much time will you need?" Dom asked.

"Vince gave me all the dope on Martino's security," Savage told them. "It was really his idea." He paused and noted, "Somebody's going to go down for taking Vince out. I liked him."

Both Lanzas stared at Savage, uncertainly. Finally Dom agreed, "We'll try it. Ben, ask for what you need." He got up and moved slowly across the floor. When he was gone, Frank ordered, "Make it soon, Savage. This thing is getting hot."

"Sure." Savage left the room and went to knock on Dani's door. When she opened it, he insisted, "It's time for a committee meeting, Boss." Stepping inside, he told her quickly what had happened. "I think it can be done," he ended.

"No, Ben," she instantly responded. "It's too dangerous."

"So is driving on the freeway." He shrugged. "If it works, we're out of here. Which I'm ready for."

She argued with him, but he remained stubborn. Finally she unveiled her greatest fear, "I've got the feeling if I tell you not to do it, you'll quit and do it on your own."

He grinned toughly. "If you've got such a feeling, Boss, I guess it's your womanly intuition." Then he sobered. "It's a tough job," he admitted, "but not much worse than what we've had around here. Ring is just the sort of hairpin to send troops in and wipe us all out. Anyway, I think I can do it and save my precious body."

Dani wanted to forbid it, but knew that he would grin and go right at the job. She grabbed his arm and ordered, "Ben—be careful!"

"Sure." He nodded. "You can have my watch, if I don't come back."

"Don't—don't joke about it!" she admonished him, and he saw that her hand was trembling. "I'm a little bit lost, Ben," she whispered. Without warning, she suddenly leaned against him, her face on his shoulder.

He stood there, surprised at her reaction. He knew her to be a strong woman, for time and time again he had seen her come up and face something that would floor most people. Now he felt a little perplexed. He put his arms around her and waited until the tremors in her body ceased. Pulling back, he looked at her steadily. "I'll be all right," he comforted her. "You mind the store while I'm gone."

Suddenly Dani realized that she was holding on to him and pulled back with some embarrassment. "Sorry to be such a crybaby, Ben," she apologized. "Guess I'm just a weak woman, even after all the things I've done to make you think differently."

215

He shook his head as he stepped back. "You're a good guy, Boss. I'll be in touch." He left quickly, and she went back to stare out of her window, noting that the clouds were blowing in to cover the face of the silver moon.

Joseph Martino was tired of the meeting. For three hours he had sat at the table, saying little but listening as his three top lieutenants tried to hammer out their disagreement. Mickey Spinelli was even more hotheaded than Johnny Ring, which was saying a lot. The thin Sicilian had a pair of hot black eyes and the morals of a cobra. Over and over again he sang one song, "Go in and take Lanza out!"

Ring was more cautious, but not much. He disagreed only on timing and methods. As always, he dominated the group, with his dark eyes missing nothing. He had let Spinelli talk, then interjected, "Mickey is right about one thing, Joe. Sooner or later Lanza is going to wake up. If Phil were alive, I don't think we'd all be in this room right now. He'd have hit us like a ton of bricks!"

"But Frank isn't Phil," L. D. Burger argued. This tall, heavy man, dressed in the latest fashion, was balding, but his tanned face remained youthful. "I say we ride it out. Just keep your guys pushing at Lanza's operation. We'll take it over with no big bang."

Both Ring and Spinelli objected violently. "No way!" Ring exclaimed, his thick body tense. "Frank ain't Phil, but he's a Lanza. The old man may be dying, but I know him! All he has to do is say one word, and we'll get hit with stuff you never even thought of, Joe! It'll be like the time your old man had it out with Dom. No, we've got to hit him hard and often."

Joe Martino got up and shook his head. "You three can sit here all night, if you want to. I'm going to bed."

"Let's let it ride," Burger agreed smoothly. He was a man who lived by compromise and deals, so he saw that Joe was not going to budge. Winking at Johnny, he promised, "We'll talk again. Right now we're all right, and I don't want any big trouble hitting the papers. We don't need any publicity at the moment."

Ring stared at him, then nodded. "All right, L. D." But a fierce determination etched itself on his round face, and his small mouth was set like flint.

Martino saw this, but was too tired to argue. "I'm going to bed," he announced and left the room. Going up the stairs, he passed Fred DeSpain, the inside guard, and greeted him, "Good night, Freddie."

"Good night, Mr. Martino," DeSpain answered. "Have a good night." DeSpain was a tall, thin man with silver hair and a pair of steady gray eyes. He was in charge of security, and every night he stood right outside Martino's door. At dawn another man relieved him.

DeSpain waited until Martino was up the stairs, then crossed to the phone on the table by the large entrance door. "Mac?" he questioned softly. "Ring and the others are leaving. As soon as they're gone, lock up, then send Al and Blinky to check the lines. No, nothing special going on, but want to keep them on their toes."

Putting the phone down, he began systematically checking all the entrances. DeSpain was an electrical genius and had nothing but contempt for most security systems. He had spent a long time designing this one, but he knew it was only strong when it was maintained and upgraded. "I could get through every bit of this system," he'd told Ring.

"And if *I* can do it, there's another guy out there who can do it. The thing to do is to keep changing it. That and put a fail-safe on every part of it."

So he had put each entrance on a separate circuit. That way, there was no chance of an intruder putting the whole system out of order. Each window and each door was independently wired and equipped with a laser beam. Anything coming through would set off the bleeper De-Spain wore day and night, as well as the central alarm in the guardhouse at the main gate.

He activated each entrance, then tested it by putting his hand in the space. Each time, he was gratified to hear the bleeper on his belt make a shrill noise. Finally he was satisfied. Going upstairs, he sat down in the special chair beside the door to the Martino's suite. At 11:20 the lights suddenly dimmed, but only for a moment. At midnight he got up and went downstairs. He waited by the phone, and when it rang, he said, "Okay, Mac?"

"Nothing happening, Fred. You want me to send the guys out again at two o'clock?"

"Sure. Keep them awake. Did the lights dim down there?"

"Oh, yeah, I got a call from the power people about an hour ago. They asked if we'd had any kind of power shortage. Said an eighteen-wheeler had ploughed into a power pole. Killed two guys and knocked out some of the relays in this area. Said they'd send a guy out to check the transformer."

DeSpain frowned. If the main power went off, he had a large generator to take over, but it was not as reliable as the main source. "All right. Be ready to kick the generator in if there's a power shortage." He hung up the phone and checked the systems again. All were working, so he had a cup of coffee and a sandwich in the kitchen, then went back and sat down in his chair. At 1:30 the lights dimmed again, and he checked with Mac at the main gate by phone.

"Yes, Fred, the guy from the power company is here. He's been up that big pole at the entrance. He's at his truck now, talking to somebody. You wanna talk to him?"

"Yes. Put him on." DeSpain waited for a few minutes, then a voice said, "Harold Dale. Who is this?"

"Fred DeSpain. What's the trouble?"

"Well, I don't think it's too serious," Dale informed him. "The main transformer had a subsidiary fuse knocked out. I put that right. You haven't had any problem since midnight, have you?"

"Yes. The lights dimmed just a few minutes ago."

Dale was silent, then he spoke doubtfully. "Can't understand that. Say, there's a smaller transformer somewhere inside the property, isn't there?"

"Yes. Your company put it in about two years ago, when we installed a lot of new equipment. You think it could be damaged?"

"I dunno. Maybe I better have a look-see. Them lights in there shouldn't have dimmed."

"Come on up. Let me talk to the guard." DeSpain waited until Mac came on the line, then ordered, "Let him in, Mac. He shouldn't take too long. Check him when he goes out." He hung up, then went out into the drive to wait. A white truck with a yellow light on top and CEN-TRAL POWER COMPANY painted on the side came down the road. DeSpain waved him over, and a man with a yellow hard hat stuck his head out the window. "Where's the transformer?" he asked.

"Over here." It was only a short distance, so DeSpain walked instead of getting in. When he stopped and pointed up, the truck stopped, and the man got out. "That's it," he declared, pointing up.

"Won't take a minute." The repairman went up the pole expertly and opened a door on the steel box. He probed at the inside, then slammed the door and came down the pole. "That's it," he said in disgust. "But I don't have the part to put it right. Have to call in." He waved at his truck. "Phone's out of order. Got one I can use?"

DeSpain nodded. "Inside." As he led the way to the house, he asked, "How long will it take?"

"When I get the part, about ten minutes." DeSpain led the way through the side door and waved at a phone on a small table. The repair man dialed, waited, then casually took a gun out of his belt and aimed it at DeSpain.

"You're going to feel bad about this, Fred," he warned pleasantly. "Now, let's have the gun."

"What gun?" DeSpain asked, his mind racing. He was very fast and considered pulling his own weapon from his shoulder holster, but something in the eyes of the man holding the magnum on him kept him still.

"Second thoughts are usually best," the other suggested. He reached out and plucked the gun from under Fred's arm, then ordered, "Turn around, easy like, and put your hands behind you."

"You'll never get out of here alive," DeSpain commented, but there was no answer. His wrists were suddenly bound with what seemed to be a piece of wire, and then he was turned around. The intruder had put his gun away and pulled a roll of duct tape from his pocket. Ripping off a small strip, he slapped it firmly over Fred's mouth. "Come along, now, and I'll put you where you can't do any mischief."

DeSpain tried to resist, but the wire cut into his wrists. He was led outside and forced into the backseat of the truck. A loop of wire was placed around his neck, then fastened to one of the bars that held the seat. "Now don't move too much, or you'll hurt yourself, Freddie," Savage advised. He got out and left, and DeSpain discovered that he was helpless. Frantically he struggled, but after tightening the noose and almost passing out, he could do nothing but lie there and curse silently.

Joe Martino was sleeping soundly. He and his wife both had taken sleeping pills, and when he woke up, it was like coming out of a coma. All he knew was that a bright light hurt his eyes, and when he threw up his hands to shield them, an iron grip forced them down.

"What's going on?" he mumbled. He tried to open his eyes, but the light was too bright. He reached out and grabbed for his wife, who was beginning to stir. "Martha? You all right?"

Mrs. Martino woke up, and cried out, "It's a fire!"

Martino tried to get up, but as he tried to rise, he felt something cold on his forehead. It was hard and round— and with all the nightmares of a thousand nights rising to engulf him, he knew it was the muzzle of a gun!

"Now, just lie still, you two," a pleasant voice commanded. "Don't try to get up."

Mrs. Martino began to moan, and her cries unnerved Joe Martino even more. He called out hoarsely, "Don't kill her! Please don't hurt her."

There was a silence, and the voice went on, "I'm glad you said that, Joe. Most men would be thinking about themselves. I'm glad to see that you've got enough manhood to think about Mrs. Martino first."

Martino lay still, and Savage moved the light from his face. Though Martino felt relief, he could see nothing. The room was totally dark—that was the only way his wife could sleep—but Joe remained terribly aware of the presence of the gunman. He waited for the man to speak, but the silence ran on. Martha reached out, and he took her hand. Finally he questioned, "Who are you?"

"Why, I'm a specialist, Joe," the voice replied. "Right now, I specialize in Joe Martino. I work for Mr. Lanza, as you've probably guessed."

Terror ran through the couple, and Martha shrieked, "I told you this would happen if you started trouble, Joe!"

Martino was not a tough man, not in the mold of his father, but he spoke steadily, "I guess you've come to kill me."

"Why, no. I've come to try to persuade you to live." A soft laugh floated on the darkness, and the voice explained, "Now, Faye wanted you killed, but I persuaded Mr. Lanza that it wouldn't be necessary." A short silence, then the speaker added, "It's really up to you, Joe. If you promise that you'll stop sending your goons to hit the Lanza family, I'll walk out of here, and that's the end of it. If you can't see it that way, it'll have to be Faye's way."

"Promise him, Joe!" Martha Martino exclaimed. "Do it now! He'll kill us both if you don't!"

Martino lay there, thinking, then asked, "What makes you think I'll keep a promise? If you let me live, I might send Ring to hit the Lanzas."

"You might, but who would hit me? You don't even know who I am, and even if you did, who would you send who could take me? If you hit Lanza, Joe, you're dead. You know that, don't you? You paid for the best security in the world. DeSpain is the best, isn't he? But here I am. I'll always be there, Joe. Mr. Lanza paid in advance. If you hit him and run to France, I'll see you there. You'll wake up some night with me sitting by your side. And it'll be too late to promise then."

The room was silent then, except for Mrs. Martino's sobs. Though the intruder exerted no pressure, Martino knew that the gun remained in his hand. He slowly agreed, "All right. You have my word."

He waited, ready to protest, to vow, to try to convince the man of his honesty. But with a sudden movement, the assassin got to his feet. He only warned, "You'll have to get rid of Johnny Ring, Joe. I think you mean what you say, but Ring won't let it alone. Get rid of him. He can't be controlled—by you or by anyone else. If he hits Lanza, it'll be you who'll wake up with me sitting beside you, not him. Don't use the phone for ten minutes. I'd have to come back."

The door opened and closed, and Martha grabbed at Joe, holding him as tightly as she could. "He let us live, Joe!" she cried over and over. Finally he reached over and turned on the light. His hands were shaking, and he stared at them blindly.

"Joe," his wife gasped, pulling at his arm. "You've got to do it! You wouldn't have a chance! That man would find you anyplace on God's earth!"

Joe Martino nodded slowly. "Yes. I'll have to do it." But he was already thinking, *But how will I get rid of Ring? He'd kill me just as quickly as the man who just left.* Slowly a plan formed, and he put his arm around his wife. "Don't worry,

Martha. We'll be out of it. It was a mistake to go against Dom Lanza. But we'll put a stop to it. I'll have a meeting with Dom, so he'll see we're serious."

"But what about Ring?" she demanded.

"I have a plan for that," he acknowledged slowly. "He got us into all this. Now he'll have to go!"

14
Rosemary's Choice

For three days Dani's nerves had been stretched so tautly that even the children had begun to notice it. She wasn't sleeping well, for the nightmares of the shooting exploded in brief but terrifying scenes that brought her awake, drenched with sweat and clawing at the sheets. Each day that Ben was away on his mission drained her. Rosemary, being closer to her than anyone else, had noticed it first.

The two of them had been sitting outside in the shade of one of the huge live-oak trees when Rosemary mentioned it. It was the twenty-third of March, and the weather was hot. On this, her first day out, Rosemary was prepared to enjoy life to the fullest. Pat napped while a young student from Tulane drilled Matt and Rachel in science. Dani had Rossi wheel Rosemary outside in a wheelchair, and for an hour the two of them had been delighting in the gusts of wind that tossed the clouds and caressed their cheeks.

Somehow Dani found herself telling Rosemary about her life. She had said little to anyone for a long time about her past, but the privacy of the moment and Rosemary's sympathetic attitude caused her to speak. Dani told how she had had her life neatly arranged, only to have it go down in flames. "I had my CPA," she recalled slowly, "and was working with the attorney general's office in Boston. But then I fell in love with a man."

She paused for so long that Rosemary asked gently, "What was his name, Dani?"

"Jerry Hunt. He was like no man I'd ever met, Rosemary! But he was very different. I mean, he was a seminary student and planned to go to Africa as a missionary. I don't know what he saw in me, but he asked me to marry him, and I said yes." Dani looked across the broad green yard to where Mel Ennis, the manager, was driving a John Deere tractor, cutting the grass with the precision of a hair stylist. Then she shared, "I don't know what we thought, Rosemary. I think both of us knew I wasn't fitted for the missionary life, but we didn't talk about it." She let her voice drop, then spoke so quietly that Rosemary had to lean forward to hear her. "He died before we had a chance to find out. Maybe it was a good thing."

"How did he die, Dani?" Rosemary asked quietly.

"It was—my fault," Dani noted painfully. "We had a fight one day, while we were driving on the interstate. I made him stop the car, and when I got out, he drove off. It wasn't a bad fight, but Jerry—" Dani struggled with the words, and finally told her, "He had an accident that killed him instantly." She paused, then took a deep breath. "It was my fault, so I decided to go as a missionary in his place."

"I never knew you were a missionary!"

"Well, I wasn't." Dani shrugged. "I was doing my work at the seminary when my father had a sudden heart attack. I had to leave school and take over his firm—that's Ross Investigations. And that's where I am now."

Rosemary stared at Dani, then said, "I knew you've been nervous lately. I thought it was because of Ben." When there was no response, she asked, "Are you in love with Ben, Dani?"

"Why, of course not!" The answer came back so vehemently and the color rose in Dani's cheeks so quickly that Rosemary said no more about it. "He doesn't even like women," Dani blurted out. "Or he likes them home, keeping house for a dozen kids. I've almost fired him a dozen times, Rosemary. He's just one of the employees."

Rosemary reached over and patted Dani's arm. A smile lit her face, and she quietly assessed the situation. "I don't think so, Dani. You've been a nervous wreck ever since he left. Nobody will tell me what he's doing, but I assume it's something dangerous."

Dani gave her a reproachful look. "Naturally I worry about one of my investigators!" She rose, her hair blowing in the breeze, and looked across the lawn. "I'm going to take a day off soon, Rosemary. There are some things I need to check at the agency. I'll wheel you inside."

"No, just have Thomas come and get me in an hour," Rosemary suggested. "I could walk, as far as that goes." She hesitated, then added, "You've been so good for me, Dani—for all of us." It was not what she meant to say, and she sought for the words to frame what had been in her mind. Finally she confided, "Dani, I was so afraid of you when you first came."

"Afraid of me?"

"Yes. You were so efficient. You took over the house and the children, much better than I ever could." She hesitated, then looked up at Dani. "And I was terrified you'd take my husband."

"Why, you shouldn't—"

"No, it could have happened," Rosemary said. "You're so beautiful, and Frank is an attractive man. And I—I haven't been a wife to him for months." Tears suddenly rose to her eyes, and she whispered, "I'd lost him, Dani! But now I think I have a chance!"

"Of course you do!" Dani smiled. She leaned over and kissed Rosemary's cheek. "It's going to be fine!"

Rosemary held tightly to her, her eyes pleading. "But I can't stop drinking, Dani! I've tried so hard, but it never works. It started when I got so afraid of where we were going, as a family. I was afraid of the life that lay ahead for the children. I couldn't talk to Frank about it. I tried, but it didn't make any sense to him. Now, he's more like he was when we first fell in love—but the problem's still there! I know I'll drink again!"

Dani glanced at Rosemary, then sat down. "Rosemary, you can't handle the drinking problem. But there is a way, if you'll take it." She pulled her New Testament from her pocket, and her face was utterly serious. She had waited for this moment and was certain that it was right for her to share the gospel with this woman. "Rosemary, it's impossible for any of us to live a good life in our own strength. You've described what I've felt many times. You try to quit doing something, but sooner or later you find that it's come back. Let me read you what the Bible says about that. It's in the gospel of Matthew, the twelfth chapter."

228

She read slowly, " 'When the unclean spirit is gone out of a man, he walketh through dry places, seeking rest, and findeth none. Then he saith, I will return into my house from whence I came out; and when he is come, he findeth it empty, swept, and garnished. Then goeth he, and taketh with himself seven other spirits more wicked than himself, and they enter and dwell there: and the last state of that man is worse than the first. . . .' "

Dani looked into Rosemary's eyes and explained, "You've tried to clean yourself, but you have never put anything in your life to take the place of the drinking. So when the urge comes back, you have an empty heart, so you let the drinking come back in." Then she turned a few pages in the Bible. "Rosemary, you need something in your heart so that when the urge to sin comes, there will be strength to resist. Let me read you a story from John's gospel, the fourth chapter." She read the story of the woman at the well and how Jesus met her need. "Every man she'd ever met had *used* her, Rosemary, but Jesus wanted to *give* her something. And do you know what He gave her?"

Rosemary was staring at Dani, her eyes filled with tears. "What?" she asked faintly.

"He gave her Himself," Dani said. "The gospel means the 'good news,' and the good news is that God became a man and that man was Jesus Christ. And Jesus died, as you know. Why did He have to die? To pay our debt of sin. And now that He has paid it, we don't have to be afraid of death or of facing judgment."

"But—how does Jesus get *inside* of me?" Rosemary asked.

"I can't explain it to you in scientific terms," Dani told

her. "In the third chapter of John, Jesus Himself could speak of it, only by saying it was like a new birth. '. . . Ye must be born again,' He told a Jewish rabbi. But even though I can't *explain* it, I can tell you that it's true. When I finally came to the end of my rope, I called on the name of Jesus, and two things happened. First, I had peace with God. The torment and guilt left. I *knew* I was forgiven! And the second thing—from that time on, Jesus Christ has been in me. I've never seen Him or heard an audible voice, but I just sense His presence. When I pray or worship, He's just there, Rosemary!"

There was such a look of joy on Dani's face, that Rosemary stared at her. "Do you think He would forgive me, Dani?"

"That's why He came!" Dani exclaimed. "He loves you so much, Rosemary!"

"How—how can I do it?"

"It's not a matter of living right. You know already that won't work. The Bible says we are saved by faith. Paul wrote, in his letter to the Ephesians, 'By grace are ye saved through faith.' And in Romans we're told how to come to God." She turned to the passage and had Rosemary follow as she read: " 'If thou shalt confess with thy mouth the Lord Jesus, and shalt believe in thine heart that God hath raised him from the dead, thou shalt be saved.' " Then she added, "Whoever calls upon the name of the Lord shall be saved."

"Just ask God? That's all?"

"If Patrick were hurting, and you could help him, what would you do if he cried out for you?"

"Why—I'd help him!"

"Because you love him. But God loves you more than

you love Pat, Rosemary. He gave *His* son so that you can be saved." Then Dani knew the time had come. "Will you have Jesus Christ as your Saviour, Rosemary? That means letting Him forgive all your past sins and live in you so that you can face anything in the future. It means obeying Him, even when you may not want to. It's not just a matter of getting out of hell, you see. It's like a marriage. Jesus will be your heavenly husband, just as Frank is your earthly husband. It may be hard, but it's worth it!"

Rosemary dropped her head and murmured, "Help me to pray, Dani!"

For the next few moments Dani did just that, until she heard with joy that Rosemary was asking God for forgiveness. Finally she gently prodded, "Rosemary, did you call on God?"

"Yes!" Rosemary lifted her face, which was filled with hope. But she asked, "Shouldn't I feel different, Dani? I thought I'd feel like shouting or something."

"You're a newborn baby, Rosemary," Dani told her. "But you're God's baby now. You'll be growing fast. Jesus will begin teaching you things. I'll help all I can. But when you called on God in the name of Jesus, that took care of your past sins, and now you have to learn to follow Jesus in every way."

Rosemary was happy, but concerned, "I don't think Frank knows anything about this. He won't understand."

"He probably won't, but he'll see a new peace and strength in you that was never there before," Dani promised. "Don't preach at him, Rosemary, just let Jesus have you—and one day He'll have your whole family!"

The scene had lifted Dani's spirits, and she watched carefully the rest of the afternoon and especially that night.

Rosemary said nothing to the children or to Frank, but the happiness in her caused Pat to say, "Mommy, you look so good!" Later, when Dani went by to see that Rosemary was all right for the night, she told her, "I'm going to be praying for you, Rosemary. Sometimes when you come to God, the devil will try to discourage you. If you start thinking that nothing happened or if difficulties come and you get down, you have to lean on Jesus. Will you remember that?"

"Yes!" Rosemary beamed. "I want to start learning the Bible, Dani, but I don't know where to start."

"Start with the gospel of John." Dani smiled. "We'll have lots of time to talk about it. Good night, Rosemary."

She left and went to her own room, but in the middle of the night, the worst of nightmares awakened her. Dani dreamed that she was shooting the man, and his blood turned into a flood that came up and was drowning her. A voice demanded, *Call yourself a woman of God? You're nothing but a killer!* She came out of the dream with a sharp cry and leaped out of bed. She was trembling terribly and did not dare go to sleep again. When dawn came, she stumbled to the kitchen for coffee, but could eat nothing. At eight o'clock Rossi came to say, "A call for you, Dani."

She took the call inside, and Luke Sixkiller's voice came through the phone. "You're under arrest, Ross!"

"Oh, what's the charge?" she asked, smiling a little. His voice was rough but a refreshing change from her thoughts.

"Resisting a police officer," Sixkiller accused. "This is what they call an off-duty arrest. It's my day off, and I'm coming to get you. Tell those ugly apes at the guardhouse if they try to stop me I'll put them where the dogs won't bite them. Got it?"

"You fool!" She laughed. "What are you talking about?"

"My ego is bruised. And the guys in my squad know you've turned me down. It's bad for morale, Ross. So you're going out with me if I have to drag you, kicking and screaming. I'll be at the front gate at one o'clock. Don't make any plans to be in early!" He hung up before Dani could answer, and when she put the phone down, she felt better.

"I've got to go into town for the day," she told Frank later that morning. "Since Ben's not here, you'd better get some more security in the house."

"Not trouble, is it?" he asked, concern on his face.

"No. I just need a break," she answered. "Will you stay close to Rosemary and the children tonight?"

He studied her, perplexed. Then he grinned. "Sure. I've gotten hooked on Monopoly. Matt's three games up on me—but Rosemary always helps him. I caught her slipping money under the table to him last night."

"I think that's sweet!" Dani smiled. Then she sobered, adding, "It's changed things, Frank, the way you've given yourself to them. They've all responded."

"I've learned a lot, Dani." He nodded. Then, with some alarm, he demanded, "You're not running out on us for good, are you?"

"No, I'll be back late tonight. Got a date with the fuzz," she added humorously. "Luke Sixkiller. Don't let your boys give him any static when he brings me home. He might bust the whole Lanza family."

"He's just about tough enough to try it," Frank agreed. "Say, that shortage you found? We had a good accountant look at it. He says the same as you. Pop and I had a meeting with Eddy and Max last night." He frowned and looked as though he tasted something unpleasant. "Turned out to be a real brawl. Everybody accusing everybody else. Could turn out to be a real family feud."

"Probably not." Dani shrugged. "Things like that happen all the time. My guess is somebody will find it under a wrong number somewhere."

She left, and the thoughts of getting away from the Lanza kingdom lightened her spirits. She found herself whistling as she showered, and when she dried off, she laid out a new outfit. It was an ivory cotton jacquard coatdress, double-breasted with covered buttons and hip pockets. There was no chance of wearing the .38, for the dress clung to her too closely. She slipped into it and admired the fit of it in her full-length mirror.

"You look far too nice for a flatfoot like Luke Sixkiller!" she told her reflection. But as she made her way downstairs she felt excited about her date. The doorbell rang just as she reached the foyer, and she opened the door to find Sixkiller leaning against the door frame.

"You going to come quietly?" he asked. "Or do I have to use force?"

"Oh, officer," she responded in a tiny voice. "Don't I have any civil rights?"

"In that dress, you'll need all you can get." He grinned. "Let's go party." He led her down the steps, and she stopped when she saw his car. It was a new Porsche, a gleaming silver color, that looked as if it was going ninety-five miles an hour, standing still.

"My!" Dani breathed in admiration as she slipped in on the maroon leather seats. "I didn't know you were so well off, Lieutenant!"

He closed her door, walked around, and slid in beside

her. "I like to make everybody think I'm on the take," he told her. "I just got the thing last week." He started the engine and tooled away from the house and down the driveway, steering with his left wrist. "Woke up one morning and realized I'd always wanted one of these little numbers. Then I thought, *If I get wiped out today, I'll die without having one.* So I cashed in all my stocks and bought it." Then he grinned at her, his white teeth gleaming against his bronze skin. "Well, to tell you the truth, I really bought it to impress you broads. Are you impressed?"

"Oh, Mr. Sixkiller!" she breathed and leaned back away from him. "I didn't think you'd bother with a girl like me!"

They carried on a light conversation all the way to the gate. When they left, Sixkiller called out, "Hey, leave a light on for us, Legs!" Then he turned and asked, "What's your pleasure, Miss Ross?"

"I need to go by the office for a few minutes."

"Sure." He drove with the same careless skill with which he did everything else, and soon he questioned, "What's going on, Dani? We got zilch on the shooting. Same on the bomb. Don't think we'll nail anyone for either of those little numbers."

Dani hesitated, then decided not to tell Luke about Ben's idea. It alerted her to the fact that she had become part of the Lanza structure. Instead she told him of Rosemary's improvement and how she and Frank seemed to be doing better. He listened, then warned, "Frank's always been the oddball in the family. The rest of them have been pretty tough. But Ring's not finished. Guys like him only stop when they get a bullet in the brain."

Dani agreed, but turned the talk to lighter things. They stopped at the office and found her father there. He brightened at the sight of her, then looked at her escort. "Are you two together?" he asked with a gleam of humor in his gray eyes.

"She chased me so long I had to break down and take her out," Sixkiller teased evenly. "I thought we'd take in the display of Etruscan pottery down at the museum."

"It certainly sounds exciting, Lieutenant," Mr. Ross agreed smoothly. "Dani's always been into Etruscan pottery."

"Makes my heart pound." Dani nodded. Then she took her father's arm and said firmly, "Let's go out for coffee. Luke, you stay here. And don't get fresh with the help."

"Oh, I don't mind, Miss Ross!" Angie Park turned her blue eyes from her typewriter to Sixkiller and commented sweetly, "I always liked the strong, silent type." She nodded at the policeman, adding, "Just sit right there, Officer, and you can tell me about your arrest record."

Dani spent an enjoyable hour with her father. Almost at once he asked, "How much longer are you and Ben going to be on the Lanza case?"

"I don't know, Dad," she confessed. "Ben's got something he's working on. If it works, we could wind it up very soon." She patted his arm. "Do you miss me?"

"Yes, and so does the rest of the family," he observed grumpily. He spent the rest of the hour bringing her up-to-date on new cases and old, and when she left he warned, "Be sure you don't break any laws. It would be bad publicity for the firm."

"I've got the law on my side." She waved at him. "Bye, Dad!"

"He's a nice guy, your old man," Sixkiller mused as they drove away. "I guess about the only straight private eye in New Orleans. Present company excepted." He took her to the Farmer's Market, and for a couple of hours they walked around, taking in the sights.

Right in the shadow of St. Louis Cathedral, they sat down, and Dani said, "Look, Luke, all the fortune-tellers!"

He followed her gesture, noting a line of small tables, each manned by a mystic. Some of them read tarot cards, others were looking intently into the palms of gullible clients. "Want to find out what's in your future, Dani?" Luke grinned.

"No. I don't like that sort of thing," she pronounced. Looking up at the beautiful church building, she shook her head. "People are so foolish! Thinking that they can direct their lives by astrology or palmistry! It makes me sad."

He took in her expression, then shrugged. "People are like that, Dani. Think of the poor schmoes buying lottery tickets, thinking they're going to hit it big. But they never do. I guess those people are trying to find out if something good's going to happen to them. Which it probably won't."

"It may, to some of them," Dani argued. "But they're looking in the wrong place." She got up, saying, "I'm hungry, Luke."

"Well, I've got big plans for tonight," he promised. "But we can get a muffuletta—the best in the world—right down the street." He led her to Central Grocery, where they sat right across from two tourists wearing cameras and sunglasses. It was a crowded place, half grocery and half restaurant. They had to push their way through customers standing in lines to buy the Italian foods, and Sixkiller sardonically remarked, "All the best Mafia folks buy here." They ate the muffulettas, and she licked her fingers.

"You got no class, Ross," Luke complained. "Use your handkerchief!"

Then they walked around the Quarter, and Dani was struck by the panhandlers and beggars. "I guess the Quarter has the classiest beggars in the world," she commented. They stopped and watched a man who could touch his tongue to his nose. He wore a stocking cap, three days of beard, and a drab olive jumpsuit. First, he did a mock strip, with a slow teasing roll of his nylon socks, taking advantage of raucous music from a nearby club. Then he threw his head back like a sword swallower and did the tongue act. Women squealed, and he passed a hat.

"His overhead is low," Sixkiller pointed out as they moved on. They stopped in front of a man in a purple and gold baroque outfit and a powdered wig. He stood on a blank pedestal in front of a government building. He changed poses, and whenever anyone put a bill in a box labeled THIS ISN'T EASY, he bowed.

Dani liked the musicians best. "There must be a law that says they all have to play 'When the Saints Go Marching In,' " she murmured, holding on to Luke's arm. She liked the woman on a corner, playing "Tin Roof Blues" on a clarinet. She wore a neat flowered dress, its puffed sleeves starched and Sunday-school proper. Dani put a ten-dollar bill in the box in front of her, and the woman smiled.

Finally she suggested, "Let's go." Luke took her to the car, and they got in. "Little early for our real late date," he said. "Let's just cruise around." He took her through the streets of New Orleans, beginning with St. Charles Street, and then they rode on the ferry, giving them a good look at the skyline.

They talked a little, and it was an enjoyable time for Dani. Finally he took her to a fine restaurant, where they had lobsters, which they picked out of a glass aquarium. There was a string quartet, and Dani found herself relaxing. They left about ten, and he drove around some more. She leaned over against him once, when he was circling the city, and dozed off. When she woke up, "Where are we, Luke?" she questioned him.

"In Dom Lanza's backyard," he uttered laconically.

Dani straightened up and saw that they were moving slowly along a broken street faced by crumbling buildings. It was very dark, and the yellow glow of street lights gave the scene a twilight atmosphere. From decaying buildings, dim, shadowy figures flitted to and fro. Dani felt the uncleanness of it all and unconsciously moved closer to Sixkiller. "This doesn't really belong to Dom, does it, Luke?"

"Maybe he doesn't own the houses," Luke allowed. "But it's his turf. See that guy over there?" Dani saw a huge black man standing in front of a building that had cardboard in the place of window glass. "That's one of Dom's higher-class employees."

Dani stared at the man. "Him? What does he do?"

Sixkiller gave her a strange look, then pulled over to the curb. "Come on. I'd like you to meet him. After all, you both work for the same man."

Dani felt a strong aversion to getting out, but when Sixkiller opened her door, she had little choice. Darkness swallowed them now, and the street light, she noticed, was shattered. Three men came out of nowhere, appearing in front of them. They all wore some sort of gang uniform, she realized.

One of them said, "Hey, looky, what we got here, man?" He was wearing a pair of jeans, a feather in a head-band, and a black-leather vest with no shirt. The three spread out, but Sixkiller interjected, "Hello, Ace. You going to shake me down?"

The tall black man's head bobbed, he leaned forward, and then took a step backward. "Hey, it's the Lieutenant, dudes! How you doin', man?"

"Doing fine, Ace," Luke responded easily. "Anything you need?"

"No, suh!" The man called Ace was frightened, and he called out, "Come on, you dudes!" They disappeared into the darkness as silently as predatory fish slide into an opening in a reef.

Dani was trembling, but Sixkiller took her arm. The large man they had seen first had watched the scene. Now he politely greeted Luke, "Hello, Lieutenant."

"Hello, Jake. How's business?"

The question seemed to trouble the man. He stood there, mountainlike, his broad face expressionless. Finally he admitted, "I'm doing very well, thank you."

"Dani, this is Jake Potter. He's a pusher for Dom Lanza." Sixkiller added, "This is Miss Ross, Jake. She works for Dom, too."

Potter stood as still as a statue. His large eyes flickered to Dani, but went back to the policeman at once. He could have crushed Sixkiller with one blow of his hamlike fist, but he stood very still. Finally he asked quietly, "Is this a bust, Lieutenant?"

"A bust? Why, Jake, you know me better than that! If it

was a bust, would you be standing there with your nose not broken? With your head not split?" Sixkiller sounded hurt, and he turned to Dani. "You see how it is, Miss Ross? We policemen have an unhappy life. Here Jake and I have known each other for five years, and he still doesn't trust me! Is that fair, I ask you?"

Dani didn't understand what was happening, but one thing was clear: The huge black man was deathly afraid of Sixkiller. She had heard that Luke was a hard man, but seeing this terror in a man who was obviously not afraid of many convinced her.

Just then a thin, yellow woman dressed in a leather miniskirt and high boots came up. She had on a low-cut blouse and was obviously in poor condition. She lurched suddenly, falling against Jake Potter. "Here's the money, Jake," she cried, and the hand that held some bills trembled violently.

"I don't know you!" Potter objected instantly, pushing her hand away. He gave Sixkiller a wild look, and added, "She's just a chippy, Lieutenant."

The woman stared at him and then began to weep. "Jake, you tole me, if I got the money, you'd give me—"

Potter's huge hand shut off her words. He cuffed her and whirled her around. "Git away, woman! I don't know you!"

Sixkiller apologized, "Didn't mean to interrupt your business, Jake. Come along, Miss Ross."

Dani followed him back to the car, and when he drove away, she let go with the anger that had built up in her. "Why did you bring me to this place, Luke?"

He didn't answer for a moment, then admitted, "I wanted you to see what pays for those nice meals you've been having at the Lanza place, Dani. That poor woman crying for a fix, she pays for it." He drove out of the ghetto and finally spoke, "Sorry, Dani. But I think you've been kidding yourself about some things. Sure, the kids are sweet, and you like Mrs. Lanza. Dom can be real cultured. Frank looks like a three-piece-suit guy working for a stock broker. But what you've just seen—*that's* the Lanza business."

Dani responded quietly, "I think you'd better take me home now, Luke."

"You mean back to the Lanza place?" he asked.

"You know what I mean!"

He shrugged and, without another word, drove through the night. When they got to the gate, Legs opened it immediately, and Sixkiller brought her to the front of the house. She got out, and he went with her to the front door. "Good night," she said abruptly.

Then he pulled her around. "Dani, why do you think I took you to the ghetto?" he asked. His dark eyes glowed, reflecting the brass lights over the entrance. He was a powerful man, physically and in other ways, and she could not pull away from him. "You think I didn't know it would hurt you? That I'm just a dumb flatfoot?"

"Oh, Luke, I don't think that!" she corrected quickly. Then she nodded and softly stated, "You're afraid I'm getting too involved with the Lanzas. That I've lost my sense of right and wrong."

He nodded. "That's right, Dani. And you wouldn't be the first. Money can do that—a lot of money. But with you it's not money. You like the old guy. He's dying, and you're sorry for him. But I wanted you to see what's underneath the Lanza empire. So I pulled back a rock and let you see some of the crawly things underneath." He hesitated, then added, "It was pretty noble of me, Dani. Here I wanted to show you what a great prospect I am, and I shove your face in the garbage can."

Dani realized that he was speaking the truth. She looked into his expressionless face, and spoke appreciatively, "I think you're noble, Luke. Thanks for looking out for the girl detective." Then she put her arms around his neck and pulled his head down. He was, for once, caught off guard, and by the time he tried to hold her, she was moving back. "There." She smiled at him. "That makes two of us noble people around here. Good night, Luke—and thanks!"

"Hey!" he protested as she closed the door, "I didn't mean to be *that* noble, Dani!"

"Call me again, Luke," she invited through the slit in the door. Then she went to her room and got ready for bed. After she had showered and put on her gown, she sat down in the chair and began to read the Bible, but it seemed so remote from what had happened. Closing the Bible, she slipped into bed and tried to pray, but her mind was cluttered with too many thoughts.

Finally she said aloud, "O God, I can't pray! Take care of Ben. Take care of Rosemary and Frank and the kids! Soften Dom's heart!" She finally drifted off to sleep, and for the first time since the shooting, slept all night without a bad dream.

15
A Trip to the Dentist

On Tuesday evening, Frank came to Dani's room. "We're having a meeting about the books. Like to have you sit in on it, if you're not too tired."

Dani wanted to refuse, but since she had been the one who had initiated the problem, she agreed, "Of course, Frank." When they got to the large meeting room, she was surprised to find the entire family there, especially Dom, who was obviously in pain.

As soon as Dani sat down, Eddy angrily attacked her, "Listen, I hear you've been spouting off about how somebody's been nibbling at the till. Well, I take that personal, Miss Ross! I've never taken a dime that wasn't mine from this operation!"

Helen Darrow was sitting by her husband, Max, staring at Eddy with suspicion. "You handle the books, Eddy," she pointed out sharply. "If something's wrong, you're responsible."

Eddy glared at her, and Dani was aware that though

they were brother and sister, little natural affection existed between them. "Your dear hubby Max does most of the juggling with the funds," he snapped. "Maybe *he's* the one who's been on the take!"

Max flushed and shouted, "Why, you little shrimp! If you were more than half a man, I'd push your face in!"

Eddy turned pale, for no one referred to his physical infirmity. Then he fixed his eyes on Darrow with such evident hatred that Dani felt certain if he'd had a gun, he'd have killed his brother-in-law.

"Keep your mouth shut, Max!" Eddy's wife, Irene, was on her feet and would have attacked the lawyer, but Frank reached out and caught her. The yelling continued, but Frank finally shoved Irene into her chair and slammed his fist on the table.

"Shut up, all of you!" he shouted. When they stopped in surprise and stared at him, he shook his head. "You sound like a bunch of kids! This is a business matter, and we're going to treat it as such. The next one who raises his voice, I'll chuck him out that door—and I'm not kidding!" Everyone—most of all his father—stared at Frank. There was, Dani saw, a thin smile of approval on Dom's thin lips as he looked at his older son.

"Miss Ross first noted some sort of discrepancy in the books, but Sam Vino checked it out. Sam's never mistaken, Eddy, and he says there's something wrong. Now, you and Max have been working on these books for a long time. I'll give you three days. Come up with some answers—or maybe I'll have some questions you won't like!"

The meeting dragged on as Frank went through details, and Dani soon tired of it. She had been impressed with the authority that Frank displayed and knew that Dom was pleased. But when the meeting broke up, she felt glad.

"Thanks for coming, Dani." Frank nodded. "I hope you don't have to get involved in this mess any more."

Dani murmured, "It would be better if I stayed out of it, Frank. This man Vino is your best bet."

Frank looked at her glumly. "Hate to think one of the family's been stealing, Dani. That's about all a man like me has—family pride."

He walked away abruptly, and Dani went to her room. She'd checked out a Dickens video, *Bleak House*, and settled down to watch it. It was very long, over six hours, and about 3:00 A.M. she turned it off. Going to the window, she stared out, wondering about Ben. Even as she did, she saw a pair of headlights come down the road. It was unusual for a vehicle to approach the house at that hour, so she watched closely. When the car passed by the large mercury light near the garage, she saw that it was Ben's.

She gave a gasp of relief and tore out the door and down the stairs. The air was cool, and when she got to the garage, she found that Ben was just getting a suitcase out of the trunk. He looked up sharply when she entered, and a grin turned up his lips. "Hello, Boss," he greeted her.

"Ben!" Then Dani could not think of what to say. The tension that had bound her had been worse than she knew, and as she stared at him she became suddenly aware of the power he had to stir her. She forced herself to say calmly, "I'm glad you're back."

"You been waiting up for me all this time?" he asked with a glint in his dark eyes.

"Of course not! I—just couldn't sleep." She brushed her hair back and inquired, "How did it go?"

"A piece of cake." He shrugged. "Let's get some coffee, and I'll tell you about it. But at the big house, not here."

Dani knew he didn't trust any of Lanza's men, so she agreed. They crossed the terrace, and soon he was munching freshly baked doughnuts, washing them down with scalding coffee.

"You never taste anything, Ben," Dani complained as she watched. "You eat so fast your taste buds never get a chance. Now, tell me."

He went through the story, making it sound easy, but she could read the difficulty and danger that he had passed through. It was a way he had, she knew, of making the difficult seem easy. And as he sat there, talking, she wondered just exactly what sort of man he was. He had always been an enigma to her, and the more she knew him, the more she became conscious of the complexity that lay beneath a seemingly simple exterior.

Finally he ended the story, "So Joe promised to be a good boy and let the Lanzas alone. Then I tippy-toed out and came home."

Dani thought about it, then asked, "Do you think he'll stick to it?"

"I think so. He's pretty jumpy, and his wife is worse. The problem is Johnny Ring, just as it's always been." He leaned his elbows on the table, and there was a light of speculation on his face. "I think Martino will have Ring tossed in the river."

"Have him killed?" Dani asked in a startled tone.

"Sure. Happens all the time. These mob bosses don't like a strong man. A guy gets too strong, he'll take over. That's what Capone did, and these big operators know what to do about that." He studied her, then remarked,

"Looks like we might be out of here in a day or two. Don't guess you'd mind that."

Dani shook her head. "I want to leave, Ben. It's been—very hard."

He knew she was thinking of the shooting. "I'll tell Dom what happened first thing in the morning, but my guess is that Martino will call early. He's really scared."

Dani got to her feet, and he followed suit. "I'm glad you're back," she told him. "I did worry about you."

He studied her, then shook his head. "Go to bed, Boss. When we get out of here, let's go fishing or something."

She smiled at him, her eyes glad, and as he left, she remarked, "Yes, let's do it, Ben. Go fishing, I mean. I need a little simplicity, I think." He left, but she sat down for a long time at the kitchen table, trying to think how it would be to get out from under the Lanza influence. Finally she went to her room, thinking, *He's arrogant enough as it is. I shouldn't have let him find out how much I worried about him!*

"Martino called this morning," Frank announced as Dani came into his office. "He wants to call the whole thing off." His eyes were disbelieving, but he suddenly smiled. "Your man Savage really knows how to scare a guy. Pop said Joe Martino was practically *begging* to get off the hook."

Dani asked, "Did your father believe him?"

"Not at first, but Joe kept picking at him. Finally my father was convinced. The two of them are going to meet. Martino even agreed to come *here!* That's what convinced Pop, I think. Joe Martino is a coward. He wouldn't stick his head in this place unless he had to."

"Looks as if my job will be over soon." Dani smiled.

"Now, don't go running away so quickly!" Frank protested.

"Not today anyway." Dani reminded him, "I've got to take Pat to the dentist."

"Want someone to drive you?" Frank asked.

"No, I can drive my own car. I've been blackmailed by your younger son." She smiled. "The only way I could get Pat to agree to go for his checkup was to promise to take him to the aquarium afterwards."

"Kid is going to be a terror when he grows up." Frank shook his head in mock despair. "He's been conning me for a long time. Now he's branching out. You can handle him alone?"

"Oh, yes. Save some dessert for us."

When Dani went to get Pat at one o'clock, she found him huddled in Rosemary's arms, his eyes large with apprehension. Playing it very lightly, Dani said, "Well, Pat, let's go get the checkup out of the way. I can't wait to get to the aquarium."

"Don't want to go!" Pat moaned, holding tightly to Rosemary.

"Of course you do," his mother encouraged. She whispered in his ear for a few moments, and Pat looked up at her with surprise. Then he pulled away and went over to pick up his blanket.

"Let's go, Dani," he called happily, racing out the door.

Dani stared after him, then wondered aloud, "What in the world did you promise him, Rosemary?"

"That's privileged communication." Rosemary laughed. Then she got up slowly and came to embrace Dani. "I've been so excited, Dani! When I go to bed, no more bad dreams. Every time I want a drink, I just do what you

249

said." Her blue eyes sparkled and she laughed. "I just tell him, 'Devil, I've put all that away and locked the door. Jesus has the key. Go get it from Him if you can!' "

"I'm so happy for you, Rosemary," Dani said. "We'll have time for a little Bible study when I get back. Maybe after the Monopoly game. Well, I'd better take him before he backs out."

Pat had waited at the door, and the pair of them left. Passing the tennis courts, they saw Ben playing tennis with Abby. Matthew and Rachel watched from the sidelines. Ben missed a shot, and Abby laughed in delight. "You're an old man, Savage!"

"Oh, yeah? You just get your breath, kid." He came over to walk beside Dani and Pat. "You sure you don't want me to come along?"

"No. You watch the store. We'll be all right." The thoughts of their meeting the previous night came back to her, and once again Dani wondered if she'd led him to think she was too interested in him. She kept her voice casual as she added, "Don't worry about me."

He gave her a strange glance, but only commented, "Keep your powder dry." Then he turned and went back to the game. It was an unsatisfying scene to Dani, but she put it out of her mind. She strapped Pat into the car and left the grounds, thinking of the possibility of getting off the case within a few days. Faye was at the gate, along with Frenchy, and as the small Cajun opened the gate, Faye questioned "What time will you be back, do you think?"

"Should be around four o'clock." Then she pulled through the entrance, asking Pat, "Would you like to play the radio?" He nodded and found a rock-and-roll station, which he turned up to maximum volume. She hated it, but it kept the child happy.

Dark clouds were building up to the south, and she hoped that the rain would hold off until after dark. The road was in poor repair, and she had to dodge potholes, which pitted the asphalt surface. The three miles of road was rarely used by anyone, the Lanza place being one of the few dwellings it led to. It wound around a large sugar-cane field, then joined another more widely traveled road and intersected the state highway, six miles to the north. As Dani made the sweeping curve around the cane field, she was forced to brake suddenly, for two vehicles blocked the road. One of them was a panel truck with DAVIDSON'S FLORIST in large letters on the side. It was right across the road and nosing into the front of it was a white Taurus. Two men stood beside the cars and appeared to be having a rather violent disagreement. One of them, a tall man dressed in a gray sports coat, had the other man by the arm. The other wore a tan uniform with *Davidson Florist* printed on his cap.

The tall man looked around as Dani slowed to a stop, gave the driver of the delivery van a slight push, then turned and came to where she was parked. He was shaking his head, and a furious expression covered his thin face. He was very tall and said something she could not understand. She lowered her window, and he bent down to tell her, "Got to get a call in to the police. Stupid clown can't drive!"

Dani promised, "I'll make a call when I get to the highway."

She started to raise the window, but suddenly a gun appeared not six inches from her eyes. "Don't try to do that—or the kid's dead."

Dani's mind seemed to freeze. The muzzle of the re-

251

volver was like a tunnel, and she could see the man's trigger finger quite clearly. All he had to do was touch the trigger, and she was dead. Suddenly her mind began racing, and she thought, *He'll have to make me get out of the car. I can get my gun out as I do that.*

"Lean forward and put your head on the wheel, slow and easy," the man ordered.

She obeyed and at once felt the muzzle of the revolver touch her head. Then she felt his other hand on her back! *He knows where I carry my gun,* she thought, and despair settled on her. She felt him yank her coat up, and then he pulled the .38 from the holster.

"All right, you can get out now. Get the kid, too."

Pat stared at the gunman with large eyes. "Who is he, Dani?" he whispered.

"Don't be afraid, Pat," she encouraged quietly. Unbuckling her seat belt and then his, she got out, and the boy scrambled out to stand beside her. He groped for her hand, and she held it tightly. "You're making a mistake," she informed the man. "My people know where I'm going. And if I don't call in soon, they'll know something is wrong."

The thin gunman grinned, but shook his head. "Nice try—but then I heard you were a cool one." Then the smile faded and he commanded, "Over to the van, and move it fast!"

As Dani walked toward the van a third man emerged from the delivery truck. He was short and heavy, with jet-black hair. "Harry, take her car. You know where to put it." The man dressed in the tan uniform had moved to open the back door of the van, and when he turned, he had a roll of silver duct tape in his hands. "Turn around," he commanded Dani. She had no choice and was forced to pull her hand out of Pat's grasp. Her hands were taped together, then she heard the sound of the tape being ripped. She gasped as another piece of tape was slapped over her eyes, and Pat began crying.

"Now the kid," the tall man's voice directed. Dani was shoved into the van, striking her knee on a sharp surface. She cried out, "Pat!" but rough hands seized her legs, and she was thrown roughly, falling on what seemed to be some sort of pad. She strained to break the tape, but it was useless. Pat's cries became louder, and then she heard a voice say, "That's good enough." Finally she felt the child's body strike her legs.

"It's all right, Pat," she comforted him. The door slammed and she invited, "Come up here and lie down beside me." The boy wriggled and came to press himself against her. "Now, try not to cry," she directed, keeping her voice as even as she could. Fear raced through her, but she knew her job was to keep Pat from sensing it. "We're in some trouble, Pat, but you remember the story I read you last night?"

His voice was muffled, for he was pressing his face against her breast, trying to get as close as possible. "You mean—about the man in the lion's den?"

"Yes, Daniel. Remember what happened to Daniel? He was in terrible trouble, wasn't he? But God saved him."

"I know! God glued up the mouths of the lions so they couldn't bite him, didn't He?"

"That's right, Pat. And God will get us out of our trouble. So let's just start right now asking Him to keep us safe, all right?"

"All right!"

He began to pray in his childish fashion, and Dani was very glad that she had taught the children how to speak to God. It had not been very real to any of them, but Pat was occupied at least. She prayed herself, asking God to preserve their lives, but she felt burdened with the knowledge that most kidnapping victims were not rescued. It was, as she well knew, too dangerous to let the victims live, for the kidnappers were very conscious that one day they might face the victims in court.

The truck door slammed, then the engine started, and at once the truck spun around and moved down the road. Dani lay there, listening to Pat and speaking to him from time to time, but with another part of her mind, she recorded as best she could every scrap of information about the route the truck was following. She could only estimate the speed of the vehicle, but she guessed that the driver would not exceed the speed limit—too much chance of being picked up by the police. She knew the country well, having lived in the area for years, and she and Ben had thoroughly covered the section around the Lanza estate. She concentrated on picturing a map in her mind and tried to see the car as a red dot moving down the highway. She knew at once when it passed the cane field, for they made a sharp left turn that led to the state highway. There was a stoplight where the road intersected the state highway. She waited as the driver stopped, then made a left turn. *Going east*, she thought, *toward New Orleans*. She could not reach her wrist to use her pulse for a clock, so she counted off the seconds, keeping track of the minutes. The traffic picked up, and she could hear the big trucks passing, their wake rocking the smaller panel truck.

Eventually, of course, she became confused, for the

truck went through a suburban area, making several turns and pausing for lights. But finally she felt a thrill when the sound of the tires on the highway changed from a high-pitched sound to a more hollow one, and the vehicle tilted upward. *We're on one of the river bridges!* she thought rapidly. *Got to be going through Algiers, down the river.*

But then she became confused, for nothing else marked the progress of the van—no particular sounds or traffic patterns—just the steady hum of the engine. She lost track of time, as well, but guessed that they had not traveled more than thirty or forty minutes since passing over the bridge. Then the truck made a sudden left turn, and five minutes later, passed on to a very rough road, so rough that it shook Pat and Dani to their bones.

Finally, the truck stopped, and the door slammed at once. Dani lay there, waiting, and the back door quickly swung open. She heard a voice say, "Everything go all right?"

The voice of the driver was assured. "Sure. Like clockwork."

"All right, you boys clear out. Here's your money."

"Yeah. See you around—"

"No names, you fool!" the other man cut him off. "Get them out and then clear out."

Dani felt Pat being pulled away. She was jerked out of the van and held upright when she swayed. "Take the boy," the speaker ordered. Pat was whimpering, and Dani comforted him, "It's all right, Pat."

Someone grabbed her arm and pulled her across a paved surface. Then the voice commanded, "Step up." She cleared the step, and once again began trying to picture everything in her mind. Already she was thinking of escape, and a knowledge of this place would be necessary. They were marched across a concrete floor, then the pressure on her arm jerked her to a halt. A metallic clanging came to her, and she was pulled forward. Her heel caught on some sort of projection, and then she was stopped again. "Get the kid in," the leader ordered. He had a high-pitched voice, but it was filled with authority. Then the clanging sound came, and the floor suddenly moved. Pat cried out in fear, but Dani soothed him, "It's just an elevator, Pat."

The elevator seemed to move slowly, and there was no way Dani could estimate how many floors it rose. *It's not a passenger elevator*, she decided. *More like one that's used to move freight.*

Then the floor stopped with a sudden lurch, and the door opened. Dani felt herself led down a hall, and heard a door opening. One of her captors firmly pushed her inside, and she felt Pat come bumping into her legs. "Don't try to take the tape off your eyes until the door closes," the man warned. "You know why, I guess."

It gave Dani some relief. "Yes. We won't try to see your faces." Unseen hands turned her around and ripped the tape from her wrists. She rubbed them and caught at Pat, who was trying to get closer to her. The door closed at once, and she reached up and tore the tape from her eyes.

She took one look around, noting that they were in a room no more than twelve feet wide and fifteen feet long and that there was one small window. Then she knelt and pulled the tape from Pat's hands and eyes. He grabbed at her, and she held him tightly, rocking him and making comforting noises.

As she held him to her breast, she studied the room

more closely. On one wall, there were two cots with blankets and pillows, a table, and two chairs; this made up the total of furnishings, except for what she knew to be a Porta-Potti, the type of commode used by campers, and a green, five-gallon water container with the *Gott* brand on the side.

She gave Pat a squeeze, saying, "Let's see what's outside." Walking to the window, which was no more than two feet square, she paused and studied it. It lacked glass, but was barred with what looked like rough steel bars, the sort used in building foundations. It was five feet from the floor, and when she dragged a chair over and looked out, she saw that the building they were in was on the Mississippi River. There was no mistaking the largest river in America.

An old warehouse on the river, she knew at once. *Probably been vacant a long time.* This was not uncommon, she knew, and even as she looked she saw a tug pushing a string of low-lying barges downstream. The river was broad, and looking down, she could see no nearer signs of life. The entrance was on the other side of the building from where their room was, and she groaned at that. *Maybe I could have dropped a note—or signaled a car, if this room looked out on that side.* Looking out across the water, she knew that no boat would ever come close enough for her to call, and she could never drop a message. Who would pick it up?

Pat said, "Hold me up, Dani. I want to see." She did as he asked, and he studied the scene. When she put him down, he looked at her and questioned in a small voice, "Dani, how long do you think it will be before God gets us out of here?"

Dani gave him the best smile she could manage. "Why,

it might seem like a long time to you and me, Pat. But God won't let us down. We just have to be patient. Now, let's see what our little house is like."

As they explored the small room, Dani shared Pat's thought: *How long will it be before God gets us out of here?*

16
Waiting

"Savage, Dani and Pat have been kidnapped!"

Ben had been summoned to Frank's office by Frenchy, and the private eye had known as soon as he walked in the door that it was bad news. Frank's face was pasty white as his father cast one agonized look at Savage. Dom seemed shrunken, almost like a mummy, too stricken even to speak.

"I got worried when they were late for supper," Frank went on, speaking woodenly. "They never made it to the dentist's office."

"You call the police yet?" Ben asked tensely.

"No!"

"It'll come to that sooner or later." Savage knew at once that notifying the police was not going to be an acceptable idea to either man. He shrugged, choosing rather to let it come when it came. "Get the call yet?"

"The call?" Frank asked almost stupidly. He was a quick-minded man, sharp in his responses, but Pat's loss had numbed him. "Oh, from the kidnappers. No, not yet."

"We don't need a call," Dom whispered. He raised his eyes, and sick as he was, a fire burned in them. "Who else but Martino? I should not have believed the scum!"

"Let's wait," Savage advised quickly. "I think you're right, but there's an outside chance it might be someone else." He shook his head in anger. "I thought I had Joe scared enough to do anything!"

"Let me make a couple of calls—not the police," he added as Frank started to protest. "Maybe she went by her parent's place or the office." He dialed the numbers and made up a story that covered the calls. "Nothing doing," he said, putting down the receiver. Taking a deep breath, he forced himself to speak slowly. "How many know about it?" he asked.

"Just the three of us," Frank informed him. "I've got to tell Rosemary."

"Maybe you should wait, Frank," Dom suggested. "If Dani and Pat come walking in, it would mean you'd put Rosemary through a terrible time for nothing."

"They're not going to come walking in, Pop," Frank stated flatly. Anger was beginning to override the fear that had numbed his mind, and he suddenly exploded. "Faye's been right all the time! We should have wiped up on that crowd long ago! And it's not too late!"

He half turned, but Savage disagreed, "Yes, it's too late now." His hard tone caught Lanza, who turned and stared at him. Savage went on calmly, "What good would it do to hit some of Martino's bunch—or Joe himself for that matter? Dani won't be at his house. She'll be far away, and there'll be a phone there. If you start blasting, Dani and Pat will go up in smoke."

Frank stared at him, then his shoulders sagged. "Sure, Ben," he agreed heavily. "I wasn't thinking. But I still think we ought to tell Rosemary. I'll stall until Matt and Rachel are in bed, though."

Dom asked suddenly, "Ben, have you ever been involved in a kidnapping case?"

Savage nodded. "Three times, all in the Denver area." He saw that strong as they were in many ways, both men felt racked by helplessness. He declared, "It's a dirty business. Most of the time, no matter what the family of the victims does, it doesn't help."

"You mean they'll kill Dani and Pat , no matter what we do?" Dom asked.

"We've got a chance," Savage insisted evenly. "But only if we keep our heads. They have all the good cards, and they know it. Get this straight right now: They'll try to break us down. They know we're hurting, and they'll try to make it worse. For instance, they'll try to scare you into moving fast."

"I'm pretty scared right now," Frank confessed dully. "What else can they do?"

"They can tell you that they're going to send you one of Pat's fingers by UPS if you don't move fast." He saw the shock rake across Frank Lanza's face, and Dom stared at him, his face frozen. "Oh, they'll say worse than that, I'd guess. It's always the same. Time is against them, and they know it. So they have to get what they want and get out quick. That's why I think we ought to call the law right now. They can do things we can't."

"No law!" Dom Lanza spoke emphatically and shook his head defiantly. "We have enough manpower to handle it. I can call in a hundred men by tomorrow."

Savage felt sorry for the old man, but there was no gentleness in him as he spoke. "Dom, this isn't a gang war. A *thousand* gunmen wouldn't help a bit. Get those ideas out of your head!" He went over and sat down and looked at the two men. "No sense looking at the phone. It won't ring for a day or two."

"What! Why not?" Frank cried.

"Look at you," Savage pointed out. "You're falling to pieces right now, and it's only been a few hours. You think they don't know that? They *use* it, Frank. The longer they let you stew, the easier you'll be for them to manipulate. By this time tomorrow, you'll be helpless."

Dom asked, "Isn't there anything we can do, Ben?"

"Sure! But none of it's going to help your nerves," Savage warned. "You've got to understand one thing—it's all a game of nerves. The first guy who blinks gets the ax. I know it's rough, but I'm telling you it's the only way to get Pat and Dani back!"

A silence ran around the room. Frank took a deep breath, expelled it, then slowly nodded. "All right, Ben. You're the man. What can we do besides wait?"

"Get an electronics man here quick," Ben suggested. "I recommend Vance Hill. He's the best."

"Get him!" Frank ordered. "What does he do?"

"Gets the phones ready for the call. There'll be more than one, and we want everything on tape. They'll threaten to kill Pat if you do it, but they'll have no way of knowing. Most kidnappers know that's going to be done anyway, so they take their precautions about the calls they make."

"Can't we trace the calls?" Frank demanded.

"You've been seeing too many movies! It takes a long

time and a bunch of special equipment for that. Chances are they'll use a different phone each time. But even if they didn't, as long as they keep the calls short, there's no chance of tracing it."

"Call that man," Frank insisted. "Tell him to name his price."

"It'll be the same as if he did it for Ross Investigations," Savage said. He made a call, spoke with Hill, and put down the receiver. "Now, nobody elected me to run this show, but let me at least fill you in on what will probably happen. You need to be ready for it. And you might as well sit down. We're not going anywhere."

As Frank obeyed, Ben went over and looked in the cooler. Picking out a Coke, he poured it in a glass, added ice, and took a sip. He was a hard, tough shape as he stood there, and both men suddenly felt glad they were not alone.

"The call will come, probably tomorrow," he guessed. "It will be rough. They make the demand: how much money. Then they'll tell you to get it, and they'll give you some rough threats. Finally they'll hang up." He took another sip and stared at the floor, thinking hard. "The second call will come maybe ten hours or so later. This time they'll give you specific instructions—and more threats. They'll want the money right away, and that's your chance to stall them. Tell them you're having trouble raising it. Stall all you can." He lifted his head and fixed Frank's gaze. "And right then is where you make *your* demand, Frank!"

"My demand?"

"Yeah. You say that Dani and Pat are probably dead already. Tell them you're not paying a dime until you talk to *both* of them. They'll try to break you down, but you can't back up. Don't try to push them around. Just keep saying you've got to know they're okay."

"What if they kill them rather than do that?" Dom asked intently.

"They won't." Savage shook his head and smiled grimly. "What could they use for leverage then? No, they'll scream, but in the end they'll have to do it. And that's our only hope."

"I don't understand," Dom complained. "Aside from letting us know they're alive, how will it help?"

Savage took several sips of the Coke, then stared at the glass. "I hate these things!" he muttered. Then he looked up, his face hard, but a light shone in his hazel eyes. "What do you think Dani is doing right now?"

"Why—I don't know," Frank stammered. "What *can* she do, Ben?"

"She's thinking, that's what." Savage nodded emphatically. "That woman is a thinking machine! Never saw anything like it. When we were stuck in that silo, waiting for that nut to bump us off, she went around fixing food and preaching to all of us, but she was thinking all the time. Never stopped! And she thought us out of there!"

"She told me that *you* were responsible for the escape," Dom objected.

"I climbed a rope, but she was the one who thought it out. I'm just a hard-nosed cop, but that lady is something else. I don't know where she is, but right now she knows that sooner or later she's going to get to say something to us over the phone."

"How can she know that?" Dom asked in a puzzled tone.

"Because she knows *me*." Savage nodded again. "She picked my brain dry a long time ago. I've told her about every case I was ever on, and she never forgets a thing. So she's figuring out how to tell us where they've got her and Pat or something else that will give us a handle on the thing. That's why we need the phone system. She'll only have a chance to say a few words, and they'll have to get by whoever's holding her. She'll have to make it sound as if it means nothing, or they won't play." He thought for a minute. "It just came to me, she'll probably give Pat something to say that will help. Those guys won't suspect a kid of doing a thing like that!"

Frank studied Ben's face, then asked, "You know Dani pretty well, don't you?"

Savage looked at him with a stolid expression. "I work for her," he commented evenly.

The phone rang sooner than any of them thought. Vance Hill had gotten there and set up the system by midnight. He had made himself a small command post in a room next to the den, where he sat with a pair of headphones on, ready with his finger on a switch. "No way they'll know I'm there," he had assured Ben and the Lanzas. "But I'll get it all."

Frank had left at eight, to tell Rosemary, and when he came back just before ten o'clock, Dom asked, "How did she take it?"

Frank shook his head. "Better than you and me, Pop." He sat down slowly, a perplexed look on his haggard face. "I thought she'd go to pieces and reach for a bottle, but she didn't. She cried a little, but then she looked at me and said, 'It will be all right.' Why, she sounded so blasted *sure!* I don't get it!"

Savage grinned. "I do. You left her with Dani too much, Frank. She's hit the glory trail."

"Religion?" Frank stared at Savage. "I don't believe it!"

"I do," Dom chimed in. He had refused to leave the room and was lying on the couch. Thomas Rossi had come and sat on a straight chair, watching the old man. He had made Dom comfortable, but could not make him take a sleeping pill. Now he looked carefully at Dom, as did Frank. "She's been working on me," Dom admitted with a smile.

"Aw, come on, Pop!" Frank exclaimed.

"You think it's pretty hopeless, a man like me finding God?" his father inquired. "Well, I think so too—but that woman will not give up!'

"Ain't she a caution?" Savage laughed deep in his throat. "She's been at me from the time we met, and no matter how rotten I act, she just goes right on telling me how God loves me." He sobered and shook his head. "You know something? I'm beginning to believe it."

Dom nodded. "Rosemary is different, Frank. You will see. It's a thing I can't understand, but she's like a new woman. Maybe this kind of faith is not for me or you, but it works for her."

"It worked for Vince," Savage put in suddenly. "He went out with a smile on his face. I think—"

The sudden sound of the phone made all of them jump, and Frank leaped at it.

"Slow and easy!" Savage warned. When Frank picked up the phone, he announced, "This is Frank Lanza!" He blinked and pulled the phone away from his ear, and the others could hear the frantic voice of a man. "It's Joe Martino," Frank told the others and listened to the tirade coming over the receiver. Finally he cried, "I don't believe you, Joe." Another burst of words and Dom finally came over and suggested, "Let me talk to him, Frank."

He took the phone, put his lips near the receiver, and rapped out, "Shut your mouth, Joe." He waited and added, "You're trying to say that you had nothing to do with the kidnapping. Maybe that is so. But to prove it, you will have to come here alone and talk to me. No muscle with you, understand. Be here in one hour. Otherwise, my friend who called on you in the night will be back for a second visit. One hour!" He put the receiver back and smiled at the two men. "You know, I think he'll come. And he'd only do that if he really had nothing to do with it."

"He said it was all Ring's idea, Pop." Frank nodded. "Said Ring won't even tell *him* where he's got Dani and Pat."

"I think he's telling the truth," Dom noted slowly. "Ring is ambitious. I've always known that one day he would get rid of Joe. Old Sal was too tough for him, but he knows he can take Joe. I think this is it. He'll get what he wants from us, and somehow he'll take over the Martino organization. He'll either scare Joe into retiring or kill him."

Vance Hill stuck his head in the door. "System works good. You want to hear it, Mr. Lanza?"

"No, just be ready," Frank ordered. Then he sat down and said, "Well, let's wait some more."

And they did—for twelve hours. It was 11:00 A.M. when the call came, and it lasted less than a minute. Frank answered and, after giving his name, had no chance to speak. As soon as the call was over, he yelled, "Vance! Can you give that back to us?"

Hill had rigged a speaker in the den, and in a few seconds, they heard a high-pitched voice that Dom instantly identified "Johnny Ring!"

"Now listen, Lanza," the voice said. "You know we have the kid and the dame. What you'll do is this, get two million in cash—old money, no new stuff! This afternoon you'll receive a Federal Express package. It'll have legal papers, contracts, and stuff like that. You sign them on the lines where your initials are. I'll call again and tell you where the drop will be. If you don't get the cash and the contracts to us, we'll send you the kid's head in a sack by mail. The woman's, too, but only after we have a little fun with her!"

There was a *click*, and both Lanzas looked at Ben. He lifted his shoulders and admitted, "Now, the hardest job of all."

"Which is what, Ben?" Frank asked.

"Get some sleep. None of us wants to, but we've got to be sharp when he calls back, and we can't do it if we're dead for sleep. Use sleeping pills if you have to, but get some rest."

Frank nodded. "I want to be with Rosemary," he said and left the room.

Thomas Rossi came over and, without instructions, began pulling Dom to his feet. Dom protested, but the tall man ignored him and led him out of the room. Alone, Savage went to the window and looked out into the bright sunshine. "Well, Boss," he murmured aloud. "I don't mind telling you, I'm pretty scared." He looked down at his hand, which trembled slightly. "Didn't think there was anything in the world could do that to me," he commented with wonder in his voice. Then he moved out into the sunshine and for a long time walked around the track, his mind working like a machine.

The first twenty-four hours had been easy.

Dani had spent much time talking to Pat, for she discovered that he had to have the sound of her voice, or he grew fearful. Hour after hour she told him stories, mostly from the Bible. Later, she found herself talking about her childhood, and though it seemed strange to her, he found it fascinating. *Why would a small boy want to hear stories about a little girl?* she wondered at first. Then she realized that Pat took refuge in them; they took place in a *normal* setting and permitted him to ignore his bizarre world.

Besides keeping Pat occupied, she monitored every aspect of the routine of the place. Breakfast had come at nine that first day. A knock had startled her, and then a voice had commanded, "Turn your backs to the door and stare at the wall! If you get a look at me, you'll be feeding the fish!"

It was not a voice she knew, but she took it seriously. She put her arm around Pat, and the two of them faced the wall. The door opened, and she heard the sound of someone entering. "Just stay right there," the man directed. After some movement, she heard the door shut. When Dani turned around, she found two plastic trays and two cups on the floor. They were from a fast-food place. The eggs and bacon were cool, so they had been purchased some time ago.

At noon, the routine was repeated. This time the meal was in a paper sack from the same place, containing two large hamburgers and two large fries. There were two large diet Cokes and a bucket of ice. Dani made a ceremony out of each meal, setting the table with napkins and plastic knives and forks and then trying to make the food last as long as possible. Pat loved hamburgers, and so did Dani, for that matter, but she saw that he wasn't eating. "Hey," she proposed cheerfully, "why don't we save some of this for a midnight snack, Pat? I always get hungry about that time. And you can stay up as late as you want to tonight."

He agreed with that, and all afternoon they played games that she remembered or invented. By pulling the table beneath the window, she discovered that Pat could see out, and this occupied part of the time.

At six-thirty, the voice came again, "All right, face the wall." Dani got Pat, and they stood patiently. But this time, she requested, "Please, could you bring us something to read? Something a boy would like?"

There was no answer, and the door slammed hard. Dani and Pat turned, and she picked up the food. "Looks like soup tonight, Pat," she reported, "and apple pie." The soup was in two large containers, and it was cool. "My favorite!" Dani blurted out. "Chicken and rice! Come on, let's set the table."

They set the table, pulling napkins out of the sack, and found two watery milk shakes. Dani talked rapidly and managed to down most of the soup; more important, she was able to get Pat to eat most of his. "Now, apple pie!" she crowed, but after a couple of bites, Pat could eat no more. "Well, we'll save these for our midnight snack," Dani decided. "Let's clean up, then we can watch the river. It'll be pretty with the sun going down."

For a while, they watched the river through the narrow aperture. "Can I sit in your lap, Dani?" Pat asked as they moved away.

He would never have done such a thing under normal circumstances, but Dani showed no surprise. "Hey, that's a good idea, Pat!" She smiled. "I'm glad I thought of it!" He climbed up in her lap and put his face against her at once. "Tell about when you were a girl," he insisted.

Dani began to tell stories, making up a few now and then, and in twenty minutes, Pat was sound asleep. Dani found herself nodding off, and coming awake with a jerk, she looked around in shock. Then her eyes fell on the soup containers, and she took a sudden deep breath. "They doped the food," she muttered. The drug must have been powerful, for she was barely able to put Pat on the cot and pull a blanket over him. She groped her way to the second cot, fell onto it, and tried to pull up the blanket, but sleep felled her, and she dropped off as if her captors had thrown a switch.

"Come on, wake up!" a harsh voice roused her the next morning. Her tongue felt thick, and Dani staggered when she tried to get off the cot. Pat, she saw, had not moved, but she called out, "All right—you can come in now."

She knelt beside the boy, keeping her face turned away, and waited until the door slammed. Straining to focus her eyes, Dani turned and discovered with a slight thrill that beside the food, lay a stack of magazines. Twenty comic books, filled the hoard, most of them terrible, but the collection included a few harmless ones. There were also some adult women's magazines—slick and mindless, to Dani's way of thinking. But there were also several news magazines and a copy of *Popular Science*.

She made up her mind instantly not to eat the evening meal. *Got to keep a clear head*, she told herself. Going to the water jug, she took a long drink. Her tongue felt dry as toast, and a terrible taste filled her mouth. She glanced at Pat, then went to the window. It was a bright day and the chocolate-brown river rolled along with the might of its flood. There were no barges in sight, but she knew they would come. Looking carefully for landmarks, she realized she faced a nearly empty landscape. This was flat country, the home of bayous and swamps. She had hoped for a large building or even a small one—perhaps a radar tower or something that would mark the spot. But only the brown river and the rolling green of trees met her eyes. The warehouse was set inside a curve in the river. At the base of the building the rotted remnants of a dock showed Dani it hadn't been used in years.

Fishermen sometimes come close in, hugging the shore as they look for fish. I could have a note ready, she told herself and began trying to find writing materials. The magazines would have done for paper, but she lacked a pen or pencil. Finally in desperation, she tore the cover from one of the magazines, and breaking off all but one tine from a plastic fork, she began punching holes in it. She made the holes large, and spelled out, *Kidnapped—Call FBI—Dani Ross*. She added her telephone number and held it up to the light. *I guess if they see it, they can read it*, she thought. She was trying to think of a container for the note, when Pat woke up.

He was thickheaded and frightened, but she cheered him up, "Hey, your favorite breakfast, Pat! Pancakes and sausage—and lots of syrup!" He awoke slowly and ate little, but as the day passed he seemed to cheer up.

All morning Dani kept him busy, using the magazines. She made games that required him to look through them, searching for certain words and pictures. The noon meal came—hamburgers again—and to her captor, she said, "Thanks for the magazines."

"Forget it!" a gruff voice responded, and this time he took the Porta-Potti with him. Dani felt a strange sense of irrational gratitude to the man, but shook it off. That emotion was common enough with kidnap victims, she knew. The victims became so anxious to please their captors that they let it get into their thinking. But Dani had no illusions: It would take a miracle to get Pat and herself free.

While Pat was taking a nap that afternoon, she stayed at the window. *The answer's got to be here*, she told herself. There was no pen to take notes with, but she filed every detail in her mind. She had spent considerable time there the day before, so a pattern of sorts was established. All afternoon she watched, and slowly she began to put together what she and Pat must do. It was weak, and doubts came at her in waves, but how else could she help Ben to find them?

She knew in her heart that Savage was sitting somewhere, waiting for a tiny clue. He would throw his life away like a trifle to save the two of them, she well knew, but now he was helpless.

He'll be waiting to hear from me, she thought. *I've got to give him something to go on! I've got to!* She prayed steadily, and when supper came, she suggested, "Pat, let's skip the soup tonight. It made me a little sick last night. We've still got some hamburgers and fries left from lunch."

Pat agreed, and she poured the soup out the window. As the sun went down, she told him, "Pat, you and I have got to give God a hand."

His eyes grew large. "I didn't know God ever needed help!" he exclaimed in awe.

"Well, sometimes He uses people, just as He used David to slay Goliath. Now, I'm going to teach you something, and it's *very* important!" She paused and put her hands on his shoulders, gazing into his eyes and saying slowly, "Pat, it's the most important thing you've ever done. Do you understand what I mean?"

Pat Lanza was only four, but he was bright and perceptive. He had seen enough television to know that danger was all around them. He slowly nodded, and Dani smiled. "Good boy! Now, here's what we must do. Pretty soon, someone will come and get us. They'll take us to a room, and they'll tell you to tell your father that you're all right."

"Daddy!" Pat parroted instantly. "I can talk to him on the telephone?"

"Just for a minute, maybe less," Dani warned. Then she began to tell him the probable scenario, how masked men would come and take them away. "You won't see their faces, but don't be afraid."

"They're bad men, aren't they, Dani?" he asked.

"Yes. But God will help us. Now, Pat, if you say *exactly* what I'm going to teach you, your daddy and Ben will come and take us home—but you must be very careful."

"What am I gonna say?" he demanded at once. His eyes were bright, and he leaned forward as she gave him the words. "Why, that's easy!" he said. "I can do that!"

"Of course you can!" Dani smiled. Then she spent the rest of the evening going over and over the message that she wanted him to deliver. Finally he grew sleepy, and she read to him. Just before he nodded off, she had him repeat the message. He did it perfectly, then she prayed with him, and he dropped into sleep. It was not a drugged sleep this time, and she was glad of that.

She lay on her bed, going over what she had planned. Though it began to sound ridiculous to her, she could think of nothing more. She prayed for a long time before dropping off to sleep.

A few hours later the door opened without warning, and two men wearing masks came in. The short, muscular man held a telephone in his hand, one of the cordless models. He spoke roughly, "You two are gonna do a little talking. You just tell them you're all right, see? Nothing else. Especially *you*, lady!"

Dani nodded and looked straight at Pat. "You understand what you're supposed to say, Pat?"

He looked at her, and her heart skipped a beat. She thought he was going to ask her if it was time to say what she had taught him. But he merely nodded, and the man lifted the phone, "All right, here's the kid."

Pat took the phone and listened; then he said exactly what Dani had told him to say. "That's enough," the man snapped. He spoke into the receiver again. "Now, here's the woman." He handed her the phone, and Ben's voice asked, "Are you all right, Dani?"

She spoke a few words before the phone was snatched from her hand. "All right, that's enough!" The two men walked to the door and slammed it with a loud noise.

"Did I do good, Dani?" Pat wanted to know.

She bent down and hugged him. "You did very well, Pat!" she whispered. "Now it's time to pray for Ben and your daddy."

"They'll come for us, you wait and see!" He nodded. Dani held him close and felt doubt clasp her with an icy grip. But she observed, "We're going to believe God to bring them, Pat!"

17
The Message

The call in which he spoke to Dani came on Friday, and all night Ben went over its transcript. Frank kept interrupting him, and by the twentieth time the concerned father asked if he'd made anything out of it. In desperation Ben said, "I'm going to take a drive and try to clear the cobwebs out of my head."

"What if they call again?" Frank asked nervously. He hadn't shaved, and his eyes were dull from lack of sleep.

"Stall them," Ben demanded tersely. "Say you can't get the money. Tell them you'll have it tomorrow." He left quickly, before Frank could protest. For an hour he cruised the back roads, then took Interstate 10 and drove to Baton Rouge. He stopped at Shoney's, on Seigen, nibbled at a club sandwich, and sat alone, drinking coffee. He pulled a typed copy of the call from his pocket and studied it.

The anger and fear that drove him were getting worse, not better. He knew time was his enemy. Ring was a killer who would not blink at two murders. *We've got nothing to tie the thing to Ring. He could kill them, get rid of the bodies, and nobody could touch him.* He stared at the single sheet of paper, willing the meaning of it to unveil itself. *She's got the answer in here—but I'm too dumb to see it,* he thought in despair. He was basically a man of action, never completely happy unless he was in motion. Though he had an ability to think on his feet and though instinct often had brought him to answers that more logical thinkers could not discover, he grew restless when confined to a problem that could be solved only by systematic methods.

He clenched the paper so tightly that his knuckles grew white, and he longed to scream at the top of his lungs—but he sat there silent and lost to his surroundings. When she brought him more coffee, the waitress said, "I'm going off duty now. Would you like some dessert?" When he shook his head silently, she added, "Thank you—and have a nice day."

The phrase lingered in his mind: *Have a nice day.* Such catch phrases, which people spouted, but that meant nothing, irritated him. *Have a nice day,* he thought bitterly. *She doesn't care if I have a nice day or not. If she really cared, she'd see I was breaking up inside: She'd sit down and let me tell her how, for the first time in my life, I'm into something I can't handle. "Have a nice day!" If one more idiot says that to me, I'm going to break his face and then walk over his ribs—then I'm going to smile that stupid, meaningless smile and say, "Have a nice day!"*

He jammed the paper in his pocket, threw a dollar on the table, and went to pay his bill. The cashier rang up his tab, and as she took his money, asked, "Everything all right?"

He wanted to yell at her, *No! My world is falling apart, and if you tell me to have a nice day, I'm going to part your hair right down the middle!*

"Have a nice day." She smiled and handed him his change.

Savage stared at her and said very slowly, "Actually, I have other plans." Her mouth dropped open, and he turned and walked away. As he drove off, he suddenly spoke to the steering wheel, "Well, do *I* care if *she* has a nice day or not?" He burned rubber as he came out of the parking lot, half hoping a cop would stop him. He had a half-formed wish that he could get into a rousing fight with someone, but by the time he was back on the interstate, he felt calmer.

On the return drive, he considered every possible move, but nothing came up right. He thought of going to Dani's father. Maybe *he'd* be able to make sense out of the transcripts of the phone calls. But Dan had a weak heart, and the news of his daughter's capture might set him back. He thought of going to the FBI, but rejected the thought. As he turned off on the Pontchartrain Causeway, he found himself dreading returning to the Lanza house. They were all expecting him to come up with some sort of answer—and he didn't have one.

As he pulled up to the guardhouse, Louie Baer came out, bent over, and greeted him, "Hi, Ben. Any news on Dani and the kid?"

"Still working on it, Louie."

"Mr. Lanza said to come see him soon as you can."

"Thanks, Louie." Savage parked the car and went directly to the big house. He found Frank and Rosemary in the office, on a small, black-leather couch, and she was holding his hand. "Did they call?" Ben asked, but already knew the answer.

"Not yet," Frank told him. He studied Savage, then

blinked his eyes and laid his head back on the couch. He seemed defenseless and vulnerable in that position. Rosemary reached out and brushed a lock of hair from his forehead, and in that simple gesture Savage suddenly saw her love for Lanza. When Frank opened his eyes and smiled at her, it was clear that the two had come a long way.

Guess they're going to make it, Ben thought. "Frank, I still say we need the law on this," he asserted.

Frank stared at him, weakening. "You may be right, Ben. Rosemary says so, but you know Pop. I don't think he'll ever give in."

"He's a sick man, Frank. Not himself. It's your decision."

"I think Ben is right, dear," Rosemary supported him.

Frank Lanza looked harried. He had spent a lifetime letting his father and Phil make the decisions. Now the pressure was piling up on him. He tried to avoid the moment. "Maybe tomorrow. I'll talk to Pop." Then he asked, "Do you think it's one of the family, Ben?"

Savage shook his head. "I don't know, Frank. It could be. Somebody knew that Dani was going to be alone with Pat and exactly *when*. Trouble is, some of the guards or the house help knew that, too."

"They're all broken up," Rosemary reminded them. "Even Eddy and Max are getting along. I haven't seen that in years."

"One of them may be acting," Frank exclaimed bitterly. "I can't believe in anything anymore." Then he gave his wife a quick smile. "Except you, Rosemary. You've kept me from falling apart."

"God isn't going to let anything bad happen to Dani and Pat," she said calmly. Her face was thinner than usual; her wound had drained some of her vitality; but both men noted a light in her clear blue eyes. She turned to Savage and remarked, "I've studied the copy of the phone calls, Ben, but I can't make anything out of them. Only that they're alive."

"We're all missing something," Savage muttered. "Dani's got the answer we're looking for in here. I'm just too stupid to get it!"

"Let's hear it again," Rosemary proposed. "Maybe it's in the *way* they said something, instead of in the words themselves."

Ben nodded, and walking to the door, he ordered, "Vance, play the call again." He threw himself into a chair and closed his eyes, his head back on the cushion as the words came out of the speaker.

Ring: All Right, Lanza, here's the kid.

Pat: Daddy?

Frank: I'm right here. Pat! Are you all right?

Pat: Yes, but I want to come home. When are you coming to get me, Daddy?

Frank: Very soon, Pat.

Ring: All right, that's enough. You've heard the kid.

Frank: It sounded like him, but it could be some child you've trained to say those things. I want proof that it's my boy.

Ring: You ain't in no bargaining position, Lanza! All right, you get one more shot, and that's all!

Frank: Son, are you being well treated?

Pat: I guess so, but I miss my programs. Dani's been telling me stories. I like the one about Rapunzel. But I'm going to miss Billy White's party. It's at 3:30 and—

Ring: (breaking in) That's enough, Lanza. Now here's the dame. (In a muffled voice) You say one word outta line, and I'll shoot the kid in the leg.

Dani: Hello?

Ben: You all right, Dani?

Dani: Well, I could do with a good Cajun meal, Ben, but I'm all right. My captors have been good to us. I'm not treated like a queen exactly, but so far we're all right. (Pause.) Ben, give them what they want! It's the midnight hour, and I'm getting a clear signal that they'll kill us if you don't come through. This is an SOS, Ben—

Ring: All right, that's it! You know they're all right, Lanza. Now it's up to you. Watch the mail. As soon as you get the instructions, do what they say. There won't be a second chance on this for the kid and the dame!

Frank: It'll take another twenty-four hours to get the money.

Ring: (Long pause.) All right, but that's it. And there'll be no more phone calls!

Silence ran around the room, as they heard the click that signaled the end of the call. Finally Frank asked tentatively, "Ben—can you make *anything* out of it? Anything at all?"

Savage lifted his head and stared out the window. "Nothing to do anything with, Frank."

"What Pat said about Billy White's party," Rosemary said slowly, "it wasn't quite right."

Savage gave her a swift look, "There's no party?"

"Oh, yes, but it's not at three-thirty. It's next week, but it's an evening party, beginning at seven."

"Pat probably forgot," Frank amended wearily.

"Maybe not," Ben said slowly. He let the thoughts flow through his mind, then added, "I think it's something Dani told him to say."

"But what could it mean?" Rosemary asked.

"May mean that it's the right time to get them out of

wherever they are. Or maybe it's a street address. She used the word *queen*, so maybe there's a 330 Queen Street. But there's no Queen Street in New Orleans. I looked it up."

"Maybe in a little town close by," Frank suggested.

"Could be, and that's the kind of thing the police could have been checking," Ben commented mildly. "The part that's got me stumped is the Rapunzel thing."

"It's a fairy tale," Rosemary recalled. "I remember it, but I didn't think Pat knew it."

Ben stirred and asked, "I'd like to read it. Have you got a copy?"

"Yes. It was one of Rachel's favorite stories. I'll go get it."

"Let me." Frank rose. "Would it be in Rachel's room?"

"I think so. You know how she never throws anything away. Try not to wake her up." When Frank left, Rosemary studied Savage carefully. "Ben," she whispered. "Is there a chance?"

"Always a chance."

Rosemary considered his words, then replied gently, "You're worried about Dani, aren't you?"

"Sure."

The brevity of his reply and the lines etched in his tough face seemed to tell her something. "I love Dani," she told him simply. "She's been the best friend I've ever had. But I know you love her, too."

Savage looked up sharply, a surprised expression fleeting across his face. He caught her gaze, then dropped his head, and shrugged. "She's a good kid," he finally admitted before barking angrily, "Drives me crazy, this transcript! The answer is right there, but I'm too stupid to see it!"

Frank came back, a book in his hand. "It's in here," he said, handing the book to Ben.

Savage got up and took the book. Glancing at it, he laughed shortly. "Guess I'll go do my reading." Walking to the door, he muttered, "I'm down to reading fairy tales! That's about my speed!"

When he was out of the room, Rosemary observed, "Ben's in terrible shape. He wants to lash out at something. Waiting's hard for a man like him."

"For me, too." Frank nodded. Then he came over and looked down at her. "You really think we'll get him back, Rosemary?"

A pleading look entered his eyes, and his wife reached out for his hand. When she took it, she nodded. "Yes, I do think so. I'm afraid, of course, but somehow there's something inside of me saying that we'll get them back."

He studied her, finally admitting, "I never believed in miracles. But now that I've seen one, I guess I'll have to change my mind."

"A miracle, Frank?"

"You," he said softly. "Not long ago you would have been dead drunk if a thing like this had happened. Now I'm leaning on you. Is it religion?"

She put his hand to her cheek, thinking hard, then shook her head. "No, not religion. I've always had that."

"What then?"

"It's hard to explain, Frank. Really, I don't think it *can* be explained," she murmured. "All I know is, I called on God and asked Him to forgive me—and to make me good. Ever since that moment, I've known that He's been with me."

Frank stared at her. "I'm glad you're here, Pet," he

283

commented quietly. "I don't think I could make it alone through all this!"

Dani knew it was the last day of March. She had no calendar, of course, but she and Pat had been taken on Tuesday the twenty-eighth. Though the three days seemed more like three years, she let no sign of her fears get through to Pat.

The two of them had grown very close, naturally. Dani had wondered how she would have fared had she been in the cell alone. Not very well, she thought, for her efforts to keep the boy's spirits up had kept her from worrying about her own plight.

The two of them had read the magazines and comic books over and over, and Dani had told every incident of her childhood that she could rake up from her memory. She had arranged the food so that they did not eat the evening meal, knowing that it was vital to be alert. For the last two nights she had stood at the window after midnight. She had made a screen of sorts from the covers of magazines, a little larger than the window itself. On the hour she tried to send a signal by covering the window, then moving the screen away. It was an awkward business, and probably useless, but she kept at it until her arms were too weary to continue.

Over and over the memory of the phone call ran through her mind, and she almost wept when she realized how vague her hints to Ben had been. She thought of better ways, but it was too late. The chances of their captor letting them use the phone again were microscopically small.

Dani slept in small naps—mostly when Pat lay down during the day—or not at all. She had asked for something to bathe in and had found a small enamel basin, along with some soap, cloths, and towels beside their noon meal. Using the tepid water from the five-gallon jug, Dani washed Pat carefully just before bedtime. After he was asleep, she removed her clothes and sponged off, using most of the water. She hated to be dirty, and the simple pleasure of being clean was enormous. *How little it takes to be content*, she thought as she washed her undergarments with what was left of the water. She hung them up and threw the water out the window.

Then she sat down and began to pray. Her communications with God had been odd, since she had been taken. At first they had been "panic" prayers: *Lord, get us out of here!—God, don't let us die!* But to her surprise, their nature had changed. Now she simply thought about the Lord, remembering verses from the Bible that spoke of His mercy and His love. She meditated on these, and as she did, she felt peace growing in her. For long periods she found herself praying for Ben and the Lanzas. Later she remembered that during those terrible days when she and Savage had faced death in the silo, she had come to pray like this.

Finally, Dani slept, but when the knock on the door came the next morning, and the voice cried, "Breakfast!" she came up from the bed quickly.

"All right," she said, going to stand beside Pat's cot. She faced the wall, and the door opened. "Thank you for the basin and the soap," she added quietly. "I used all the water."

There was no answer, but she heard the man's steps moving to the spot to her left where the five-gallon water container was located. A sudden crash made her turn instinctively to see what had happened.

The short, muscular man with the high-pitched voice had fallen to the floor. There was a soapy puddle, and his foot had slipped. Dani began, "I'm sorry—"and stopped abruptly.

He was not wearing a mask, and she was looking right into his face. She knew him at once, for Dom had shown her his picture. It was Johnny Ring. He had a round face, dark eyes, and a small mouth, and a feral air about him.

He stared at her, and Dani knew with a sudden alarm that she had made a terrible mistake. She wheeled at once to face the wall, apologizing, "I'm sorry. I should have cleaned up that mess."

There was no answer, and his silence somehow terrified her more than a threat. She listened as he moved out of the room, and when the door closed, she thought: *He'll never let me go now! I can identify him!* Fear, thick and strong, constricted her throat, and when Pat greeted her, "Hello, Dani," she could not answer for a moment.

"Is it pancakes this morning, Dani?"

She stared at the boy numbly, automatically replying "You can go see, Pat." Then she stood still, trying to think, but her analytical mind raced. *He'll have to kill me, even if he gets what he wants. And it will be tomorrow or the day after. He can't wait any longer!*

Pat came back with the plastic trays. "Aw, it's eggs again. I hate eggs!"

She could not eat more than a few bites, and of all the days in Dani's life, that one, March 31, was the worst. She could only pray, *Lord, give Ben some sense—and don't let anything happen to Pat, no matter what happens to me!*

18
Midnight
Incident

Abby sat between her mother, Irene, and her aunt Helen at the table, thinking that it was about as close to each other as the two women had gotten in a long time. Years earlier Abby had learned that her aunt Helen was jealous of her father, and she understood now that it was because she and her husband Max had no children. Her father and Max got along very well, but their wives never had and never would. Abby toyed with her food, wishing that she could leave, yet at the same time morbidly interested in the scene. It was the first time they'd all been together as a family since the kidnapping, and she noted that Frank and Rosemary were completely changed.

Frank Lanza had never, Abby knew, been a demonstrative man, but there was a new quality in the way he leaned close to Rosemary. Despite his lined and weary face, a light shone in his eyes for his wife. And Rosemary—Abby could not believe the change in her aunt! For a long time she'd had nothing but contempt for this woman, and when she'd heard that her aunt had gotten religion, she'd scoffed, "See how long *that* lasts!" But in just the short time since Rosemary had been shot, Abby'd been forced to admit that she'd changed. Abby had waited for her aunt to try to convert her, but that had not happened. Yet the younger woman sensed a new spirit of happiness in Rosemary that could not have been counterfeited.

"Where's Grandfather?" Abby asked her father.

"Not feeling well enough to get out of bed today," Eddy explained briefly. He looked at Frank and asked, "The doctor come to see Pop today?"

"This morning." Frank shook his head, adding bitterly, "A waste of time, but what else can we do?"

"I'll go up and sit with him," Helen offered quickly. She rose, but paused on her way out to put her hand on Frank's shoulder. "Try to get some rest, Frank. You're not going to last, if you don't." Then she hesitated for one moment. Awkwardly she touched his cheek, whispering, "We'll make it, Frank!"

She left quickly, her head down. As soon as she was gone, Max remarked, "She's taking it harder than anything I've seen. Not just Dom, but the rest of it." He stared down at his plate, his thin face looking almost cadaverous. Then he tried to smile. "I guess we're all pretty low."

Eddy nodded. "The terrible thing is—there's nothing to do. Nothing at all!"

They sat there silently, nobody really interested in the food. Finally Frank announced, "I'm going to call in the police. Should have done it earlier, but you all know how much Pop is against such a thing."

Irene asked, "Isn't kidnapping a federal offense?"

"Yes, and Savage said all the time we should have had

them in." He hesitated before continuing, "But I was too much of a coward to make the decision."

"Aw, come on, Frank!" Eddy interjected, his sensitive face working with emotion. "In a thing like this, nobody knows for sure what to do."

Frank looked at Eddy and Irene, then shifted his gaze to Max. "I'm not tough enough." He shrugged. "If it had been Phil, he'd have—"

"He'd have had every man we had out gunning for Martino!" Irene responded firmly. "And you know how much good that would have done!"

Abby didn't want to listen to any more. "Mother, can I go to my room?" she whispered. When Irene agreed, she made her way out of the house. The afternoon sun was covered by clouds, and a stiff breeze ruffled her hair as she walked along beside the hedges. She strolled to the gym and found Rachel and Matt knocking a Ping-Pong ball listlessly over the net. "Is Ben around?" she asked.

"He's doing something to his car," Matt informed her. Suddenly he smashed the small white ball with all his might, driving it over the net. It hit Rachel on the arm and fell to the ground. "I'd like to *kill* those guys!" he declared between clenched teeth.

Rachel bit her lower lip, then tossed her paddle on the table and ran out of the gym. Abby watched her go. "Hey, Matt, why don't you try to cheer her up?" she demanded.

Matt stared at her angrily. "Cheer *her* up? Who's going to cheer *me* up?"

Abby shook her head. "You're tougher than she is, Matt. And she's just a little girl."

Matthew flushed and flung off, throwing over his shoulder, "Oh, all *right!*" Abby left and found Ben in the garage, but he was not working on the car. He was standing in the doorway, looking out over the level green lawn. He turned when she came to stand in front of him, but said nothing.

"Hello, Ben," Abby greeted him.

He was wearing a pair of old jeans and a faded blue shirt, and on his feet were a shabby pair of loafers.

"I guess there's no news, is there?"

He shook his head and then offered, "Haven't seen you much lately, Abby. How've you been?"

"Oh, all right, I guess." She hesitated. "You know, I found out something about myself, Ben." She thought hard, her pretty face as serious as Savage had ever seen it. "I found out I'm not as rotten as I thought."

This brought a quick smile to Savage's lips, and he remarked, "That's a good thing to find out about yourself. How'd it happen?"

"When Dani and Pat were kidnapped," she told him slowly. "It was awful! I—I guess I just didn't know how much I loved the little guy! I've been with him all his life, Ben. He's just like a little brother. And when I heard about—about it—" Tears rose in Abby's eyes, and she dashed them away quickly. "Well, I guess I've been so busy feeling sorry for myself, that I haven't had time for anybody else."

Ben looked at her carefully. He suddenly reached out and gave her a hard hug. "You know, Abby, growing up isn't always a matter of months and years. Sometimes we muddle along for a long time and don't seem to be getting anywhere—and then something falls right on our heads, and we get a little older."

Abby didn't move for a second, and she began to cry.

290

He put his arms around her, holding her until the storm of weeping was over. Finally she pulled back, and asked, "You have a handkerchief?" She took the one he offered, wiped her face, and then blew her nose. "I'd better keep it," she suggested. Then she looked at him and gave a wan smile. "I've been trying to get you to pay attention to me ever since we met, Ben Savage, and here I blubber like a whipped cur, and *then* you cuddle up to me!"

Ben shook his head. "You're going to give some guy all he can do, Abby. You've just had a bad start." He looked over the estate, then added, "This is no way for a young girl to live, all surrounded by walls and cut off from everything."

Abby asked curiously, "What about you, Ben?" She suddenly gave an impish grin. "Maybe you ought to cry on *my* shoulder! I know you and Dani are close. I know you two fight all the time—but I've seen how you look at each other sometimes."

Savage ruefully protested, "You see too much, Abby." Shaking his head, he added, "I'm up against a stone wall. And time's running out." He pulled the transcript of the call from his shirt pocket and opened it. "It's all right here, Abby, all we need to find them—but I can't get at it."

"What's that, Ben?" she asked.

"It's the record of the call the kidnappers made," he pronounced gloomily. He handed it to her. "I know Dani gave us some kind of key to where she and Pat are being kept, but I can't find it!"

Abby read it quickly. "I don't guess it could have anything to with the *Cajun Queen*? You'd have thought of that, first off."

Savage stared at her, and she saw his eyes fly open. He

snatched at the paper and read it. "The *Cajun Queen*? That's the paddle wheeler that tours the Mississippi, isn't it?"

"Why, sure! I've gone on it a couple of times. It makes two tours every day," she explained, sensing his rising excitement. "It goes out in the morning to the river plantation, then in the afternoon it goes to the Bayou country, out to where the Battle of New Orleans was fought."

Savage was reading the paper as if he'd never seen it before. His lips moved, and he suddenly shouted and picked Abby up in a bear hug, spinning her around. Putting her down, he gave her a hard kiss right on the lips. "You're beautiful!" he shouted and then ran out of the garage at full speed.

Abby stood there, her lips tingling. She swept around and hit the trunk of Ben's car with her fist. "Blast!" she cried loudly. "At last I get a kiss out of him—and I don't even know how I did it!"

Frank and the others looked up as the door suddenly burst open and Savage rushed in. His eyes were bright as he called out, "Frank! I've got something! Come on!"

Leaving the table, Frank followed Savage to the study. "What is it, Ben?" he asked eagerly.

"Time to call the fuzz!" Ben announced, and he spoke rapidly for the next few moments. A sense of urgency surrounded him, and when he finished, Frank nodded. "It's the right thing, Ben. Do you want me to call the FBI?"

"No, let me get Sixkiller," Savage suggested. "It's in his backyard, and the feds like people to go through channels." He whirled, picked up the phone, and dialed a number. "He'd better be there!" Then he demanded, "Let me have Lieutenant Sixkiller. This is Ben Savage, and it's urgent!"

*   *   *

The rotors of the police helicopter beat the air steadily, throbbing like a giant heart. The brilliance of the halogen lights mounted on the side of the concrete block building lit up the scene in stark black and white, creating canyons out of crevices and mountains out of rivet heads. Nearby Ben hunched his shoulders and wished Sixkiller would hurry, but he understood the problem: Dealing with the FBI or the CIA is never an uncomplicated process.

Wish it was just Luke and me, he thought as the blades churned the air, sending scraps of paper flying and a fine dust settling over everything. But there was no way the lieutenant was going to stick his neck out that far. Sooner or later the case would be dragged out, and the first question his superiors would ask Luke Sixkiller would be: *Why did you leave the federal officers out of it?*

Savage took a piece of gum out of a package, unwrapped it, and watched as the wind whipped the wrapper into the darkness just outside the perimeter of the helicopter pad. He doubled the gum up, and as he chewed it, thought about the scene he'd had with Sixkiller. The dark eyes of the policeman had turned cold when Ben had informed him of the kidnapping four days earlier.

"Good how quick you reported it." Sixkiller had bitten the words off. "We love that sort of thing up at the station."

Ben had explained that Dom wouldn't permit it, but he knew the excuse sounded feeble. He got nowhere until he informed the policeman, "Luke, it's not just the Lanza boy. They took Dani, too."

That made a difference, and after Luke had cursed him a little more for being an idiot, Ben had finally told him,

293

"Look, you can do whatever you like to me, but later. We've got one shot at getting them out, and the timing is close."

Luke had listened to his full explanation. "All right, Ben, but we'll have to let the feds in on it," he warned.

Now Savage looked up and saw Sixkiller coming out of the low building, another man following him. Ben threw the gum away and straightened up as Sixkiller stopped and performed introductions: "This is Ben Savage. Savage, this is Pedro DeSilva."

DeSilva stared at Savage coldly. He looked like a villain in an old swashbuckler movie—slender, with an aristocratic face, a trim moustache, and a pair of steady brown eyes. "Savage, after this is over, I'm going to have your license."

"Sure. But later, all right?"

DeSilva shook his head. "You think I won't, but I've made a career out of busting hot dogs like you. Let's go."

He turned and walked to the helicopter. The three men climbed in, and the pilot yelled, "Who's going to aim this thing?"

Savage nodded and moved to the seat beside the pilot. "We want to cruise down the river. Start out right over Jean Lafitte State Park. You know it?"

"Is the pope Catholic?" The pilot grinned. He lifted the craft off the pad, wheeled it in a sharp circle that made Ben's stomach ache, then sent the chopper forward through the darkness.

"Ben, maybe you can tell DeSilva what's going on," Luke suggested.

"Sure." Ben pulled the transcript out of his pocket and handed it back to DeSilva. "That's the only call we could

294

set up," he shouted. "I think it tells us how to find where they're stashed."

DeSilva read it and frowned. "Pretty obscure," he commented. "What did you get out of it?"

"Nothing, for a long time," Ben told him. "Then a few hours ago I think I got it. That's when I called you, Luke."

"We certainly appreciate your prompt response," Sixkiller snapped grumpily. "Now, tell the man your little secret."

The whirring pulse of the chopper was loud, so Ben had to turn his head and speak above it. "She knew she only had a few words, DeSilva, so she put in as much as she could. And the words aren't in a pattern of any kind. Ring might have spotted that. So she just threw them in, hoping that we'd sort them out."

"What have you come up with?" DeSilva warned, "It better be good."

"I finally came up with the *Cajun Queen*. Then the rest of it made a little sense."

"What's that—the *Cajun Queen*?" DeSilva demanded.

"Cruise boat for tourists," Ben explained. "A paddle wheeler copied from the old Mississippi River boats. So as soon as I put the idea of a boat together, the figures came at me—3:30."

"Let me guess," DeSilva insisted. "That's the time the *Cajun Queen* goes by where they're being held."

Savage stared at him. "That's right. I'm impressed. The only FBI people I've known would have had to run that through a computer to get it."

"I'm better than most," DeSilva applauded himself evenly. "So you checked on where the boat would be?"

"Right. We'll be over it in a few minutes. Hey!" Ben called to the pilot, "Do you know Irontown?"

"Irontown?" the pilot asked. "I think so. It's just north of West Pointe a la Hache. That where you want to go?"

"Yeah. Stay in the middle of the river. Let me know before we get there." He looked at his watch and said, "Twelve-fifteen. Just about right."

"How do you expect to find anything in the middle of the night from a chopper in the center of the river?" Sixkiller asked.

"The boy mentioned a fairy tale, *Rapunzel*," Savage shared. "It's about a young girl who was kept prisoner in a tower. Somewhere close to Irontown Dani could see the *Cajun Queen* at 3:30. I'm betting she's up in some kind of building, not on the first floor, but higher. Held prisoner in a tower, like the story."

"That's great!" DeSilva exclaimed sarcastically. "We do our hunting in the middle of the night!"

"Yeah, but the rest of it is that Dani said 'It's the midnight hour.' She took a chance putting that in. Ring might have caught it."

"I don't get it, Ben," Sixkiller admitted. "What happens at midnight?"

"I think she'll make a signal. She said 'This is an SOS.' Ring thought she was talking about the spot she's in—but I think she was telling us that at midnight she gives a signal that we can see."

The three men were quiet, and then the pilot reported, "Coming up to Irontown."

Ben wheeled around. "It may not be very visible. Everyone watch the shore."

The chopper sank down to within fifty feet of the water, and Ben called out, "Hold it there! And take it slow."

"Right!" The pilot was good. He eased down the middle

of the channel, hardly moving, but keeping the chopper on an even keel. Desperately Savage peered into the gloom, but could see nothing. "Many buildings around here?" he asked the pilot.

"Not many. A few summer camps. Few old warehouses."

They were all watching, but nothing showed. The pilot told them, "We're past Irontown. Want me to turn around?"

"Go another three minutes," Savage ordered. When the three minutes were up, he said, "Now let's go back."

They made the return trip, again moving slowly. Savage's eyes ached from his efforts to pierce the gloom. Finally the pilot spoke again, "We're about two miles past Irontown. What do I do?"

Ben sat there, trying to decide. Finally he directed, "Go three more minutes. The boat probably wasn't all that regular. Maybe we're too far downriver." But they saw nothing at all. "Let's run over it again." he commanded. "Take us up higher."

The chopper rose to a hundred feet and moved forward. When they passed the town again, Ben looked at his watch. "It's nearly 12:30," he announced. "Maybe someone's with her. Maybe she can't signal."

DeSilva shrugged. "Maybe. Let's stay at it."

He had not finished his sentence when Sixkiller yelled, "There it is!"

"Where?" Savage threw himself around and saw where the policeman was pointing. Very small and dimly three short dots of light, then three longer ones, and then three more short ones appeared.

"That's her!" Savage yelled. "We've got them!"

"Want me to get closer?" the pilot asked.

"No!" DeSilva responded instantly. "Might draw their attention. Can you fix that building for us?"

"I don't know it, but it's right across the river from Davant—that's the little burg there, see those lights?"

Ben peered at the building, noting that the signal was still going on. "Looks like the only building in sight," he observed. "Put me down somewhere!"

"No, take us back to New Orleans," DeSilva ordered sharply.

"But—"

"You want to be in on this or not, Savage?" DeSilva demanded. "You've violated your license by not informing us of the kidnapping. You've done a good job of finding the location. But now I'm running the show."

Savage nodded. "All right. But I'm going in after them, DeSilva. If you think different, you'd better have some better boys on your side than I've seen in the past!"

DeSilva smiled and stroked his thin moustache. "I'm always glad for a little cannon fodder. We can let them fill you full of holes while we get their position."

"You thrill-hungry private eye!" Luke Sixkiller snorted. "Always out to grab all the glory! I hope Johnny Ring stomps on your ingrown toenail!"

"He'll probably try," Savage agreed slowly. Already he was thinking of a way to get into that window where the yellow signal had scored the darkness.

The argument had grown heated, and finally Savage exploded. "You federal types are all alike!" he spat out in a voice that betrayed his raging anger. "You don't care anything about the victims! Oh, no! All you want is to see that your little plans go smoothly!"

DeSilva, Sixkiller, and Savage were standing in front of a police car, and farther off was the team that DeSilva and Sixkiller had assembled. They had tumbled out of the chopper, and for the next two hours the New Orleans Police Department saw activity! Savage had wanted to call Frank, but DeSilva vetoed that idea.

"He'll be no help. And he could be a liability," he had stated flatly.

Sixkiller had argued. "It's his kid, DeSilva. He's got a right to be here. I say call him."

But the agent remained adamant. "There's no time. You say that yourself, Savage."

Ben had reluctantly agreed, and they had all gone down Highway 23 to a point about a mile north of Davant. "They could be watching this road," DeSilva warned. "We walk in from here." He had led them through some brush-covered country, staying clear of the road. Finally he pulled up. "There it is," he reported quietly.

Ben shoved forward, peering through the early morning darkness. An old building, shabby and weather-beaten, loomed against the sky. "There's a car in front," he told the others quietly. "Got to go in from the back."

"No way." DeSilva shook his head. "We'll have to get as close as we can, and then make a rush."

Savage stared at him. "Dani and Pat are on the fourth floor. The first thing they'll do is kill them. There's no way you can get inside and protect them from the front."

An argument had started, and finally DeSilva demanded, "Stay out of this, Savage."

Ben looked at him, then turned and picked up the knapsack he had brought. He slung it on his back and pulled the .44 magnum from its holster.

DeSilva at once grew alert. "That won't help you. That's stupid!"

"I'm going to get them out," Savage announced quietly, almost conversationally. "If you try to stop me, I'll probably be dead, but so will you and a few more. Now, I'm going to climb to the top of that building. When I get there, I'll give you a signal, like this—" He raised and lowered his arms three times. "That means I'm going in, and you've got ten minutes to get in place. When I get Dani and Pat on the roof, I'll signal again, and you can take Ring and his gang." He stared at the agent, turned, and walked away.

DeSilva pulled his gun, and two of the officers came rushing forward. One of them held a shotgun. "Want me to pot him, Mr. DeSilva?"

DeSilva glared at the man, then put his gun away. "That would be nice, wouldn't it? Announce that we're here to the kidnappers." His anger was a raging thing, and he snapped, "Sixkiller, you did this. You'll be hearing more about it."

"Sure, DeSilva." Sixkiller nodded. "Good thing you didn't try to use your gun on Savage. A good FBI man is hard to replace." He slid his own weapon back into its holster and gave DeSilva an expressionless look.

Suddenly DeSilva grinned. "Is he any good, Luke?"

"Pete, he's the best there is at what he's doing right now!"

Savage's back was tense as he walked away. DeSilva might be mad enough to put a bullet in his leg; but he trusted Sixkiller to watch for that. As he squirmed through the underbrush, he closed his mind to everything but the job in front of him. Even as he was forced to leave the shelter of the brush and walk across open ground, Ben remained aware that he might be taken out with a rifle bullet at any second.

But no sound, none at all reached his ears, and he skirted the side of the old building, heading for the back. The river lapped at the foundation stones, and looking up, he saw that there was only one line of windows, one on each floor. *They've got to be in the room at the top*, he thought.

The sides of the old building were unbroken, and he saw no way to climb the face of it. Pulling the knapsack from his back, he took out a thin nylon cord. From a pouch he took out a series of hooks, which he bolted together to form a small grappling hook with three points. Carefully he tied the line to the grappling hook, then looked up. It required a long throw, and the hook would make some noise. It also seemed unlikely that he would make it with the first cast. But there was no other way, so he moved back around to the side where there were no first-floor windows. Carefully he took the loops of cord in his left hand and began swinging the hook in a circle with his right. He made the best judgment he could and released the hook. He followed through, but turned to watch the hook rise as the line played out of his left hand.

At first he thought it was going to be a good one—but the hook struck the top of the building with a ringing noise, then fell back to earth. Ben stood there, hand on his gun, waiting for a voice or a shot. But there was no sound, so he gathered his rope and tried again.

This time the hook sailed over the edge of the building and disappeared. He heard it hit the top of the building and again waited. He thought he heard a voice inside, but it was muffled and faint. Carefully he pulled on the cord, holding his breath, hoping the grappling hook would catch.

It did catch! A smile touched his lips, and he bent over and put on the knapsack. Then he grasped the rope and started the climb. The rope was so small it was hard to hold, and finally he had to resort to a different approach. He would pull himself up, then loop the cord around his palm, then pull himself up another few inches and repeat the sequence. By the time he got to the top of the building, his arms felt made of lead. He pulled himself over the edge, then rolled on the roof with a gasp.

But there was no time to waste. Already the clear light of morning touched the trees. He moved over and stood on the front of the roof. He could see no one, but he knew the policemen would be setting their watches.

Ten minutes. He quickly slipped to the rear of the building and looked down. The window of the fourth floor was farther down than he had thought, maybe ten feet. He felt tempted to call so that Dani would not be taken off guard, but could not risk it.

Grasping the grappling hook, he looped it around an iron stanchion that rose up out of the roof, then carefully dropped the line over the side. It fell not a foot from the line of windows, which was exactly what he wanted.

Going back to the knapsack, he pulled out a set of heavy-duty bolt cutters with a ring on one handle. He clipped the ring to a ring on his belt and loosened the gun in his holster. Carefully, he dropped over the side, this time wrapping the rope around his leg and rappeling down. Though the rope cut into his leg, he ignored it. He lowered himself until his upper body was even with the top window, then stopped. Carefully, he inched his head to the right and got a look into the room.

Dani lay on a cot, with Pat huddled next to her. He looked at them for a few long seconds, knowing that when he grew to be an old man, he would be able to pull this memory out of his past—Dani's face touched by the rosy tint of the rising sun, beautiful even though marked with fatigue and suffering, and the maternal cast of her broad lips as she held tightly to Pat Lanza.

As sounds came from inside the building, Savage called, "Dani!"

Her eyes opened at once, and she looked around wildly. He spoke her name again, and she came off the bed, stumbling as she rushed to the window. Her hands reached through the window, touching his face, and tears filled her eyes.

"I knew you'd come, Ben!" she whispered.

He reached through the bars with his free hand and caught a handful of the great mass of auburn hair. He held to it tightly, then huskily managed, "Good morning, Boss!"

They were still for a moment, before Pat cried out, "Ben!"

"Pat!" Savage called quickly. "Be very quiet!"

Dani watched as he made some sort of harness out of the line he was dangling from, so that he soon had both hands free. Then he removed the bolt cutters and put their jaws around one bar. He began to squeeze, but the steel was tough. He gave it all he had and was just beginning to give up, when the bolt cutters suddenly sheared through. He gave a deep sigh of relief and, working quickly, snipped through the other bars.

"I'm going back up," he told them. "When I let the rope down, it'll have a slip knot in it. Pat, you get Dani to help you in it and come out the window. Don't look down; look up at me. All right?"

"Sure!" Pat cried, his face shining.

"Good boy! Then I'll send the rope down again. Put it under your arms, Dani. Let yourself out the window feet first. May be a tight fit, but don't worry, I'll have you."

"I won't worry, Ben." Dani smiled.

He looked at her, then nodded and went hand over hand up the rope. Quickly he made a slip knot and lowered it. When he saw Pat's sturdy body coming through the opening, he began to pull, and soon Pat stood beside him, holding onto his leg.

"Quiet, now," Ben warned. "We've got to get your nanny out of there." He lowered the rope, and Dani pulled it in. Her legs came out awkwardly, scratching against one of the steel stubs; then her upper body followed. She slipped and gave a small cry as she plunged downward, but Savage was ready and took the shock of the fall. The rope slipped through his hands, burning them, but he tightened his grip, ignoring the pain. As soon as he had brought her to a stop, he pulled up, then reached down and took a new grip. She was much heavier than the boy, of course, but he had her up to the top of the level of the roof and was able to grab her by the wrist and haul her up. They sprawled on the flat roof, and for one moment he embraced her as they lay there, gasping for breath.

Her lips were only inches from his, but he threw the moment away. "Next time we do this," he teased, "I wish you'd go on a diet."

She knew he was letting the moment pass, for he was a man who drew back from emotional display. She simply pulled his head down and gave him a light kiss on the cheek. "Thanks for the ride," she whispered.

Then he rolled to his feet and looked around. The roof was perfectly flat, with only one break—a square wooden affair in the middle. That had to be the exit to the roof from the inside. Savage went to the front of the building and held his hands over his head, then pulled them down three times. He ducked back and moved to where Dani and Pat stood.

"Come over here," he ordered. "There may be some shots before long." He led them to a spot near the rear, where he had a full view of the trap door leading down. "They'll be coming up that way, maybe," he warned.

Dani and Pat both moved closer to him. Ben put his gun away. "Let's sit down." He pulled Pat close with his left hand and did the same for Dani with his right. "I got your message, Boss," he informed her quietly. "You did fine."

"So did you," she congratulated him. There was a strange feeling in her breast, a rushing tide of joy as the fear left. "I've been praying for you to come," Dani stated.

"Me, too!" Pat exclaimed. "We've been—"

He was cut off by the sound of automatic rifle fire coming from the front of the building. After a pause a voice announced over a bull horn, "Surrender now, Ring, and you'll be all right."

But as soon as DeSilva spoke, the morning air was broken by several weapons being fired. Some of them, Savage knew, were shotguns, and he guessed that the police would be putting tear gas inside the building.

The fight went on for some time. "They're inside now, the swat team," he said. "Won't be long now."

And it was not. There was a furious burst of fire from somewhere inside the building, then a silence. It ran on and on—and then the trap door began to open!

At once Savage drew his gun and put himself between Dani and Pat and the door. He held the gun steadily on the door. Finally it fell back and a man stepped out.

"Don't shoot." Sixkiller grinned as he stepped out on the roof. "It's only us lawmen." Then he saw Dani and went to her. She fell against his broad chest and held to him tightly.

DeSilva came up then and, taking in the scene, declared, "Well, Savage, you messed up my little bureaucratic plan, just as I thought you would."

Savage stared at him. "How's that, DeSilva?"

DeSilva's thin face was expressionless, but a gleam lit his dark eyes. "Ring and his two helpers, they made a fight of it." He shrugged eloquently, a thoroughly Latin gesture. "No trial, no glory for me. Just three graves. Too bad."

Savage just stared at him. "Yeah, it's tough. But you can still get your kicks by pulling my license."

"You think I've got nothing to do but waste my time pulling rank on two-bit gumshoes?" DeSilva snorted. "I won't waste my time. A hot dog like you won't last long, anyway."

Dani came out of Sixkiller's embrace. "Pat and I are so grateful to all of you," she told them. Coming forward, she put her hand out, and DeSilva took it. "You did a wonderful job!"

DeSilva stood there for a moment, then nodded. "Thank you, Miss Ross. Now, let's get you both out of here. Are you ready to get to your home, young fellow?" he asked Pat with a smile.

Pat had been holding on to Ben. He looked at the FBI agent and nodded. "Sure! I'm sick of hamburgers every day!"

Ben laughed and picked him up. "You're going to be a very popular young fellow when you get home. Everyone's been worried about you."

After some thought, Pat asked, "Ben, it would be a pretty good time to ask Dad for that Power Wheels I've been wanting, wouldn't it?"

Ben squeezed him and winked at Dani. "I think you could ask for the moon, Pat."

"I don't want the moon," Pat argued as they climbed down the ladder. "Just a red Power Wheels. I think I'll ask Mom for it," he added confidently. "She'll get Dad to buy it for me, I bet!"

Ben rode back to town with Dani on one side and Pat on the other. As the car moved through the early morning, he reached out once and pressed Dani's hand.

"Boss, don't do that to me again!" He said no more and released her hand, but she smiled, knowing what he meant.

19
A Little Therapy

Dani folded the coffee-colored blouse and laid it carefully in the suitcase lying on her bed. Then she picked up the .38 in the brown harness. She stared at it for a few moments, then placed it on top of the blouse. Taking a deep breath, she closed the suitcase, snapping the catches. The sharp *click* of the latch seemed to be a final point of some kind or perhaps some sort of fork in the road, a turning that would control her life in the future.

She picked up the suitcase, took one final look around the room, then lifted her chin and stepped outside. Thomas Rossi had just turned the corner of the hall. "Mr. Lanza would like to see you for a few moments before you leave," he told Dani. He put out his hand and took her suitcase. "You've been good for him."

"I've grown very fond of him, Thomas," Dani said. They walked down the hall together, and when they came to the door, she put her hand out and smiled at him. "I'll be coming back to see him, Thomas."

Rossi's stern lips suddenly turned upward in a smile. "That's a good thing, Miss Ross. We'll all like that." He opened the door, then stepped back. "Go right on in."

Dani entered the room and found Lanza sitting in his favorite chair. He was looking out the window, but his head turned toward her as she came to stand beside him. When he spoke, she noted that his voice was weaker than before, and his lips were drawn back in the manner of the very old or the very sick. "Ah, you are leaving us," he commented. "Well, that must be."

Dani asked quickly, "Have you heard what the FBI found?"

"No. A man named DeSilva left a message for me to call him, but I have not."

"Do it, then," Dani encouraged him. "You've been worried that a member of your family has been unfaithful."

"There *has* been a traitor among us," he insisted.

"Yes, but not of your blood. I talked to DeSilva this morning. Ring left a lot of evidence behind—including plenty of it concerning how he got his information." She paused and spoke quietly, "It was Faye Dietrich, Dom. DeSilva has letters in his handwriting. Apparently he and Ring were out to gain control of your business as well as Joe Martino's. You really had no security, Dom."

Lanza considered that. "I knew the man had ambition, but I had not thought him a traitor. I will have to deal with him."

"No, the FBI's taken care of it," Dani corrected him. "He's a party to the kidnapping and will stand trial and will be convicted. You don't have to do anything." She hesitated, then added, "And the shortage, Frank told me that the accountant finally found it. It was a laundry thing."

"Not the kind that washes clothes, I'm afraid." Dom shook his head sadly. "It was a 'laundry' for money, Dani. You know about that, I'm sure."

"Yes. It's a way to get illegally gotten money into circulation."

"Well, it can get to be very complicated. Eddy and Max were juggling operations around, and I guess they got an account buried." He shrugged, adding, "The one bright spot in the whole thing is that the family is not stealing. Stupid, yes. But not stealing. Faye is different. I will have to deal with him."

Dani wanted to take his mind off Faye. She sat down and reached out for his hand. "Don't think you're rid of me," she warned with a smile. "My office is too close for that. We've got a lot of talking to do, you and I, Dom Lanza."

He stroked her smooth hand, looked down at it, and lifted his eyes. "I wish I had met someone like you a long time ago. Maybe if I had discovered love and kindness outside the family, things would have been different." Then he cocked his head, studying her with his dark eyes. "I have never known such a thing, the way you have made such a change in people in so short a time. Rosemary—she is a new person. And Frank, he is different, too. Not to speak of the children."

"I've changed, too, Dom," she admitted slowly. "Sometimes I think we are the sum total of the people we meet. They say we are what we eat, but I think the real part of us is made by others." She looked down at his hand, thinking of the past weeks, then softly noted, "You and I are very different, Dom, but God has given me a great love for you."

He studied her shining auburn hair, appreciated the smooth curve of her cheeks, and noted again how strength and beauty were so well united in the woman. He wanted to say many things, but he chose the one element that had become most pressing to him. "Dani, you have saved my family, and you have made me aware of God." He paused, then added, "I thought that God could never be a part of my life. Now, you have opened up my heart. I read about Jesus Christ, and if what I read is true, He draws no lines."

"Never! Jesus came to show us what God is like," she explained. "One of his disciples once said, 'Lord, show us the Father.' " And Jesus answered, " 'He that hath seen me hath seen the Father.' Jesus *is* God, Dom. What we read in the Bible about Him is what He wanted to show us about his Father."

Dom replied, "I am much closer to God, Dani, than I ever thought I'd be—yet I am still troubled."

"We all have questions, Dom," Dani comforted him. "Let's go on together. I'll come back, and we can talk." She hesitated. "I always get a little nervous when someone says, 'God told me to do thus and so.' Maybe that's right, but I don't get such a direct message. But sometimes a certainty comes into my heart, and I just *know* that God is speaking to me. I've had that kind of certainty about you," she insisted. "God is drawing you, and He will have you in the end."

"I—I will look forward to our meetings," he declared. Then he picked up her hand and kissed it with a humble and eloquent gesture. "Now, give me your blessing before you go."

Dani prayed a simple prayer for him, then impulsively leaned over and kissed his withered cheek. "I'll see you

311

soon," she said, then not trusting herself to keep the tears back, she left the room quickly.

She found Frank in his study, and he got up from his desk at once. He took her hands, questioning, "So you won't change your mind and stay?"

"No, Frank. It's tempting, but I've got an agency to run."

"Well, Dani, I wish you would stay." A peculiar expression ran across his face, and he suddenly asked, "Would it make any difference if I told you things are going to be different around here?"

She looked at him inquiringly. "Different, Frank?"

"Yes!" he shrugged his shoulders and began to pace the floor. "This thing has shaken me up, Dani. Made me see things differently. Rosemary and I have had some long talks about things—you know, the kids and the way we have to live. Well—we decided there are things more important than money."

"You're leaving the family business?" Dani asked in surprise. She and Rosemary had talked about it, but it had seemed unlikely that Frank would ever think of such a thing.

"That'll be up to Pop, I guess." Frank shrugged. "We've got a lot of legitimate things going—more than I'd thought. I'm pulling out of the rackets, everything that's brought all this trouble. Eddy and Helen can do as they please, but we just want to live normal lives." He laughed shortly. "I guess Pop will kick me out on my ear. Maybe I can learn a trade. Think I'm too old to learn to be a good plumber, Dani?"

She smiled and put her hand on his arm. "You'd be good at anything you took up, Frank. But I don't think your father will be too hard on you. As a matter of fact, after the shock is over, he'll be glad, I think."

"Yeah, he's different now. That's more of your doing, Dani. I never saw him accept an outsider the way he has you."

"You're going to be fine, Frank." Dani smiled. She put out her hand and added, "I'll be seeing you pretty often. When I said good-bye to the children, I had to promise some frequent visits. I'll come see your father, too."

"I'll count on it," Frank pledged. "Send us a good fat bill, Dani. Money won't pay for what you've done, but it's a start."

Dani left the house and walked rapidly toward the garage. She found Ben and Abby waiting for her. "Well, all set?" Savage asked.

"I guess so." Dani nodded. Then she put out her hand. "Look out for the kids, Abby—and for yourself, too."

"Sure, Dani." Abby shook her hand, and then a mocking light came into her eyes. She turned and threw her arms around Ben's neck. Pulling his head down, she gave him a long kiss, then turned and grinned at Dani. "I thought I'd better do that, Dani," she explained. "He won't get anything like that from an iceberg like you!"

She whirled and ran out of the garage. Dani stared at her, then looked at Ben. He had lipstick all over his mouth and a confused look in his eyes. But he intervened quickly, "Well, Boss, I guess we better get moving."

Dani spoke stiffly, "I'll see you tomorrow at the office."

"Can I bum a ride with you? Can't get my heap started."

"Come on," she snapped. "I don't see why you don't get a decent car."

Savage got in beside her and leaned back in the seat.

"Don't like to waste money on things like cars. Rather spend it on important things like wine and women." He knew his remarks irritated her and said nothing until they were on the causeway. "What say we have an orgy, Boss? Let's go eat at Christian's," he suggested.

She gave him a critical glance. "Do you know what it costs to eat at that place?"

"As the French say, *Pomme de terre!*"

"That means 'potato.' " She laughed.

"Yeah, but it's the only French I know." He shrugged. "I'm hungry. I figure we have it coming to us."

"All right," she gave in. "I don't think you'll get past the door. You're not in proper dress." She looked at his jeans, Nike shoes, and white knit shirt. "You can wait in the car while I eat."

"Not to worry," he murmured, his head laid back. "I got an in at Christian's. I had a date once with one of the waitresses. She's so crazy about me, she'll convince them I'm an eccentric celebrity."

Christian's Restaurant was on Iberville Street, in mid-city. It was an old renovated church with beautiful stained-glass windows, a cathedral ceiling with exposed beams, and lots of greenery. The hostess looked carefully at Ben's outfit, but he slipped something into her hand, and at once she smiled and said, "This way please."

When they were seated, Dani scoffed, "Had to bribe your way in, didn't you?"

"Bribe?" he looked at her with a hurt expression. "No such thing! I slipped her a note and told her I was asking her out sometime soon." He studied the menu, then tossed it on the table. The waiter came at once and he ordered, "Bring me a platter of sauteed crawfish tails, collard greens, and some of that good bread."

Dani smiled at his order, then gave hers, "I'll have the duck breast with wild mushrooms."

"And the wine?"

"A margarita for me and an RC Cola for the lady."

The waiter looked shocked. "An RC Cola? I don't believe we have it."

"Send out for it!" Savage snapped. "Call this place a restaurant and don't stock RC Colas!"

Dani giggled at the expression on the waiter's face. "Iced tea will be fine." When he left, she said, "You fool! He probably doesn't even know what an RC Cola is!"

"Ignorance is no excuse," Savage proclaimed. A waiter brought two salads, and as Savage picked at his he remarked, "Well, I hope we made a bundle from this case."

"We did very well." Dani shrugged.

He watched her eat, then demanded, "You still have bad dreams about plugging that guy?"

She glared at him. "You have such a pleasant way of putting things!"

"Sorry. Have you had any reoccurring detrimental effects resulting from the experience involving your distressing moments with Mr. Roy Dusenburg?"

Dani glared at him, speechless with anger. "No!" she declared. "And I don't want to talk about it."

"Save you a lot of money if you do," he shrugged. "Sooner or later you'll have to go to a shrink. He'll charge you a hundred bucks an hour. I, on the other hand, am free help."

"And you're so highly qualified to advise me on this thing!"

"Better than him." Savage looked at her. "I've been where you are now. I doubt that your shrink ever shot

315

anyone." He took a sip of the margarita, then spoke quietly. "You might not believe it, but I've had some bad moments about things like this: in the corps, after my first action; when I had to stop a guy in Denver, who was holding two kids captive."

Dani looked at him and started. Savage was so hard, she had never considered that he suffered remorse from such things. "I didn't know that, Ben."

"Well, you know it now," he murmured. "I had to make a separate peace, Dani. Either get out of the business or learn to live with the fact that sometimes I have to use force." He gave her an intent look. "You'll have to do that, too, and it may be too hard for you."

She didn't know how to answer, and soon they were eating their food. He said no more, but began talking about the Lanzas. When she told him about Frank's decision, he claimed, "He can make it. Frank never had the killer instinct. What about the kids?"

Dani bit her lip, then shrugged. "It's a bad time for them, Ben. But they've got a chance, especially with Rosemary to help." Then she gave him a barbed jab. "I don't know about Abby. I suppose you have plans to offer her therapy?"

"Ben Savage, boy psychiatrist," he answered. "She'll have to find her way, just like the rest of us. Hope she makes it. She's not real happy."

Dani nodded and steered the conversation around Abby. She ordered some of Christian's homemade ice cream, and Savage wolfed down something awful called chocolate suicide.

When they left, it was dark. Savage offered, "Let me drive."

"You probably can't after that terrible dessert," Dani said, but gave him the keys to the Marquis. She leaned back in the seat and closed her eyes as he started the engine. "Just go to your apartment," she advised. "I'll drive myself home."

He didn't answer, and she kept her eyes closed. The large dinner had made Dani so drowsy that she paid no attention to his driving. She actually dozed off and came awake with a start when he stopped the car with a slight jolt. Sitting up, she stared around. "Where in the world—?" she stammered, then it came to her. Dani whirled in the seat to face him, "What do you think you're doing?"

"Thought you might like to go parking."

Dani glared at him. They were in the exact spot where they'd been weeks ago—on Lakeshore Drive on Lake Pontchartrain. The moon was full, as it had been on that night, and the waters of the lake were rippled in silver. "If I wanted to go parking, I'd let you know!" she cried. "Now, start the car!"

Savage turned to look at her. "You know, maybe you really *are* an iceberg, just like Abby said," he remarked.

That angered her, as he had known it would. Her eyes flashed, and she stated, "I am not interested in what that girl said! Now get this car started!"

He put his hand on the wheel, gave it a tug, then explained, "Well, to tell the truth, I promised Sixkiller we'd stay here for a couple of hours."

Dani stared at him. Her mouth opened, then she asked in an outraged tone, "Are you trying to tell me you agreed to a blasted *stakeout?*"

"Just for a couple of hours," he corrected quickly. "I mean, he was really a good guy about the kidnapping, so when he called yesterday, I couldn't put him off."

317

She would have argued, but at that moment the head-lights of a car came over the rise to the north. Savage barked, "Got your gun?"

"No! It's in the suitcase."

"Well, I've got mine. What do you say?"

Dani slammed her purse down on the seat and turned to him. "Oh, all right! But after this little stunt, I'm even with Lieutenant Luke Sixkiller!"

She moved close to him, and he slipped his arm around her. "Won't be too bad. Luke said he'd relieve us at ten. He just didn't have enough teams to cover the ground."

She didn't answer, and he held her as the car approached. It passed them without stopping, and at once Dani moved away from him. Ben chatted freely, appearing not to notice her stony silence. Several times in the next half hour cars passed, but none of them slowed. Each time Dani would slide close to him, then as soon as possible would jerk away from his embrace.

At 10:45 a car approached more slowly than normal. "Looks like he's going to stop," Ben commented. He pulled the magnum free, and Dani slid into his embrace. He could feel the steady beat of her heart as she leaned against him. The car passed, but he said, "Stay here a minute. Something funny about that one."

She lay passively in his arms, her face against his neck. He was very still, and finally she called out, "Ben?"

"Yep?"

"Do you think Abby was right? Am I an iceberg?"

He put his hand on her head and turned it so that she was facing him. Though the moonlight caught the gleam of his eyes, she could not read his expression. "I'll have to check," he murmured. She did not resist as he bent to kiss her. For so long she had been feeling lonely and cut off, and there was strength in his arms. Dani suddenly put her hand on his cheek and added her own pressure to the kiss. For the moment she forgot the days gone by and the uncertainty of the future. She gave him that part of herself that she had kept locked away, and she knew that at heart he was gentle, not hard and demanding.

Finally she drew back and whispered, "Well? Was Abby right?"

He studied her and started to answer, but at that moment the car returned. It pulled up beside them, and the door slammed loudly in the silence. Dani tensed, until she heard someone call out, "Hey, Ben, what's happening?"

It was Luke Sixkiller. Dani pulled away from Savage at once. She was rattled as Luke put his head down and grinned at the pair. "A little extra duty, huh?"

Dani exclaimed petulantly, "Never mind that. You can take over now."

"No need for that," Sixkiller stated cheerfully.

Dani stared at him. "What does that mean?"

"Why, we picked up the guy this morning. The old Midnight Mangler is behind bars." He grinned and added, "I left word for you, Ben. Didn't you get the message?"

Savage looked directly into Dani's eyes. "I forgot," he said.

Sixkiller burst out laughing. He slapped the car with a hard hand. "Yeah, you always had a terrible memory. Well, good night."

Dani sat there with clenched fists as the squad car roared off. Then she turned and screeched, "You are a *beast*, Benjamin Davis Savage! I hate you!"

Savage considered her carefully. "Well, I hate to hear that, because I don't hate you, Boss."

"I know you!" she accused bitterly. "You only think of one thing!"

"Now that's not so," he answered quickly. "Actually I think of two things. One, I think of you as a beautiful woman. Can I help that? Would you want me to?"

"I know all about *that!*" Dani exclaimed in a grating tone. "What's the *other* thing?"

"Well, I think about how fine you are," he said quietly. "Aside from being just about the best-looking woman I've ever known, you're the bravest and the most honest."

He did not move, nor did she. She knew him so well, yet she had never heard him speak so simply about her. Quietly, Dani pondered the two of them, knowing that no matter whom she met in the future, no man would ever know her as well as Ben Savage.

Finally she sighed, "Ben?"

"What?"

She sounded like a little girl anxious for approval, he thought, as she asked, "Was Abby right?"

Savage smiled and put his arm around her. "Don't have enough evidence yet. Have to do a little more scientific experimentation."

The moon washed over the lake, making the tiny waves glitter like silver. A great horned owl glided soundlessly over the lake. His shadow passed over the windshield of the Marquis, but the couple inside never noticed that the moon was blocked for a fleeting instant. The lonely hunter wheeled on downy wings and left the car behind, parked beside the quiet lake.